RUBY RED
FLAWS

RUBY RED FLAWS

A GRAYSON DYLE MYSTERY

JOE GOLEMO

LEVEL
BEST BOOKS

First published by Level Best Designs 2025

Author Photo Credit: Picturesque Productions

First edition

ISBN: 978-1-68512-886-9

This book was professionally typeset on Reedsy.
Find out more at reedsy.com

To Louise and Leo Golemo, thank you for inviting my brother, sister, and me into your lives with open arms and loving hearts. And to Melissa, I love you Always and Forever!

Praise for Ruby Red Flaws

"*Ruby Red Flaws* is a captivating rollercoaster of suspense and intrigue! This skillfully constructed murder mystery keeps you on the edge of your seat from the first page to the last twist. With remarkable characters, a riveting plot, and a trail of unanticipated clues, this is a must-read for fans of the Grayson Dyle mystery series. You'll be second-guessing everything and everyone until the shocking, heart-stopping ending!"—Anthony Scarpelli, Chief of Police (retired) – Skokie, Illinois Police Department

Chapter One

Bishop Tom Brennen's solicitation hit me out of the blue.

I had just finished the trek from Minneapolis across the Mississippi River, and I arrived at St. Celestine's Rectory in St. Paul to pick up my girlfriend, Kate Larson, right on time.

Kate was a finance consultant who oversaw the church's books as a part-time volunteer. As such, she interacted with the bishop on a regular basis. He held the Rectory door open for her as I drove up, and my pulse quickened when I saw her. To say she was attractive was an understatement, and her presence melted my heart. I got out of the car, gave Kate a quick hug, and greeted Tom, as he insisted we call him, with a firm handshake.

If I was honest, being on a first-name basis with someone at the pinnacle of the Catholic Clergy hierarchy was a bit mind-numbing. It only made sense if you knew that my brother Dean and I had recently discovered that we'd been adopted at birth and that the bishop was our birth father. Only a very small number of people knew our family secret, so an unspoken agreement had evolved to avoid any public displays of familial affection. This was especially relevant in Dean's case, who was as likely to deck Tom as to hug him.

"Hey, Kate. Hi Tom. Busy day cooking the books?" I chided them with a grin.

Kate's wide mouth and full lips produced a broad smile, which she flashed at me as she turned to the bishop. "Oh, great. He knows. Now we have to cut him in." She had a way of making everyone feel at ease, even him.

"Hi, Grayson. Nice to see you." Tom said in a commanding voice. He could be a bit awkward with the quips and usually avoided them.

"Did you tell him about your new CFO gig?" I asked. Kate had been the Chief Financial Officer at a prestigious law firm in downtown St. Paul. Unfortunately, one of the firm's Senior Partners had been brutally murdered while she was in another office hiding from the shooter, and even though I had unmasked his killer, the remaining Partners made it clear it was time for her to move on. After that, she set up a consulting firm and now was a part-time CFO for a handful of small companies, the latest being Ruby Ray Enterprises.

"Sure did."

"So, what do you think, Tom?"

"I've known Ruby Ray Dixon for many years." Of course, he did. It seemed as if Tom's network extended to every noteworthy individual within a one-hundred-mile radius of the Twin Cities. "He's a good man. I'm not sure how well his food enterprise has been doing lately, but maybe he will turn it around now that Kate is there to help."

"I've only been there a few weeks, but I've found some ways he can reduce expenses, which should shore up his balance sheet and free up some cash to reinvest in the business." Spoken like a true CFO.

Tom chose this moment to make his plea. He was a couple of inches taller than average, with green eyes, black pants, a black shirt with a white collar, and graying hair, which conferred the command-and-control presence that one would expect from a senior clergy member. It would be difficult to say no to anything he requested. He raised his hand to scratch the back of his head, which made it seem like he'd had a sudden, spontaneous brainstorm. It occurred to me later that he knew I'd be picking Kate up, and the only reason he walked her to the car was to enlist our aid. "Hmmm, now that I think about it, maybe you can do me a favor."

"What did you have in mind?" she asked. Kate was my dream girl. Even though she wore a simple white blouse, light blue jeans, and black flats, she looked like she'd walked off the pages of a magazine. Add to that pale blue eyes, blond hair, and a turned-up nose, and I still couldn't believe she liked hanging around with me.

"There is a former deacon from our parish named Marcel Galland who has been holding Sunday services at one of Ray's restaurants. I believe they call it the Supper Club. He claims that he is trying to serve those members of the community who are put off by organized religion. If that is truly what he's doing, I wouldn't intervene, although his ministry would be best led by the Church. But I've been hearing some troublesome reports about the approach he's been taking and the things that may be happening there. If they turned out to be true, the Church would need to intervene."

"How can he be holding church services at a supper club?" I wondered out loud.

"It's really not a problem," Kate jumped in. It was just like her to quickly get on top of her client's business operations. "The Supper Club closes at one a.m. Saturday night and Marcel holds his service at ten a.m. Sunday morning. His stage crew arrives early to set up and throw drop cloths over some of the racier paintings. Ray is happy to rent it because no one else is going to use it at that time. They also pay us a small fee to use the empty field next to the club to grow veggies. It's quite the operation."

Other than Marcel needing a stage crew for a church service, I couldn't see anything untoward with the arrangement. "Seems pretty magnanimous to me."

Tom furrowed his brow. "On the surface, it all seems very innocent. And, if he were not affiliated with us, there wouldn't be any issues. However, I've heard he claims to represent the Church in a way that we can't, so his members can still claim to be Catholic without having to attend mass. I've also heard shady things are going on behind the scenes. It's very worrisome."

A familiar pattern was starting to emerge. Was Tom concerned about a rogue deacon preaching a bastardized version of Catholicism? Or was he worried their donations weren't going into his Church's coffers? "Maybe this is something Frank can look into?" I offered. I'd had a previous run-in with one of Tom's staff named Monsignor Frank Scarpello, a charming fellow who officially was an ambassador of the Church but unofficially was a 'Fixer.'

He took care of potentially unsavory business behind the scenes so the good name of the Church wouldn't get sullied.

Tom glared at me, apparently unsure if I was sincerely trying to help solve his problem or if I was giving him crap for having a Fixer on his staff. "The Monsignor can't help with this one. He's too well known, especially by Reverend Marcel, as he calls himself these days." Tom's voice was dripping with disdain.

"What sort of shady things have been happening?"

Tom thought about it for a minute. "I don't want to say too much because I don't want to prejudice the situation. But Frank told me Marcel is using psychological manipulation and undue influence to convince people to leave the church and follow him instead. I hope none of this is true, but if it is, that would be most unfortunate."

Psychological manipulation? Undue influence? Isn't that what charismatic leaders used to keep their adherents in line? And how different was that from what the church does, I wondered. Did Frank suspect Marcel was running a cult?

Tom turned to Kate. "Now that you're working there, maybe you can spend a few minutes looking into him for me?"

Kate looked at me for reassurance. I couldn't let her go into a potentially worrisome situation without backup, so I jumped in. "We'd be happy to look into it."

"Thanks, you two. I knew I could count on you."

Kate flashed me one of her trademark broad smiles. "Yeah, thanks, Gray."

Kate was all-in, as I knew she would be. One thing I'd learned about her over the past year was that she liked to know things. I wouldn't call her a gossip because she didn't repeat most of what she'd learned. She just wanted to know what was happening with the people around her, and this request was carte blanche to learn about her new company.

I thought we were done and turned to go, but Tom grabbed me by the arm and stopped me. His face assumed the severe look that clergy members always employ at solemn events like funerals, ribbon-cutting ceremonies, or ordering food at a restaurant. "One more thing, Grayson. Not a word to anyone else about this." He paused for effect. "Not one word." With that, he turned to go, and we were done.

He'd acted this way before, and I never knew if he was trying to impart some clandestine message or if he just liked being dramatic. Either way, I had a sudden sense of foreboding, which only heightened my discomfort at him being a birth father—mine or anyone else's—and I suddenly realized I'd been trying to decide how I felt about him for a long time. On the one hand, Tom committed some flagrant sins against his ecclesiastical vows in his youth. On the other hand, neither Dean nor I would be here if he hadn't. He'd also arranged our private adoption by Ben and Linda Dyle, a young Catholic couple he had personally selected for the honor, and they'd raised us as their own. I couldn't imagine two more warm and loving parents. So, 'Let he who is without sin cast the first stone,' right?

* * *

Two days later, Kate and I were at my condo in Minneapolis's somewhat trendy Uptown area, prepping for a recon mission at Ruby Ray's Enterprises, aka RRE.

My one-bedroom unit was on the eighth floor of a building at the corner of Lake Street and Knox Avenue South, just off Lake Bde Maka Ska, the largest lake in Minneapolis. (It had been renamed from Lake Calhoun, a change that had caused no small amount of consternation from the locals.) The Worldwide Headquarters for the twenty-person product design company I co-owned, Design By Dyle, was conveniently located on the second floor.

Kate had been spending more and more time at my place, so I coughed up a few extra bucks for a second stall in the underground parking area to symbolize my dedication to our relationship and her personal safety. I didn't mention to Kate that the spot also provided our clients with convenient parking and was a tax write-off, but she probably knew. She sat on one of the counter stools at the kitchen island while I poured us some water and sat beside her.

"So, what's the plan for tonight?" I asked.

"Well, I've been doing a bit of research...."

"Otherwise known as snooping."

"No. No, definitely not. Snooping is when you gather intel to potentially use against someone in the future. I'm doing this to help Tom. Remember him, your birth father? The Bishop? The guy who asked us to look into the supper club church thing?"

Sure thing, Kate, whatever you say.

"I figure the best place to start looking into Reverend Marcel's operation is by talking to the man himself. And the best way to have a casual, disarming discussion is over a meal. So, the best place to meet him is at one of the Ray's restaurants."

"There's more than one?"

"Yep. There are two options. One is Ruby Ray's Aussie House, which is a deli that is only open for lunch. They serve authentic Australian food. We should go there sometime. I've heard the meat pies are amazing. You'd probably love it."

With Kate working nearby, I felt I would be sick of meat pies in a few months, but I said, "I'd be willing to give it a try."

"Great. But it's loud in there, and a lunch meeting with Marcel won't give us enough time to talk. The second option is Ruby Ray's Supper Club. It's only open for dinner and still has the same sixties-style menu and floor show that made it popular in its heyday. They even have a girl on a trapeze who does tricks as she swings and a large deck at the back where they serve dinner when the weather permits. It's very scenic. You can see the entire Mississippi River valley and both downtowns from there."

"Wait a minute. They have a girl swinging over the crowd on a trapeze during dinner?"

"Yeah, doesn't that sound great? It's not a very long show, so we can talk afterward."

"That doesn't sound so great to me. It sounds like a health code violation."

"I don't think so. It's not like she's dropping things on people's heads. Besides, she only swings over the dance floor. They've been doing it for years. Anyway, I heard from the receptionist at our business office that

Reverend Marcel was planning to go to the Supper Club for dinner tonight, so I called the Maître D and left a message to book us a table for four and seat him there when he arrives. Then I called Marcel and said we'd treat him to dinner to thank him for renting the space from us." Kate was very proud of her line of reasoning and subterfuge.

It was an elaborate plan, and I couldn't believe I would be part of it. Dining on 1960s-style fare in a once-famous supper club while interrogating an undoubtedly innocent Reverend and dodging the swing girl's feet? No wonder she spent all this time wearing me down with the backstory. "I was hoping we'd do something low-key tonight. We could have a nice dinner at one of the umpteen new restaurants around here and then take a leisurely stroll around the lake." I was about to say she could count me out when she looked at me and smiled, conveying that I was the best boyfriend in the world.

I sighed. "Fine. When do we leave?"

Kate looked at the time on her phone. "Can you be ready in an hour?"

Alrighty then.

As I was in the bedroom changing into supper club clothes, whatever that meant, I called out to Kate. "I have to tell you how impressed I am that you landed this consulting gig so quickly. How did you do it?"

"You know, the usual networking. I think it was a friend of a friend that suggested I meet with Ray."

"Really, who was that?"

"No one that you know."

I had been making small talk but suddenly got the impression that my girlfriend of over two years was stonewalling me, which was not like her. I finished changing and came out of the bedroom when she abruptly changed the subject, which seemed like confirmation that she was covering something up. I let it go for now but made a mental note to cross-examine her again.

"So, should we meet my mother over lunch or dinner?"

I just stared at her. Ever since our first anniversary, Kate had started dropping hints that her mother, Mrs. Elizabeth Larson, never Liz, Beth, or Betsy, wanted to meet me. At first, I delivered noncommittal responses while wishing the whole idea would disappear. But, by the time we'd been dating for eighteen months, Kate was getting more insistent, and the vague answers weren't cutting it anymore.

On the one hand, I supposed it was about time. On the other, couldn't we wait a few more years? I never did well meeting 'the parents' when I was a kid. Would I do any better now that I was a grown adult and business owner? But, what really bugged me was that the question was an assumptive close, a trick that car salespeople use to get you to presume you've already decided to buy but just need to decide on which one. 'Would you like the black or navy-blue model of this really expensive, luxury SUV on which I will make a large commission?'

But there was no more putting it off. I decided that this time was going to be different. I would research Elizabeth Larson to know what I was getting into. At least I'd have a few new topics to bring up during lulls in the conversation. "Lunch will be less stressful, and we can always make an excuse to leave early if she doesn't like me."

"She's going to like you just fine, Grayson."

That was only mildly reassuring, but there was no reason to belabor the point. "Let's just go."

Kate came over and delivered a big hug. I smiled despite myself. Why was I such a pushover when she was around?

Chapter Two

Friday Evening, May 5

As we drove to the Supper Club, we discussed her new gig with Ruby Ray.

"So, how do you like working for Ruby Ray?"

"He's great. Very flamboyant. He loves to tell stories, especially about life in Australia. And his wife Sheila is a hoot. It feels like we've been friends for years even though we just met."

"Why do they call him Ruby Ray?"

Kate looked at me as if I'd lost the plot. "Because he found the ruby, of course."

"What ruby?"

"What ruby?! The Poona Ruby! The largest ruby on record found in Australia. Ray discovered it in 1987 and brought it to America. Don't tell me you've never heard of it."

"Wait, there actually is a ruby? I thought that was just a legend. Is that why everything is called 'Ruby Ray's?'"

"Yep. There actually is a ruby, and apparently, it's worth a fortune. Years ago, he and Sheila decided that his name would be the focal point for the brand because it highlights the fact that the ruby is real and increases his mystique as a world-renowned treasure hunter. The fact that Ruby Ray rolls off the tongue much better than Ruby Sheila was just a side benefit."

Kate lowered her voice conspiratorially. "Guess who the trapeze girl is?"

Since she'd only named one female, it seemed obvious. "Sheila?"

"Got it in one." Kate smiled and sprung her last surprise. "And guess who else I invited tonight?"

Despite the subterfuge and weird surroundings, I was hoping to salvage a nice dinner, so I stayed away from the snark. "I really couldn't say."

"DeeDee, of course."

All I could do was shake my head. DeeDee Miller was a relative that I met through an ancestry website right after Dean and I found out we'd been adopted. She had connected me with the Brennen family, which eventually resulted in Dean and I discovering Tom was our birth father. I'd hoped to figure out exactly how we were related to DeeDee one day, but it didn't seem to matter as we had become fast friends. Most people got the strong impression she was a bit dotty, but in reality, she never missed a thing.

"You invited DeeDee? How did you know I'd say yes?"

"I was hoping I could sweet-talk you into it. Besides, we needed someone for the fourth seat."

"What about Harry?" I asked.

DeeDee was a semi-retired crematorium worker who liked bringing her work home. Literally. Her home was currently the final resting place for at least forty fully loaded funeral urns, some of which contained the ashes of people she actually knew in real life. Her favorite urn contained her second husband, Harry. It doesn't matter if she's going to church, to the store, or bingo night — she never leaves home without him. Unless they're fighting, in which case it's 'see you later, honey.'

"If you didn't want to go, he would have used your ticket. Now, I guess he'll have to watch from the floor."

We soon arrived at Ruby Ray's Mall. It had been built in the small town of Lillydale along Highway 13 at a bend in the Mississippi River. I could see the Aussie House and the Supper Club that Kate had mentioned on the first floor. The mall's façade was styled after an old-fashioned mining town from the Australian Outback. It was undoubtedly intended to look rustic, but the maintenance budget must have been slashed because now it just looked tired. A fresh coat of paint was sorely overdue, and they needed to straighten up the rooster-shaped weather vane if they expected it to turn with the wind again.

I parked facing the Supper Club and noted a building called the Aussie Museum sandwiched between the two restaurants. I was a bit skeptical. "There's a museum here?"

"Of course," Kate said. "That's where they display the ruby so people will know it's not just a legend." That sounded like a dig from my earlier comment, but I let it go.

"Isn't it odd to have a whole museum with only a big ol' ruby in it?"

"That's cute. It actually contains a wide variety of exhibits, including dinosaur bones and wildlife from the Outback. Ray is obsessed with authenticity, so all of the artifacts were brought in directly from Australia."

"Wow, I had no idea."

"Yeah, that's part of the problem. No one seems to know we're here."

As we got out of the car, I asked, "So, where's your office?"

Kate pointed toward the top of the complex. "There is a suite on the second floor above the Aussie House and Museum. Ray's private office has large windows overlooking the river, and the view is outstanding. I'm only there part-time, so they stuck me in a small office overlooking the parking lot. The view is only outstanding when you're in it."

That was nice of her, but it made me wonder if she would hit me up for something in a few minutes.

When we arrived at the restaurant's reception deck, the Maître D let us know there were no tables for four available since we called on such short notice, but they had a table for six. Would we mind sharing it with another of Ray's business colleagues? He said he'd already shown the rest of our party there. Kate said that was fine, and he showed us to a table where DeeDee was sitting. As he handed us the menus, the Maître D suggested we order drinks and dinner as soon as the waiter stopped by to avoid interrupting the show.

DeeDee got up to give Kate and me a hug. I had to lean over pretty far as she was about five feet two with short, curly white hair and hazel eyes. I noticed she was wearing the same light blue dress with the overwhelming pattern of small red flowers as when we first met at her home over a year ago. It must have been one of her special occasion outfits. A large, heavy-duty canvas tote bag was taking up the seat right next to her with the top of an urn sticking out of it. It looked like she already had a seat for Harry, and she'd even had the courtesy of putting him in the location with the poorest visibility on the stage.

Through a previous Google search, I recognized Reverend Marcel Galland, who had been chatting with DeeDee. He looked over six feet tall with dark brown hair and was sporting a black shirt and slacks, in keeping with his Reverend status. The quizzical yet pained look on his face undoubtedly meant he was both fascinated and terrified by DeeDee's stream-of-consciousness rambling. Most people are. We introduced ourselves to him next, and he seemed thankful for the opportunity to break away.

The last person at the table was someone I didn't recognize. Kate and I introduced ourselves, and he told us his name was Scott Dimond, a business colleague of Ray's. With his well-coiffed salt-and-pepper hair, light blue button-down shirt, vintage Rolex watch, and nicely contrasting brown and blue sports jacket, Scott projected an aura of influence and success, not to mention a high net worth. I got the sense it was an image he carefully cultivated.

As the others studied the menu, I couldn't help but look around. If the mall's theme was an Outback town, the Supper Club was its saloon. The female wait staff wore low-cut showgirl outfits with a laced-up bodice and a double-layered overskirt trimmed with ruby red satin ruffles and matching satin armbands. The male staff wore similar striped shirts and ruby red satin armbands.

The dance floor was about twenty feet long and twelve feet wide, with a raised platform for a stage at one end and a bar on the other. It was flanked on each side by three rows of café tables with some longer tables near the bar for larger groups. The kitchen door was off to one side behind the stage. We were seated right next to the dance floor about halfway down. These looked like great seats, and I wondered if the Maître D was trying to curry favor with the company's new CFO. I looked up, trying to spot Sheila preparing to perform on the swing, but the ceiling was shrouded in darkness.

"DeeDee was just recounting your sleuthing expertise in exposing your father's murderer. Sounds like you're quite the detective," said Reverend Marcel, who looked as if he was still trying to pry himself away from DeeDee, who was oblivious to his social cues.

"The police were never going to get it," DeeDee said with a bit too much enthusiasm. "James Brennan was such a fine attorney. He helped me with my legal issues and never charged me a dime. Grayson was just like Sherlock Holmes in how he figured it out."

I turned toward Kate so only she could see my exasperated eye roll, but she still chimed in. "I have to admit, it was impressive," she said to Marcel. "I used to work for an Attorney's office in St. Paul, where James was a Senior Partner. The police were convinced he was killed by a random junkie looking for drug money, but Grayson didn't buy that. He kept at it until he found the real killer. It was all over the news."

Marcel nodded. "I did hear about that. What a tragic story." He turned toward me. "I didn't hear that you'd solved the murder, though. That is very exciting. I'd love to hear all about it."

I finally realized that Kate had jumped in to gloss things over so that DeeDee wouldn't blurt out the actual version of events and possibly expose my relationship with the bishop. I'd have to thank her later.

"It was nothing really. It sounds more impressive than it was." If anyone started asking questions, the cover story would start breaking down. I needed to change the subject quickly and scanned the area for a diversion. Then, I noticed something odd about the item on the seat next to DeeDee. Other than being an urn on a chair at a nice restaurant, I mean. "Wait a minute, DeeDee. That's not Harry's urn. You're not cheating on him, are you?"

DeeDee knew I was kidding her and smiled. "Cheat on my Harry? After he saved my life? Never!" She was very proud of her urns and relished any opportunity to show them off. She opened the tote bag, hoisted the new urn from the chair, and held it up for us all to admire. The urn was easily twice as big as the one she usually used, and it had a silver finish, whereas Harry's had been dark blue.

"This was a spare that never got used at the crematorium. It was originally ordered by the family of a man who weighed over eight hundred pounds, so it had to be custom-made. We had to cut the deceased into two pieces to fit him into the cremator, but he still generated so much heat that the cremation room caught fire. After the fireman left, we couldn't tell which ashes were from his remains and which were from the building, so the family just said to forget the whole thing. They didn't want the urn back either. Anyway, Harry is using this one while his is in the shop."

There was a stunned silence at the table. This was not unusual for an event where DeeDee was telling tales. She leaned over to Marcel and lowered her voice conspiratorially. "You see, someone was shooting at Grayson and me, and they hit the urn instead. Harry took a bullet for me. He saved my life. I couldn't have him leaking out everywhere, could I?"

Marcel was clearly confused about whether to agree or not when I interrupted. "Maybe we should look at the menu before the waiter stops by."

"Good idea," said Kate, listing off a few items on the menu that she'd heard were delicious. Just then, and with perfect timing, the waiter came to take our drink and dinner orders. He said the first act would start soon, and he would bring our meals after we'd had a chance to enjoy the drinks.

"So, Reverend Marcel, I've seen your name on a few of the Supper Club rent payments. How's that been working out?" Kate asked.

"Please. Call me Marcel. It's been working out great. We start with worship services in the Club every Sunday morning, and the entire group goes out to tend the gardens. We have over fifty raised beds on the undeveloped field next to the Club. We sell the flowers at the St. Paul Farmer's Market and fresh, organic veggies to Ray's restaurants. Anything we can't sell, we donate to a food bank. It's a great way for people to feel like they're part of a cause bigger than themselves, and it connects church services with giving back to the community."

"What denomination are you?" I wondered.

Marcel emitted a small chuckle. "Officially, I'm a Catholic Deacon, but I'm a bit estranged from the church at the moment. They don't like me taking the process of worship in a new direction without their approval."

"Did you join another religious sect then?" Kate must have decided this would be an excellent opportunity to grill him, but the question felt forced. A religious sect? She made it sound like a cult, and she seemed to have done it purposely. Was she riffing on Tom's concern that psychological manipulation was occurring?

Marcel stared at her for a moment. It seemed as if he knew exactly where the question was going. "You can't believe everything you hear." Then, it was his turn to change the programming. "I have a question for you, Kate. As Ray's new CFO, when are you going to get some decent café tables? The ones in the Club are horrible."

Even though this would further diverge from Kate's interrogation, my design sense started tingling, and I couldn't help but jump in immediately. "What's up with the tables?"

"You know how those cheap coffee shop café tables usually are. After a few years, they wobble like crazy, and you have to shim the legs with folded-up napkins so you don't spill your drinks."

I'd been frustrated with café tables for years, and finally, someone confirmed they were a problem. And, where there were design flaws, lucrative new solutions can sometimes be developed to fix them. One of my favorite examples occurred in 1959 when a Volvo engineer realized the two-point lap belt system was woefully inadequate at saving lives in car crashes. He invented the three-point safety belt that went over the lap and shoulder, which reduced deaths dramatically. Volvo patented the design and could have made a fortune through increased car sales and product licensing. Of course, they chose to give the patent away for the general good of the driving public, so that part of the example doesn't work as well, but still.

"I couldn't agree more. Everyone knows café tables are tippy as hell. I've been grumbling about them for years." This sounded like a design flaw my company could work on. And we could use Ray's club to test out a few prototypes. Come to think of it, the lunch with Kate's mother could provide another opportunity to assess the table situation. An idea for our next big product was coming together, and I couldn't wait to share it with my business partner, Paul Cameron. Maybe Kate's dinner plans would pay off after all.

I was about to ask more questions when the waiter stopped by to serve our drinks and open a bottle of wine for Kate and me. I realized I could use the café tables issue as an excuse to meet with Marcel later, so I decided to connect with our sixth guest instead. "So, what line of work are you in, Scott?"

"I do private equity investing. I've been helping Sheila and Ray with their finances for many years." He continued talking to me but turned to stare at Kate. "I have to tell you, it's nice having Kate on board. She's a quick study and has already identified ways to save money using lower-cost suppliers. By the way, Kate, I'd like to introduce you to a couple of other clients if you're looking for more work." There was something creepy in the way he said this that I couldn't quite identify. I was going to have to watch this guy.

To her credit, she just smiled and nodded. "That sounds good, Scott. But let's see how well Ray likes my work first. I'll need him as a reference anyway, right?" That's one of the reasons I loved her. She shut him down without him even realizing it.

Scott turned towards me. "How about you, Grayson? What do you do when you're not solving murders?"

"I'm co-owner of a small product design and engineering firm." It occurred to me that Scott would definitely leave Kate alone if he thought there was an opportunity to work with my partner and me. So, I decided to lay it on a little thick. "We've been around since 2010, and it's been going well, but I've often wondered if a cash infusion would let us reach more customers faster. Is that the kind of thing you help companies with?"

"Absolutely. We should talk sometime soon." Scott extended his hand with the palm up to show it was empty, then performed a quick bounce, and a business card appeared in it as if out of nowhere. "Here's my card. Feel free to reach out any time."

It was a smooth move, and he must have practiced it for a long time. But it was also a bit cheesy, especially for someone who dealt in high finance. "Wow, great sleight of hand. You'll have to show me how you did that the next time we meet."

"Sure, just give me a call."

Our waiter and a food runner arrived with our dinners. I was pleasantly surprised that they looked much better than the average supper club fare. Maybe it was going to be a good night after all. As if on cue, the Maître D, who must also serve as the Master of Ceremonies, took to the stage and grabbed a mic. His attire matched the male wait staff with the addition of a maroon tuxedo jacket with ruby red sequins along each arm and a matching lapel flower. The lights were lowered, and the spotlight on him got everyone's attention.

"Our first act tonight, ladies and gentlemen, has been playing a unique combination of jazz, blues, and percussion for over thirty years. He's a two-time Minnesota Black Music Award winner, and he's been our opening act at Ruby Ray's for over five years. Please join me in welcoming….Patter Patterson!" He started clapping, and the rest of us followed along.

Patter, who looked to be at least seventy-five, slowly sauntered onto the stage and sat at an upright piano. With his rumpled sports coat, dark gray suspenders, and graying beard, he looked exactly like a senior jazzman.

I was mesmerized as he started to play, not just because of his mastery of the twelve-bar blues, reminiscent of Muddy Waters, but because of how he used the piano to keep the beat. As his right hand played a jazz melody, his left hand alternated between playing chords and patting out the beat on the keyboard cover, the piano sidearm, and the bench he was sitting on. Anything it could reach was in play.

I leaned over to whisper in Kate's ear. "Wow, this guy is awesome. And I love the way he uses the piano to keep time."

She leaned back toward my ear. "That's why they call him Patter—it's his signature pitter-patter move. That and his last name, of course." Kate leaned in a little closer. "Sheila warned me to stay out of his reach when I started. Apparently, he gets a bit frisky with the ladies sometimes, which might be another reason for the name." I was a little alarmed to hear that.

* * *

After a half-hour show, Patter stopped playing, and the MC retook the stage. "How about a big hand for Patter Patterson!" he said to much applause. Marcel used this moment to excuse himself from the table, citing the call of nature and saying he didn't want to miss the main show.

"And now, our featured act tonight is Ruby Ray's infamous Swing Girl. An act that is renowned all over the country for its fearless feats of derring-do. It's a combination of aerial acrobatics and contortions, all performed for your enjoyment. Please stay off the dance floor during her set, but don't worry, ladies and gentlemen, we haven't lost a customer yet. Please welcome Ruby Ray's very own Swing Girl, Sheila Dixon!" Just as Marcel was returning to his seat, Patter started playing a circus music tune that made his piano sound like a pipe organ. The applause swelled, and the audience looked up in anticipation.

The spotlight moved to Sheila, who was poised to start swinging with her right arm already up and waving to the crowd. She wore a fancier version of the saloon girl outfit with ruby red sequins along the bodice, bright ruby arm bands, and fishnet stockings.

Just as the swing started its downward arc, there was a sudden commotion in the kitchen. It sounded like someone had dropped a tray full of dishes, and the noise it created was almost deafening. Sheila kept swinging, seemingly oblivious to the clatter below her.

She seemed to be looking down and not putting much enthusiasm into it. Maybe years of two shows a night every weekend did that to you, but it seemed like something was off. The only thing moving was her right hand, which flew back when she swung forward and flew forward when she swung back. Each swing was slower than the last, and the arch was shorter. It looked like she would soon stop swinging altogether.

After a few more passes, it was clear that something was wrong as she wasn't moving a muscle. The MC also seemed concerned. He motioned to Patter to stop playing, found the release for the ropes, and let the swing down to the dance floor right next to us. Sheila's face was white, and her body was still. It was obvious she was dead.

Chapter Three

Friday Evening, May 5

A stunned silence overtook the diners for a few seconds until a small child a few tables down started sobbing at seeing the dead body. The crowd began muttering among themselves, and cell phones started coming out. Some people could be overheard talking to a 9-1-1 operator, and some of the others were taking pictures of the corpse on a swing that they undoubtedly would share on social media. Within a minute, the MC took stock of the situation and made an announcement apologizing for the inconvenience and asking everyone to please remain in their seats and to put their cell phones away out of respect. Most people complied.

I was fascinated by this new development and wanted to know more. Kate and I left our table and moved toward the scene. DeeDee started getting up, too, probably to give someone her business card and offer to perform the cremation. But she stopped when I motioned for her to stay seated. The MC initially tried to block our way, but then he let us through when he realized Kate worked there. She tried to shield the body from gawkers as much as possible while I inspected the swing and its occupant.

Sheila had been bound to the swing with wires. The swing seat hung from two cables connected to the ceiling by hangers, and her legs were wired to the seat to prevent her body from falling off. Her left arm was wired to one of the cables, starting at the elbow and going up to the hand, which was loosely wrapped around the cable. This was the position it would usually be in when she was swinging. Her right arm was similarly wired, except the hand was left free so it would fall into a perpetual waving motion.

Initially, I thought maybe she'd suffered a heart attack. But if that were the case, she would have fallen off the swing onto the dance floor. Then I realized she couldn't have performed aerial acrobatics tied to a swing. She must have been murdered and trussed up by a killer who was trying to make some weird statement. But there were no apparent wounds, so it was not clear what had killed her. Unless the Supper Club had a spool of strong, thin wire lying around the back room, someone must have brought it with them, making it seem like this was a premeditated act. If she had been shot, she would have left a gory trail of blood below her, so she must have been dead before she was tied to the swing. I didn't see any defensive wounds on her hands or arms, which confirmed this idea.

Patter came over carrying a blanket. "Here, help me with this," he said to me. "We've got to cover her up." I took one end of the blanket, draping it over her the best we could.

Now that Sheila's body was covered, I turned to the MC and whispered, "This is obviously a murder, or she wouldn't have been wired to the swing. The killer could still be somewhere in the building, and they may even be sitting here right now. We need to make sure no one leaves so the police can decide who to question before they can clear the building." I considered warning him that the killer might be just outside waiting to prey on a flood of panicked evacuees, but it wasn't necessary as he nodded in agreement. He used the mic to make an announcement saying the police were on their way and asking everyone to remain in their seats until they arrived.

Kate's eyes suddenly got wide. "I've got to check the office right away."

I was shocked. "Wait a minute. That's not a good idea. Did you hear what I said about the killer?"

"What if someone murdered Sheila to misdirect attention away from the safe so they could steal the ruby? I need to check to make sure it's still there."

I grabbed her arm. "Isn't that above your pay grade?"

Kate pulled away and shot me a look. She was going to check no matter what I said.

"Okay, I'll go with you." I wasn't sure what difference I would make. It wasn't like I had a gun in my pocket, but it seemed like the right thing to do. She headed towards the stairs, which seemed odd. "I thought you said the ruby was in the Aussie Museum."

"It's only there when the museum is open and it's on display. Otherwise, it's kept in a floor safe in Ray's office."

Kate opened the doors with her pass card as we hurried up the stairs to the private offices. We navigated through the cubes to the office closest to the river. Kate dashed through an open door with the words 'Ruby Ray Dixon' inscribed and ducked behind an oversized desk. As I followed, I noticed the view of the Twin Cities through the large windows was truly remarkable. The sound of police sirens in the background reminded me of the time I'd found James Brennan dead behind a desk like this one right after he'd been shot.

There was a look of shock on Kate's face. "Oh no. I knew it." I looked down to see the safe with its door wide open. I couldn't tell if someone had forced it or if they had known how to open it. Kate reached in and took out a large, expensive-looking velvet jewelry case that was also open. She showed it to me. "The ruby…it's gone!"

Just then, an older man stormed in. "Kate, what the hell are you doing? Get away from there!" With his wild blond hair, ruddy complexion, royal blue Ruby-Ray-logoed shirt, and huarache sandals, I figured this must be the infamous Ruby Ray himself. He suddenly seemed to notice I was there. "Who are you?"

"Grayson Dyle, Kate's boyfriend." I automatically put out my hand to shake, but Ray had already raced by me. As he noticed Kate was holding the empty jewel case, he blanched.

"Where is the ruby? What did you do with it? Is this what I get after trusting you with the combination to the safe?"

I wondered if he knew his wife was no longer among the living. Kate seemed flustered from being accused of theft and wasn't saying anything. "Have you heard about Sheila?" I asked.

"Yes, I just came from the dining room. When I saw my Sheila strung up to the swing, I knew someone was after the ruby. I just didn't know it would be you," Ray bellowed as he pointed at Kate.

Kate finally stood up and found her voice. "I didn't steal it. But I was worried just like you and wanted to make sure it was safe. But we got here too late."

"I can vouch for her, Ray. The safe and jewelry case were already open when we arrived."

"How do you know she didn't palm the ruby before you could see what she was doing?"

I couldn't believe the unfounded accusations he was slinging at Kate, but considering he'd just lost his wife, I figured it was his grief talking. "You're just going to have to trust us on this."

"How do you know she didn't kill my wife and then string her up so she could sneak off and steal the ruby?"

I found myself raising my voice and speaking slowly. "Because I was with her the whole time."

"Maybe the two of you are in this together, and I should search your pockets for the ruby right now."

"Ray, you need to calm down. You just lost your wife and your ruby, and you're not thinking clearly."

Just then, a St. Paul police officer entered the office. He seemed to know Ray, which wasn't surprising considering how long Ray had been in the area.

"Officer Schmidt, it's about time you got here. You need to arrest Kate Larson right now for the murder of my Sheila and the theft of my ruby."

This guy had really lost the plot. "Officer, that's ridiculous, I was with Kate..."

Officer Schmidt held up his hand for silence. "We don't just go around arresting people, Ray. We will look into both crimes and take the appropriate actions based on the evidence." It was good to see someone acting rationally. "Now, if you will all follow me, we need to talk about what happened tonight."

Ray followed the officer, so Kate and I brought up the rear. "You didn't palm the ruby, right?" I whispered.

"What!?" If looks could kill, there would have been two murders that night.

"Of course not, Grayson." She was trying to whisper but not having much luck. "I can't believe you asked me that."

"Sorry, Kate. Don't know what I was thinking."

She stormed past me to catch up with Ray, and I followed. What was I thinking? Then I realized it was a flashback to Kate's brother. He was a conservation officer with the Minnesota Department of Natural Resources, and he'd suffered a serious work-related back injury. He'd gotten hooked on Oxycontin, but after his prescription ran out, he turned to buying drugs off the street. Kate moved him to an inpatient treatment center, but it was expensive, and she'd gotten in over her head. As the CFO, she couldn't really ask her company for help. So, she 'borrowed' the money, fully intending to pay it back over time, which she did before anyone realized it was missing. I had discovered her secret while solving the previous murders, and, in my mind, I'd forgiven her. Or had I?

I'd have to resolve that later because Officer Schmidt had led us back to the Supper Club straight to my old friend, Detective Aaron Copeland, from the St. Paul Police Department. Since he was the lead detective on the previous murder cases I'd solved, I took it as a compliment that he wanted to interview me personally, convincing myself he wanted to hear my analysis of the crime scene. Of course, he was more likely trying to figure out how to pin the whole thing on me. And possibly Kate, too. We spent the next few hours holed up in separate conference rooms, being interviewed by Copeland and various other police detectives. As much as they tried to trip me up, it wasn't hard to keep my story straight. All I had to do was tell the truth, and I did over and over again late into the night.

* * *

By early Monday morning, I had finally caught up on my sleep. I took the elevator from my unit to the Design By Dyle office. Since I lived in the same building where I worked, I usually arrived first and had to make the coffee. As I was grinding the beans, my business partner, Paul Cameron, arrived and leaned against the kitchen door. A dull orange sleeveless jacket and light blue work shirt hung loosely on his thin frame and were complemented by light blue jeans, cowboy boots, dark hair, and three-day-old stubble. He looked like he could be posing for the cover of *Design Guy* magazine, if there was such a thing.

When we first started our business, it was just us two entrepreneurs saving money by slaving away on the first floor of my duplex on Fremont Ave. in Minneapolis's Uptown area. We were bidding on product design work and losing far more deals than we won. But we paid attention and learned as much about what didn't work as what did. Then we hit a bit of luck. A former college roommate, who happened to be the CEO of a local medical device start-up, called us with a thorny design problem. Paul and I devised an innovative solution that catapulted their product to success. Word of mouth spread, and the work soon became steadier. In a few years, we hired more designers and moved into actual office space, which made us feel like a real company.

"Hey, Grayson. The murder at Ruby Ray's is all over the news. Doesn't Kate work there now?"

"Yep. She started there a few months ago." I didn't see any reason to go into the drama between Marcel and the bishop, so I provided an abbreviated version of the evening. "She took me to the Supper Club for dinner on Friday night, so we were sitting right next to the dance floor and saw the whole thing."

"You and Kate were there when it happened? That must have been unnerving."

"Now that you mention it, I probably should have been scared. But everything happened so quickly. It never occurred to me. Guess who insisted on interrogating me?"

"No! Not Detective Copeland. I'll bet he was happy to see you, right?"

"Yeah, right. He didn't seem too pleased to see Kate either. Did the news—"

Paul cut in. "Is he married? Copeland? I'd be all over that man if I weren't already spoken for."

"I'm pretty sure he's straight, Paul. Did they say anything about a famous ruby on the news?"

"No. Wait, what? What ruby? There's a famous ruby? I love rubies. I thought that was just an urban legend."

Wow. Paul was usually on top of peculiar news items, and he normally would have known all about an actual famous ruby in our midst. If he hadn't known that Ruby Ray's enterprise was based on one of the largest ever found, Ray clearly needed to get a new marketing team stat. I assured him there was an actual ruby and described Kate's mad dash to save it, Ray's insistence that she or we had stolen it, and the police grilling us for the next few hours about the theft of the ruby and the murder.

"Why didn't they mention that on the news? That story is just as interesting as the murder. I can't wait to tell Richard."

Richard was Paul's life partner. Despite Paul's propensity to act like he was interested in strong, handsome men like Copeland, he and Richard were in a very committed relationship. They would soon celebrate their tenth anniversary together.

"I'm not surprised they kept that quiet. Don't the cops always hold certain facts back to verify the credibility of any tips they receive? And they probably don't want the general public searching for a stolen ruby. But Paul, please don't tell Richard. We really don't need word getting out. Kate is in enough trouble as it is."

Paul was incensed. "He won't tell anyone." But I'd said too much and could see he realized what I'd meant by the way he scrunched up his face. "Oh my god, you're going to start investigating, aren't you? Dammit, Grayson, you promised me you wouldn't do that anymore. I know you solved the murders the last time, but that involved your family, so it sort of made sense."

No wonder Richard called me Paul's 'work wife.' He was nagging me like we were an old married couple, and his voice was getting louder with each sentence to the point where he was almost shouting. "And we almost lost the business. I can't afford to have you gallivanting around town pretending to be Sam Spade."

I could truthfully say I wasn't planning on investigating anything—at least not at the moment. "You don't have to worry about me, Paul. I'm sure Copeland will do fine without me on this one." I knew I could avoid any further debate by dangling some new information. "Besides, it's a damn good thing I went to that dinner because I got a great idea for a new product line."

"Really, what's that?" Paul crossed his arms, apparently ready to squash any new idea I might come up with just for spite. When I told him about the café tables, his attitude completely changed.

"Oh my god, you're right. Café tables are the worst, especially the ones with a single post in the middle. Your drink always sloshes around whenever anyone gives them the slightest nudge. Why didn't we think of this before?"

Good old Paul—why didn't 'we' think of this before?

He got up. "I have to go design something," he said on his way back to his office. Apparently, I'd been forgiven, at least for now.

Chapter Four

I'm still not sure how it happened, but Kate talked me into having lunch at Ruby Ray's Aussie House only six days after the murder. The Supper Club was still closed out of respect for Sheila's passing and to give the police time to finish their investigation. It felt like returning to the scene of the crime but not being allowed to enter.

I arrived at about eleven-thirty and waited for Kate just inside the entrance. I noticed Ray had done a nice job differentiating the Aussie House from the Supper Club. It had a food truck vibe before food truck vibes were all the rage, with large neon signs facing the road and signed pictures of celebrities enjoying the food. One wall had vibrant murals of the Aussie Outback, and another was filled with brilliant images of scuba divers and snorkelers navigating a bed of coral. He even had the Triple J radio station piped in.

In the center of the room sat a large acrylic fish tank with a sign that christened it 'The Great Barrier Reef Marine Museum' and informed the public that it was filled with over one thousand gallons of ocean water, coral, and a live tropical fish community imported directly from Australia. Was it legal to import part of the Australian coral reef? I wondered.

The large, brightly colored menu on the wall behind the counter offered Aussie dishes, such as meat pie, Vegemite sammies on toast, and beetroot hamburger with cheese. He also offered traditional American fare using

Australian-themed names such as Mini Wallaby Burgers, Dingo Dogs, and Roo Steaks.

I spotted Kate walking in. Every time I saw her, I got a thrill and wondered who that ravishing woman was and if she was seeing anyone. Then I smiled to myself and wondered what she saw in me.

"Hi, Kate."

"Hey, Grayson, you look good today." She said that a lot, but it was always nice to hear.

"That makes two of us."

After ordering and paying, we soon picked up our food in vintage, 1930s-style Coca-Cola serving trays with Ruby Ray branded liners and found a place to sit.

Kate seemed a bit down as she stared at her vegemite sandwich. At first, I wondered if she regretted ordering it. I mean, vegemite was basically brewer's yeast and veggies, right? I was giving it a hard pass, but she took a bite and seemed to like it. I wasn't even sure if I wanted to kiss her after that.

"Everything okay?" I asked while digging into Harry's Tiger Pie, a beef pie topped with mashed potatoes, overcooked peas, and gravy.

"I'm just missing Sheila. I can't believe she's gone. I really liked working with her."

"That must be hard. Everyone has been saying such nice things about her. I would've liked to have met her. It's a shame you had to get wrapped up in all this." I realized we never finished our earlier conversation. "So, you were going to tell me how you met Ray."

Kate was about to take another bite but put her sandwich down. "I was?"

"It sure seemed like it. What's up, Kate? This isn't like you."

"If you must know, one of Ray's friends is a guy I used to know named Chadrick Chabot. He recommended me for the job."

"Chadrick Chabot. Why do I know that name?" After a moment, it came to me. "Isn't he one of those inspirational celebrity spokespeople like Tony Robbins?"

"They're motivational speakers, and he goes by Anthony Robbins now." Wow, you think you know someone. I had no idea she was into this genre.

Frankly, it was a little scary.

"So, how do you know Chadrick? And why does he use a last name as his first name?"

"We used to date for a while." Kate was now turning red, a color I don't recall seeing on her. "But it wasn't serious," she was quick to add. "He told me he hated his name growing up because his classmates picked on him incessantly. But as he got older, he turned it into a source of strength, driving him to help others overcome their shortcomings. He's been living up to that legacy ever since."

Wow. It sounded like she had really bought into his line of bull. "Interesting. How did Ray know Chadrick?"

"When they were both just starting out, and Ray's business was doing better, he used to bring Chadrick in to do pep talks at company meetings. They've stayed in touch over the years." Kate suddenly frowned, which was an unusual event for her. I'd obviously struck a nerve. "Why are you grilling me about this? I don't want to talk about it anymore."

I put my pie down, too. This was so odd. We hardly ever argued, and it felt like a gut punch when we did. Better move on, I thought. "So, what's the latest about Sheila?"

Kate perked up a little. "Ray must be really sorry about accusing us of staging Sheila's murder so we could steal the ruby because he stops by my office every time he hears anything new. It's probably his way of saying he knows we didn't do it, and the police will soon figure it out."

"Yeah, so what did he say?"

"He said the Medical Examiner determined that Sheila had been poisoned. And it wasn't just any poison. It was something extremely toxic that causes paralysis, which means you slowly asphyxiate. Can you believe that? Who would do that to someone?"

"Yeah, killing someone so gruesomely just to divert attention from a ruby heist." I just shook my head in disgust.

Kate looked down and must have been imagining what Sheila experienced. "What a horrible way to die."

Then, the wheels in my head started turning. "What if the killer had a severe grudge against Sheila or even Ray? Maybe they were trying to send a message using an especially gruesome murder, and stealing the ruby was just a final affront?"

Kate raised an eyebrow. "Interesting theory. I hope Copeland thought of that. Anyway, the ME will be releasing the body soon. Ray wants to have Sheila cremated, so I recommended the crematorium where DeeDee works."

"Nicely done." I was about to add, 'kill two birds with one stone,' but then thought better of it.

"But get this." Kate was never blue for long, and it was good to see her roaring back. Was she enjoying the drama just a little bit too much? I wondered. "Copeland came back and re-interviewed Ray. He asked about the fish in the Aussie House tank. Ray told him the Great Barrier Reef Marine Museum contains over one thousand gallons of ocean water, coral, and a live tropical fish community imported directly from Australia, just like the sign says."

"He never stops promoting, does he?"

"Nope. Copeland asked him if it contained any poisonous fish, and Ray said he would never import anything potentially harmful to his guests. Copeland pressed him, and Ray admitted there were a lot of poisonous fish on the barrier reef, so something might have hitchhiked in with one of his shipments of Australian Rainbow Fish. But he said the marine museum was locked at all times to keep out the tourists except for feeding and cleaning. Copeland asked to inspect it, so Ray took him there, and they realized the lock looked authentic, but it didn't actually work. Anyone could have gotten in there."

This was all starting to make sense. "The Medical Examiner must have determined that Sheila had been poisoned by someone using the venom from one of the former occupants of the marine museum." 'Marine museum,' now she's got me saying it. "That would explain why there were no visible wounds or bruises on her body. My money is on a cone snail. They're one of the most toxic animals on earth. One could have easily been overlooked when restocking the tank because most are small. If someone did steal a snail from the tank, extract the venom, and use it to kill Sheila, they must have really hated her. Was Copeland looking at anyone in particular?"

"No, but you know how the police work. They're going to focus on family members, friends, disgruntled colleagues or lovers, sworn enemies, you know, the usual suspects."

I finished the pie and Coke and leaned back in my chair. "I don't know anything about importing wildlife, but it seems like whoever is packaging and shipping live Australian Rainbow Fish would double-check to make sure they weren't accidentally including anything highly venomous. If it was a cone snail, is there any chance that Ray obtained it illegally just to make the tank seem more Aussie-ish?" Not that anyone would notice, I thought.

"I know you've only met Ray briefly, but it's a matter of pride for him that people believe the Marine Museum is authentic, just like the ruby. I wouldn't put it past him."

Kate moved closer, so I figured there was more coming.

"That's not even the craziest part." She leaned in further to make sure no one could overhear. "Ray is underwater. He's been losing money for the past few years. If he doesn't turn things around, I'm not sure how much longer he can stay in business."

"No kidding. I guess the restaurants and the ruby museum have run their course."

"I know, right? Some strange things are going on with the financial reports, too."

Now I was getting interested. It didn't seem like slowly declining sales would be a reason for murder, but someone cooking the books sure would be. "Like what?"

Kate leaned back in her chair. "I'm afraid I can't give you any specifics, Grayson, due to the confidentiality agreement I signed. I should be able to give you a general idea as soon as I figure it out." Apparently, the dirt session had ended.

Then she got a bit pensive, and her voice got quieter. "Why can't I trace the money? And what is the deal with those cash flows? They don't make any sense. If I could only find a few more of Sheila's files, it would probably clear everything up."

Just then, Kate's phone buzzed, and she returned to the present. It was a text from Ray. "Ray is wondering when I'm coming back to the office. Do you mind if I let him know?"

"Not at all."

Kate texted that she was finishing lunch and would be back in a few minutes. "Hey, you should come with me. I'll bet Ray would like to meet you under more pleasant circumstances. He may even apologize for the accusations. But don't count on it."

"Sounds good. I'd like to look at some of the café tables in the club if you don't mind."

We cleared our table and headed back to the offices. Ray, who looked grim, met us at the main office door.

"Grayson met me for lunch at the Aussie House, and I thought I'd give him a proper tour this time."

Ray half-smiled as we shook hands. "Hi, Grayson." Then he got a serious look again and turned to Kate. "The tour will have to wait. There's a Detective Copeland here to see you. He'd like to meet you in your office. I told him you were out for lunch and I would send you over as soon as you returned. He's waiting for you outside your office."

That's not good. If he's waiting outside her office, he's probably looking for something specific, and he doesn't want to be accused of planting evidence, nor does he want anyone to go in before he's had an opportunity to search the place. The three of us walked down to Kate's office and met a small police team outside of it.

"Kate Larson, I'm Detective Aaron Copeland." He was a six-one black man in his mid-thirties in a navy blue suit, white shirt, and light-orange tie. Kate and I first met the Detective over a year ago, so his formal manner was a little unnerving. "We've received an anonymous tip that we've deemed credible." He handed her a set of documents. "I'm serving you with these warrants to search your office and electronic devices for evidence. I need access to your text messages and call history, as well as your emails and computer files. So, I need to take your cell phone and computer with me."

As she slowly reached for the phone in her back pocket, Kate looked at me with an expression that said, 'Do something.'

"Can I see the warrants, please?" I'd read somewhere that you have the legal right to read the warrants before a search begins, but wasting police time while exercising that right would not help your cause. You also have the right to request that the search wait until your attorney arrives. Unfortunately, despite my recent tendency to investigate the odd murder or two, I haven't gotten around to retaining one. I was pretty sure Kate didn't have one either, not that it would do any good. I couldn't imagine what she would be hiding in her office for them to find.

Kate handed them to me, and I scanned the contents. I'd never seen search warrants before and was surprised at their scope. In addition to the devices, they covered carriers for phone, text, and cell tower data, app data from social media posts and messages, and any other app that may have a messaging or GPS-type feature, such as a gaming app where chat was provided. Any worthy perpetrator would know not to use their phone's chat because that would be the first place the police would look. But there were so many chat apps in use these days, such as WhatsApp or Signal, and so many others that included chatting, such as Facebook Messenger, Teams, or Discord, that a broad search was mandatory. I wondered if there was a bulletin board in a police HQ's back office where particularly juicy or bizarre texts would be posted for entertainment.

The warrants were so interesting that I had to fight the urge to study them in detail. But there was no time and knowing Copeland, I was certain it would be legit. "Looks like you have to turn your phone and laptop over, Kate." I thought it best not to mention that her personal and work messages would also soon be exposed. Good thing we kept our romantic messages below a PG rating. She handed her phone to Copeland, who placed it in an evidence bag, which he then sealed and handed to one of his associates, who must have been an evidence tech.

"Mr. Dyle, please wait right here. This shouldn't take too long." I knew we had the right to monitor the search, and so did Copeland. I got the impression he wanted us there so we would serve as witnesses when he found something incriminating. Ray stayed to watch the show, too. "Ms. Larson, I'd like to collect your computer, please." I glanced at Kate, who had a defiant look but was fidgeting nervously nonetheless.

Kate's office was about eight by ten feet with an average-sized metal desk in the middle, a credenza along the wall to the left, and windows overlooking the parking lot to the right. The usual accumulation of papers, knick-knacks, pencils, and pens was on the desk. I was pleased to see a framed picture of Kate and me, too. We'd been strolling around Lake Nokomis, and she'd asked a friendly-looking passerby to take our picture with her phone. It caught us both at just the right angle, with sailboats and a vivid blue sky in the background. It was my favorite picture of us together.

She entered the office and went around the desk, where she unhooked her laptop from the monitor and reluctantly handed it to the detective. He placed it in another bag, which he sealed and gave to the tech. The smug look on the detective's face gave me the impression this was some kind of payback for me showing him up during our previous encounter.

Copeland put on heavy-duty rubber gloves and scanned the desktop but must not have seen anything of interest as he opened the next desk drawers. He rooted around the center drawer and then moved to the three side drawers. He found something small at the bottom of the largest drawer, withdrew it, and held it out for all of us to see. It looked like someone had softened a sheet of brightly colored plastic with a stained-glass pattern and wrapped it around a small funnel.

"So, it was a cone snail." I accidentally blurted out. Kate threw me an angry frown that said, 'Not helpful.' Maybe not, but this confirmed my theory about how Sheila had been killed. No wonder he was using industrial-strength equipment—he didn't want to be poisoned. He took a small bag made of thick plastic from his suit coat pocket, dropped the snail into it, and sealed the top.

Kate's eyes went wide open. "You have got to be kidding me. Was that the tip you received, that I hid a cone snail in my desk after using the poison to kill Sheila? How dimwitted would I have to be to do that?"

Following typical police etiquette, Copeland completely ignored the outburst. "Ms. Larson, I'd like you to accompany me downtown, please." She looked at me and raised her eyebrows, apparently hoping I would conjure up some brilliant way to stop this from happening, but I had nothing. "Since you were there when both the murder and the theft were discovered, I'd like you to join us, Mr. Dyle."

I knew protesting was futile, but I felt it necessary to say something. "I don't suppose it would help to say that neither Kate nor I had anything to do with the poisoning, the murder, or the theft of the ruby."

Copeland stared at me momentarily as if to question my sanity and ignored the comment. "My team has been researching this little guy," he said, holding up the bag. "They are highly toxic." To underscore his point, he produced a larger, thinner bag, put the small snail bag into it, then took off his rubber gloves, stuffed them in, and tied a knot in the top. "And we're checking with the Fish and Wildlife Service to determine if importing or possessing cone snails in this country is legal. If not," he looked at Ray, "I will be referring this item to them."

Ray, who had previously been trying to blend into the background, suddenly came back to life. "Okay, Detective, yes, we have a very authentic marine museum, and all of the aquatic life is native to Australia, which is in keeping with our theme. They are all shipped here directly. I mean, look at that thing. It's so small it must have accidentally been included with a previous shipment. I certainly wouldn't want one, and who would ship it to me anyway?"

Copeland just scoffed. "Someone out here knew what it was and how to use it." He looked back at Kate and me. "Okay, let's go."

Kate and I followed him to his unmarked but easily spotted police vehicle, and he drove us to the Police Department headquarters in Saint Paul. I thought it was probably best not to say anything and was seriously considering lawyering up. I figured one of the lawyers from Kate's previous firm would be willing to help us.

But Kate couldn't help herself. "Look, Detective, this is a big waste of your time. I just started working at Ruby Ray's a few weeks ago. I've never even heard of a cone snail before today, let alone know how to get anything out of it without poisoning myself. Why would I kill Sheila anyway? She and Ray are the ones who hired me for this position." Copeland didn't respond.

Then Kate said, more to me than Copeland, "The funny thing is the Supper Club is now fully booked for at least a couple of months out even though we haven't reopened it yet. People have been calling the Aussie House to make reservations at the club and asking who the next swing girl will be." I wondered if Kate realized this made it look like Ray had a motive, although killing your wife in a public setting to drive traffic to your restaurant seemed pretty extreme, even for a flamboyant guy like him.

* * *

After being grilled for over two hours by Detective Copeland and others, Kate and I were finally allowed to go home. Copeland offered to have a policeman give us a ride back to Ruby Ray's in a squad car, but neither of us wanted anything more to do with the police that day. I set up an Uber instead.

"Well, that was brutal," I said to Kate with a long sigh as we waited for our ride to arrive.

"No kidding. I thought I held my own, though, as much as they tried to get me to implicate myself. Of course, it wasn't that difficult when you actually are innocent." Kate reached for her phone and must have suddenly realized her situation regarding technology. "Dammit, giving up my laptop is bad enough, but how am I going to get in touch with my clients without my phone?"

Based on the warrant, I guessed it would take a few months for the police even to consider returning her phone or laptop, but I didn't want to make an already bad situation worse. "You'll probably have to get a new laptop and one of those cheap burner phones, too. Although you should probably tell your clients your phone was lost or stolen instead of saying the police confiscated it because you are their number one suspect in an investigation where you are being accused of killing another one of your clients." Even though I said it with a smile, a sharp elbow to the ribs told me the last comment might have gone too far.

After a few minutes, Kate said, "I wonder if Ray will want to renegotiate the contract due to the increased traffic." I gave her a quizzical look, and she realized I needed more context. "Ray and Sheila always hoped one of their kids would take over the business so they could retire, but neither of them is interested. Ray's been trying to sell the business and the property for a few years and finally has a firm offer. It's a lot less than he was hoping for, but he'll probably sign the contract so he can finally retire and get the restaurants off his back."

"From what I know of Ray, he is shrewd enough to know the current notoriety won't last. And it will be difficult to repeat." Kate nodded in agreement. "Do you know who the offer is from or what the terms are?"

"Nope. The only thing Ray told me is that the offer expires on June 13, which is about a month from now. Not a lot of time if it means signing your life away." Kate looked down and frowned. "Buyers sometimes have their own CFOs. I wonder if the new owners will have a contract position for me."

Kate seemed lost in her concerns, which gave me time to return to one of mine. Her revelation that she used to date a motivational speaker named Chadrick Chabot had been weighing on me. It wasn't like her to keep secrets, and the degree to which she suddenly got upset and wanted to change the subject when I asked about him told me there was a lot more to learn here. I'd never felt threatened by another guy's interest in Kate, and I didn't want to start now, and it was getting harder to avoid idle speculation. But this didn't seem like an opportune time to begin grilling her again, as she put it, so I didn't say anything. Kate filled the gap. "Anyway, I checked with my mom. We are both open for lunch on Monday, May 22. Does that work for you?"

There was that question again. One thing I liked about Kate was that she had never nagged me about anything. This was coming close, but I decided to let it go. And, I had to admit that, based on our relationship's current trajectory, I needed to plan a road trip to Rochester for Kate and me to meet my mother, too. I realized I still needed to research Elizabeth and made a mental note to do so ASAP. "I think so, but I better check my schedule. I'll text you to confirm."

"Not until I get a new phone, you won't," she said with an ironic grin.

Chapter Five

Friday, May 12

I was at the office early Friday morning, trying to forget about crime and misadventure and focus on activities that could be billed to clients, just to mix things up. Paul shot me a dirty look when he arrived, probably because I hadn't returned to the office the previous afternoon. As I was leaving, I told him I was having lunch with Kate, and then I planned to gather valuable input for our new design project by inspecting the café tables to see why the legs were failing. He didn't say anything, but he probably suspected she convinced me to take the rest of the day off. I thought about telling him what had happened but decided against it as it would just get him going again. It was best just to move on.

My phone kept pinging to say new text messages were arriving. I tried to ignore it, but after the eighth one, I caved. The texts were from DeeDee, who was getting increasingly frantic because I had not been responding. A new text arrived pleading for me to come over immediately as she had urgent news. I really didn't want to leave the office, but I'd always had a soft spot for her. I figured a quick visit would only take about ninety minutes round trip. So, I texted back, saying I would be there shortly, and she texted her profuse thanks. I assumed she wanted to tell me about some new celebrity relative, so I packed up my laptop to take along. There was no way I would sit there while she surfed the web using her ten-year-old PC, which would probably be as slow-moving as the car in front of you when the traffic light changed to green. I filled my travel mug with coffee and headed out, making sure to avoid Paul's office.

On my way to the car, I texted my brother Dean. **Heading to DeeDee's place now**

As a major technophile, Dean always had the latest gear, and it was always within reach. He quickly texted back. **You're a glutton for punishment, aren't you?**

She's panicking about something - care to join me?

There was a pause before his next text. It was not like him. Maybe he was considering it, I thought. Then I realized he had probably gotten distracted by a bug in some code he'd been working on or something like that.

A few minutes later, he replied. **Nope, I'm good.**

That figured. Still, it would be good to discuss the investigation with him. **Want to meet for coffee afterward?** He would know I meant the coffee shop just down the block from my office.

Sure, let me know when you leave her place.

* * *

Twenty minutes later, I was pulling onto the gravel driveway next to her house. DeeDee lived in a small gray bungalow with a detached one-car garage and a small deck on the front. I walked to the front door and rang the bell. She must have been waiting near her door because it opened almost immediately.

"Grayson, thank you so much for coming over!" She was wearing a dark blue dress with a tight pattern of small white flowers. The combination seemed to form one of those Magic Eye puzzles that were popular in the nineties, where you could find a hidden shape if you unfocused your eyes properly. I thought it best not to do a bug-eyed stare at her dress to see if it would work. She stood on her toes for an awkward hug. "Come on in. I've just made a fresh pot of coffee."

I'd visited her home once before to discuss our DNA results and family tree, and I noted that her vast collection of funeral urns was still prominently displayed. There were at least ten in the living room alone, each on an individual doily, with fake plastic flowers and various religious items affixed. It was not a place for being squeamish about the deceased.

I'd also learned that DeeDee took her missionary causes seriously and sent small donations to many religious organizations every month. Unfortunately, they thanked her by sending more religious artifacts, which she could not bring herself to throw away. Her home was festooned with them. Most of the urns had plastic rosaries draped over them, and some had holy cards, each carefully laminated in plastic, leaning against them. She'd previously unloaded a large box of them on me, and I was determined not to let that happen again.

"Sit right here at the table, dear. I've got your coffee all ready, just like you like it."

The curio cabinets lining the dining room contained more decorated urns and left little room to maneuver. I had to squat and scoot across the chair to sit at the dining room table while trying not to disturb the copious newspaper clippings, pictures, and scraps of paper with notes scribbled on them. I knew this was her treasure trove of family tree information. I put down my backpack and took a sip of coffee. "Thanks, DeeDee." I'd already had my fill, but it was easier just to accept the coffee so as not to risk breaking her heart.

Heavy velvet drapes stopped every last ray of sunshine from entering the dimly lit dining room. They were initially a deep purple, but a dusty coating made them look more lilac. It must have been difficult for her to vacuum them. I wondered what their purpose was – did she want to keep out the sunshine or a neighbor's prying eyes? I started to take the laptop out of the backpack. "So, tell me about our new relative."

She was obviously distraught, and I could see the tears that she must have been holding back starting to form in her eyes. But she gave me a quizzical look. "New relative? This is not a time for jokes, Grayson."

"Sorry, you didn't say why you wanted to meet, so I assumed you had some new ancestry information."

"No, it has nothing to do with that. And I didn't want to tell you anything over the phone in case the line was bugged."

At first, I thought she was teasing me, and it was all I could do not to roll my eyes. Then I noticed the worry lines on her forehead were more deeply creased than I'd ever seen them, and her face was full of tension. Holy crap, she seriously thought whatever she was about to tell me was such a deep dark secret that some person or group unknown would be interested in hearing it. I put the laptop away since we wouldn't need it and turned my full attention to her. "What's going on, DeeDee?"

DeeDee steadied herself and said, "That nice Detective Copeland rang my bell at eight this morning. He said he had questions about Sheila Dixon, so I let him in and made him coffee. I offered him some fresh rolls, but he said he didn't want anything to eat. I thought that was very strange. He's always looked a little too skinny to me. Anyway, he started asking me about the cremation. Was there anything unusual about the body, and did I notice anything afterward? Well, of course, I said everything was normal. I mean, what was I going to say?"

I wondered where Copeland was going with the questions but didn't want to interrupt.

"It's a good thing it was me who cremated Sheila because there was something unusual. People want their loved one's ashes to look like a nice fine powder. But that's not what they look like when they come out of the crematory. Some of the ashes are quite coarse, and there are still pieces of bone here and there. So, after the oven has cooled, I have to put the remains in the Cremulator to pulverize them. But I have to check for surgical or dental metal first. Otherwise, the gears can get clogged. Only this time, as I was sifting through the ashes, I found this." DeeDee handed me a large red stone. "It must have been inside of her somewhere."

It was about an inch and a half long by an inch wide and could be none other than the gemstone that was Ray's namesake. It must have been the infamous Poona Ruby, the largest ruby found in Australia on record. I brought the stone to the light to appreciate the color and clarity, then realized where DeeDee said it had been and decided it would be better to examine it while it was on the table.

I had been studying her face and noticed the tension broke as soon as she let go of the stone. I thought about clutching it to my bosom and screaming, 'My precious' while imitating Gollum's voice, but this didn't seem like the right time for levity. She seemed to trust me, and I didn't want to disappoint her, but what would I do with a hot stone with such a dodgy provenance? Bury it in the backyard or hide it in a cave in the Misty Mountains, maybe?

DeeDee continued with her story. "It looks like Ray's ruby, and since it made it through the cremation process, I believe it's the real thing."

I sat back, trying to take this all in. "So, if the stone was hidden somewhere in Sheila's body when she was brought to your facility, the Medical Examiner must have missed it during the autopsy, right?"

"That's what's been troubling me. Since Sheila was murdered, they would have done a thorough postmortem examination and should have found something this big. The only thing I can figure out is that she was forced to swallow the stone, and it got caught in her GI tract because the poison slowed down her system. The MEs are so overworked these days with the city's budget cuts. Maybe they figured there was no need to cut it open and skipped that step."

As unlikely as that was, it was the only answer that made sense.

The worry lines in DeeDee's forehead scrunched up again. "The thing is, I just got scared and lied to the police about this. If I turn it in now, it will look like I was hiding it. That's why I want you to take it."

"What?!" I figured this was where the discussion was going, and my temper started flaring. I didn't want to take it out on DeeDee, because she was as much an innocent bystander as I was. But still. "Wait a minute, what am I supposed to do with it? It will look even weirder if I turn it in. Where would I have gotten it from? I can't say I just found it in the parking lot at the mall. And I couldn't tell them I got it from you, or you'd be right back in the frame. It will look like Kate and I had stolen it and then decided to turn it in to avoid any further suspicion."

Tears formed again in DeeDee's eyes, which was the last thing either of us needed.

"You have to help me, Grayson. I don't know what else to do or who I can turn to."

Why does nobody call Dean in these situations? "No worries, DeeDee. I'll take care of it."

She managed to smile. "Thank you so much, Grayson. I knew I could count on you."

"You're welcome," I said with a slight nod while having no idea what to do with the damn thing.

That seemed to relieve her a bit further. "Oh, there's one other thing you should know. As soon as the body was released, Ray called me to say he didn't want his wife to suffer from any more indignity, and he demanded I do the cremation as quickly as possible. I told him we always do everything we can to meet our client's needs, and I would be happy to start the process right away. Then, he warned me not to tell the police about his request."

"Oh, that's not good." DeeDee and I stared at each other briefly while we sipped our coffee. "I'm glad you didn't say anything to Copeland, as it makes Ray look guilty."

"You think?" For DeeDee to be snarky, she must be distraught.

Why did I care if the police moved on from Kate to Ray as their prime suspect? He was probably on the shortlist already. Maybe it would have been good for DeeDee to tell Copeland after all. I thought I'd run that idea by her. "DeeDee, what if you called Copeland back and said you remembered that Ray asked you to perform the cremation as quickly as possible?"

DeeDee was aghast and looked at me in horror. "Oh no. I could never do that. I swore to Ray that I would take his secret to my grave."

It was an odd turn of phrase, but I got the idea. "Okay, never mind." Then, another thought occurred to me as I sipped more of the coffee I didn't want in the first place. "How secure is the crematorium? Does it have surveillance cameras?"

"We have an alarm system that gets turned on at night, but there are no cameras. That would be inappropriate for our clients. Why do you ask?"

"Whoever hid the ruby in Sheila at the restaurant might have been waiting for you to finish the processing work so they could sneak in to steal it again."

Her eyes widened. "Oh my. I didn't think of that. Am I going to be in danger?"

I didn't mean to upset her further. "No, they probably didn't know you were going to process the body so quickly, so they weren't there to break in." It was all I could think of at the moment, and she seemed to relax a bit, so it must have placated her.

I desperately wanted to avoid another "oh, there's one other thing you should know" moment and decided it was time to bale. "Well, I have to get back to work. Thanks for the coffee, DeeDee."

"Are you sure you don't want to stay for lunch? I can whip up some lovely fish sandwiches in a jiffy."

"Maybe next time, DeeDee." Only one guilt trip per visit, I thought as I hugged her, grabbed my laptop, and headed out, my entire body vibrating from too much caffeine. As I got in the car, I realized I had escaped without a care package of religious iconography to dispose of, which made me smile.

* * *

Clear, I texted Dean from the car. **See you soon**

Sounds good, was the reply.

The Caribou Coffee, where we usually met, was three short blocks east on Lake Street from my apartment and office building, so I got there early and placed our standard order of a large light roast for me and a dark roast for him. I was about to take out my laptop when Dean arrived.

Dean was dressed in a black polo shirt, light blue jeans, and white sneakers, while I wore a light blue polo shirt, black jeans, and white sneakers, which must have produced a weird mirror-image effect as our resemblance was so close. Even before Dean and I submitted spit samples to an ancestry website proving we had the same biological parents, we were obviously true brothers. When we were kids, strangers at the grocery store would stop Mom and ask if she was exhausted from raising identical twins. Dean's growth spurt at ten stopped those questions, but we still looked remarkably similar, with green eyes, chestnut blond hair, and the same prominent jawline. He inherited our father's height, while I never reached five foot ten.

Of the two of us, Dean was the only one to have taken the plunge. He married early, and things seemed to have been going great. But something happened. I still don't know what. I guess there are things that even brothers don't share. The divorce was amicable, but I could tell that he thought he'd be married for the duration, and it made him feel like he'd failed one of life's biggest tests. After considering his priorities, he decided a modest lifestyle suited him better. He let his ex-wife keep their upscale home in the swanky Twin Cities suburb of Edina and moved into a relatively pedestrian split-level ranch house in Eagan, a suburb on the south side of the Twin Cities metro.

He didn't mind the twenty-minute drive from his place, and he liked this location because it got him out of his suburban existence. And I suspected he planned to hit Lake Bde Maka Ska after we wrapped up to enjoy a beautiful summer day in Minnesota and possibly meet the girl of his dreams on the walking path. Hope springs eternal, I guess.

He clocked our drinks, grabbed them, and brought them to the café table where I was sitting, along the window by the parking lot. The table shifted as Dean put down his cup, and coffee sloshed out. My first reaction was to give him crap for being so clumsy, but then I realized this was further proof of the wobbly café table plague that Paul and I needed to cure. Dean grabbed some napkins off the counter and started wiping up the spill. I folded my napkin and stuck it under one of the feet to stop the rocking.

"These tables suck," said Dean.

I just smiled. "That, my friend, is the muddle of money, the disorder of dollars, the jumble of…something. I'll have to get back to you on that one." Then I explained the table idea, and Dean's face lit up.

"You may be on to something this time." This time? I decided to let that go. "So, how did it go with DeeDee?"

I explained the situation to Dean and asked him what I should do with the ruby, hoping for a brilliant idea like chucking it in the bushes in front of Ray's office building.

He took a long drink of coffee, and I was hoping he was working on a brilliant plan. "Hell, if I know," was all he eventually said. "Maybe you should turn it in and say you found it in the bushes in front of the building?" It was weird how alike we thought sometimes.

"Nah, that won't work. Copeland would assume it was Kate, me, or both of us who had stolen the ruby and were now trying to turn it back in to avoid suspicion. Who else would go through an elaborate process to steal the stone only to return it?"

Then I described our latest adventure with Copeland searching Kate's office, interrogating us both, and accusing her of murder. After Dean stopped snickering, he said, "Okay, yeah, maybe you shouldn't turn it in. Why don't you leave it somewhere and phone in a tip?"

That thought occurred to me at the same time, but I rejected it. "It's the same issue – Copeland will still assume we did it, and we just copied the anonymous tip idea from someone else. Besides, if the cops have the stone, they will make a big announcement to take credit for recovering it, and it's probably best that the killer doesn't know that the ruby has been found."

"Why is that?"

"If the killer didn't know Sheila was going to be cremated or didn't know the stone would be found during the cremation process, they probably believe they've gotten away with the whole thing. This will make them less wary and easier to find." I had a small smile of satisfaction as I took a sip of coffee. I expected Dean to say something complimentary. Instead, he started rubbing his temples.

"Oh God, here we go. You're going to start investigating, aren't you?"

It was scary how well he could read me, but that was not the reaction I had hoped for. "No, of course not. *We're* going to investigate. I can't do this without you."

"I should have known you were up to something when you invited me to coffee. You know I can't—"

"...do anything untoward. Yes, I know, you've told me that a hundred times." As a home automation consultant, Dean had access to his client's residences or offices, and he sometimes needed to access them when the owners were out of town. So, he was obsessed with maintaining his reputation as a trustworthy professional. This was admirable, right up to the point where it interfered with making sure justice would prevail for my girlfriend. And Sheila, too, of course. "Huh, well, that's unfortunate. I thought you liked Kate."

Dean scoffed. "I like her a lot. What does that have to do with it?"

"I was hoping you'd help me clear her name, that's all. No big deal." A little old-fashioned Catholic guilt went a long way with Dean, and I could tell he was on the brink of caving in. "Look, all I'm asking is that you help me from behind the scenes, just like last time. You know, researching, reconnoitering, or hacking into something." I knew he loved all of these things and wouldn't want to be left out of the action, especially when he thought he would be twice as effective as me in doing them.

"Fine. But I'm not doing anything untoward."

"Agreed." I paused for effect. "Now that you're on board with the investigation, would you mind hanging onto this?" Dean had been finishing his coffee and just about sprayed dark roast all over me as I handed him the ruby.

"Damn it, Grayson. Don't wave that thing around in public." He palmed it and put his hand under the table. I was a bit surprised. When we were kids, he would have chucked it back at me.

"Seriously, I can't hide it in my home or office in case Copeland gets another anonymous call and decides to search them. And there's no one else I can trust with it. Besides, he's not going to rummage through your place. You're too far removed from things. He'd never get a warrant."

The frown on Dean's face told me he had given in. He snuck the ruby into his pocket. "Whatever."

Mission accomplished. "Thanks, Dean. I appreciate it. Well, I better get back to work."

As we got up to toss our empties away, I overheard him mumbling to himself. "Reconnoitering? Who talks like that?"

I started walking down Lake Street back to the office but flagged down Dean before he left the parking lot. I put my backpack on the ground and leaned in through the passenger window. "Have you ever heard of someone named Chadrick Chabot?"

Dean thought about it for a minute. Then realization spread across his face. "Isn't he one of those 'hip-hip-hooray for life' guys who go around separating people from their money?"

"Yep, that's him."

"Why do you ask?"

I was embarrassed to admit this, but I went ahead anyway. "Chadrick is a motivational speaker Kate used to date. It turns out he has tons of followers who seem to love him. I can't figure them out. I know I'm probably just paranoid, but I keep wondering how well I'm going to compete with this guy."

Always the practical one, Dean said, "It's not like you never dated anyone who was really attractive, right? Anyone over sixteen is likely to have a dating history, some of which may be embarrassing and some noteworthy, so what's the issue?"

I regretted mentioning anything and wanted to get off the subject. "Yeah, I guess you're right."

"Do you want me to do a deep dive on Chadrick and see what I can find out? A guy like that is bound to have some dirt in his past. Maybe we can figure out why they broke up?"

"No, it's not worth your time."

I waved goodbye, and Dean took off. As I grabbed my backpack, the zipper opened up, and an infestation of religious icons spilled out over the parking lot. I don't know how she did it, but DeeDee managed to pawn off more of her swag on me. It looked like another trip to my favorite dumpster was in order.

Chapter Six

A t my request, Kate set up a time for me to meet with Ray to discuss the events of the past week. I arrived at Ruby Ray Enterprises a few minutes early for our ten a.m. meeting and let myself into the main entrance. Ray met me there and showed me up the stairs to his office. He offered me a coffee or water on the way, but I turned him down. We walked through a few rows of cubicles, and now that there was no crisis to deal with, I could finally look around. Unlike the workspaces of our office staff, which were covered with all manner of design-oriented bric-a-brac and tchotchkes from dozens of trade shows and conferences, these offices were rather spartan. It looked like some desks had been occupied for years as they were covered with family pictures and various office supplies. Still, others looked like temporary visitors were using them as they had only pads of paper and pencils next to the computer keyboards and monitors.

Ray's office, on the other hand, was colorful and jam-packed with Aussie artifacts. Along with the oversized desk and the large windows with the phenomenal view of both downtowns, there were posters of Sydney's famous opera house, several other Australian cities, and the Outback on the walls. The credenza and filing cabinets were covered with shells, fishing nets, starfish, and even an authentic-looking oilskin outback hat that I was sure would make me look dashing. The desk was covered with the usual assortment of paper and pens and pictures of his family and what looked like Ray posing with various celebrities. I would be nervous working in this disarray, but Ray relished it. "Don't mind the clutter. Any of the thingos we retire from the museum or the restaurants seem to end up here." He still had a slight accent, which was really kind of pleasant.

"No worries, mate." I blurted out before I could catch myself and immediately regretted it. At least I hadn't tried to imitate his inflection. Ray either didn't notice or was used to visitors quoting what may or may not be actual Aussie phrases, as he didn't react.

We exchanged a few more pleasantries, and Ray got down to business. "I'm glad you came out, Grayson. I've been recollecting the night of the murder, and it was unfair of me to accuse you and Kate like that."

I guess that was an apology of sorts. "That's okay, Ray. You'd just lost your wife, and I'm sure you were upset."

"Too right. Thanks for understanding. I do feel bad about teeing you up with the coppers, though. I hope that hasn't been rough."

"It's all good." Was it really all good, I wondered? Ray didn't sound too contrite. If he knew the number of times the police had questioned me for simply being a spectator to a crime, he would have been more apologetic. But, if I called him on it, it would shut down the interview. "We've dealt with them before, so I wouldn't worry about it. I have some questions for you if that's okay."

"Kate said you had a few things to chat about."

I decided not to mince words. "Now that you know Kate and I are innocent, who do you suspect is the murderer?"

"Couldn't say. No one I can think of. Sheila was a real beauty, and everyone loved her. And we don't have any known enemies if you're going to ask me that next."

Well, check that box with a no. "Okay. What about security cameras? I thought I saw some covering the parking lot. Are there any others on the property?"

"A few years ago, some of our patron's cars were getting broken into, so we installed a few cameras on the light poles. Truth is, they're dummies that don't record anything. But I got the nice, high-quality fakes with the blinking red lights, so they look real. They worked too because the break-ins mostly stopped, so I didn't see any need to install real ones."

"Makes sense." But your decision probably has more to do with your current funding situation, I thought. "Ray, as I said, I've worked with the police before..."

"Kate told me how you solved your parents' murders when the police couldn't do it. Good onya."

"Thanks. That's what I'm trying to say—we can't always wait for the police to solve a murder. They tend to go through their established process, and sometimes, that just doesn't work. Like in this case, they've had a rush to judgment that Kate and I are somehow guilty and won't let it go. I'm concerned they won't look at enough other suspects to find the real killer. I'd like to meet with your staff and probably your family to ask a few questions and see what I can find independently."

Ray looked at me for a minute as if considering my offer. Finally, he decided. "Can't see how that would hurt anything. Kate's been talking you up lately, and you seem like a real smart guy. I'll let our team know you might be poking around a bit and not to get their nose out of joint if you wantta talk to 'em."

"Thanks, Ray. I appreciate it. By the way, what's the real story behind the ruby? I know it's been on display in the Aussie Museum, and I've heard one of the biggest ever found in Australia. Is that right?"

Ray was suddenly beaming. "Righto! I found it in the Aga Khan Mine in Western Australia in 1987. A lot of my mates thought that area had been mined out. But I spotted a rock formation I'd worked in the past, and I figured there might still be some life left in it. I worked that line for days until I found the right vein. It wasn't more than an hour or two, and I had it in my hands—the great Poona Ruby."

Ray was obviously very proud, and his enthusiasm was contagious. It made me want to grab his oilskin hat and jump on a plane to the Land Down Under. Unfortunately, that was not going to happen anytime soon. Maybe I could talk Kate into a vacation there in the next year or two. "Any idea what it's worth?" I was fairly sure Ray would not consider it a tacky question.

"Well, it's invaluable, of course. And you never really know what something's worth until you sell it. But I've had appraisers say it would fetch well over a million U.S. dollars at auction."

"That certainly is impressive. I have a few other quest—"

Ray was on a roll and wasn't about to be sidetracked. "I've got big plans to rebuild the business. My finance guy, Scott Dimond, is going to introduce me to some marketing people to revitalize the brand. Get us connected to the millennial crowd, you know, those websites the kids use like that Tick Talk thing—that's where the money is these days. They'd come flocking in if they only knew about the museum." An idea must have popped into his head. "Tell you what. I've got a few minutes to spare. How about we do a quick run-through? You can see everything up close and personal."

Oh boy. That sounded like someone offering to show you all of the two-hundred-plus selfies they took on their European vacation. And, with the main attraction safely tucked away in my brother's house, I wondered what was left to see. But I had more questions to ask, so I couldn't really say no. "Sure. That sounds great."

"Great! Let's go." We went down the stairs to the first floor and walked around to the museum's front entrance. Ray opened the door with a key and hit a few switches on the wall to turn on the lights. We entered a large room with multiple displays that were highlighted by spotlights.

"I'm not going to give you the full tour, Grayson. For that, I'd have to charge you $12.50," he said with a smile. "I just want to give you a feeling for the place."

Thank God for small favors.

Ray walked us through the room, pointing out various items, including dinosaur bones, fossils, and the boats and nets used by Australia's Salt Water People. His knowledge of the subject matter was impressive. Either he was a master showman who could whip up excitement in a crowd with his sheer enthusiasm, or he really did get a thrill from the stuff in his museum after all these years.

He had an impressive display of Australian wildlife, such as the iconic Koala, the extinct Tasmanian Tiger, deadly snakes, and giant spiders. "These are just replicas, of course, but the kids love the animals. The more dangerous, the better. They're our best-selling items in the gift shop."

As we approached the back of the room, a large sign with an arrow pointing to the right stated, 'This Way to Ray's Famous Poona Ruby!'

We entered the next room, and Ray turned the lights on to reveal what could only be described as an anti-chamber. According to the signs, there were large acrylic cases that contained the prospecting equipment that Ray had used all those years ago. "This is the actual gear I used to find the ruby." There was camping gear, mining tools, and various apparel, including a mannequin that had been adorned with a blue cotton shirt, jeans with oilskin chaps, a bush ranger jacket, leather boots, and an oilskin hat. It was holding a pickax and was about to strike a vein of reddish material in the ground beneath it. This must have been a recreation of the moment Ray found the ruby.

Ray pointed to it and laughed. "Not sure I'd fit into that get-up these days."

Another large sign over the door leading to the next room simply said 'Ruby Room.' The idea was to build excitement for the final reveal of the infamous ruby, and it sort of worked if you were into that sort of thing. It probably helped if you were twelve years old, too.

We entered the final room, and Ray didn't bother turning on the lights as we walked by the case that would have held the ruby. "Nothing to see here, unfortunately. Well, that's the tour. How'd ya like it?"

"That was a lot of fun. Thanks, Ray. I'll have to come back to learn more about Australia."

"Yeah, you should. Well, let's go up and see if Kate's gotten here. It'll be faster if we take the back way."

Ray led us to a set of double doors that opened into a large room that must have been the museum's storage area. A strong, musty smell hit me immediately. He didn't seem to notice, but I had to stifle an impulse to cover my nose to avoid offending him.

"Don't mind the mess back here. We're just like the Smithsonian. We only display a small portion of our collection and rotate the pieces to keep the museum fresh so people will come back again and again."

It was great to hear that Ray had aspirations for his business, but based on what Kate told me about its current state of affairs, the notion that anyone would return to the museum after their first visit was reality-free.

The room contained over a dozen heavy-duty storage racks, each of which held a bewildering array of items and a row of pallets that held numerous larger objects of interest. It would have been fun to look at a few of them, but Ray was hell-bent on returning to his office, and we tore through the room at top speed. He burst through the double doors at the other end of the room and held one open for me. As I was trying to catch up, something on one of the shelves caught my eye, primarily because it didn't have a thick layer of dust like most of the other artifacts.

"Hang on a second, Ray. I want to see something." Tucked away at the back of the shelf was a small fish tank containing a couple of pairs of tweezers and some small glass vials covered with a plastic liner.

"Ray, I know what this is. After discovering Sheila had been poisoned, I watched a few online videos about cone snails. When it senses a fish nearby, it spears the prey with a hollow tube and uses it to inject its venom. This paralyzes the fish so the snail can reel it in and swallow it whole. The gear in this tank was used to extract the venom from the cone snail."

Ray was incredulous. "What? No way. Not here in my museum."

"Yes, Ray. Right here." I pointed to a pair of tweezers. "These hold a small bait fish, so the cone snail will try to attack it." Then, I pointed to the glass vials. "As soon as the cone snail deploys its spear, the bait fish is withdrawn and replaced with one of these. The snail spears the plastic top and injects its venom into the tube instead of the fish. It's pretty simple, as long as you are patient enough." I noticed one of the vials had a thick liquid in it. "Look at this one, Ray. It still has venom in it. We would have found the snail here if someone hadn't planted it in Kate's office."

No wonder the murderer used the museum warehouse to extract the venom and store the rest of his supply. No one would bother them back here, no matter how long it took. They probably thought they had found the perfect hiding place. I was suddenly happy that Ray had been so exuberant about his museum.

Ray frowned as he examined the tank and then looked at me. "I think you're right, Grayson. Can't believe I didn't notice that sitting in plain sight."

He was about to pick it up when I stopped him. "You should probably let Copeland know about this so he can check it for prints."

Ray nodded. "Righto."

"And, we probably don't want to alert the murderer by announcing we've found their stash of poison. You should have Copeland visit after hours when everyone else has gone home."

He smiled. "You're always detecting, aren't you, mate?"

Was that a compliment or a complaint, I wondered?

Chapter Seven

Tuesday, May 16

Ray led us back to the second-floor offices, where we stopped at the front desk. A woman sat there working at a computer. "Have you met our office manager, Cheryl?" he asked me.

"No, I haven't had the pleasure."

"You must be Grayson Dyle," said Cheryl with a weary look before Ray could make a formal introduction. She wore a light yellow short-sleeved blouse with dark blue jeans and looked about thirty years old, although her somewhat jaded demeanor made her seem older.

"You must be Cheryl," I answered in a weak attempt at humor. We shook hands.

"Grayson is our resident detective," Ray said. He was almost beaming, which was a bit embarrassing for me.

"Have you seen Kate?" I asked her.

"Nope. She's not in yet."

"Okay, thanks."

Ray turned to me. "Well, it was good talking to you, Grayson."

I didn't want to wear out my welcome, but I didn't know when I'd get another opportunity to talk to Ray one-on-one, so I decided to press on. "I was hoping I could ask you a few more questions."

He looked a bit surprised but finally agreed. "Let's go back to my office." I followed him there, and after we got settled, Ray said, "Fire away."

"I've heard so much about Sheila, and I'm sorry for your loss, but would you be willing to tell me about her? What was she like?"

Ray leaned back in his chair, tilted his head back, and got a bit nostalgic. "She was lovely. And she had a bloody wicked sense of humor. One time, Sheila was using a large kitchen knife to pry open a can, and she broke about an inch of the tip-off. Most people would have just binned it. But not Sheila. She took out the ketchup and sprayed it around the counter. Then she poured it on her hand and held the knife so the broken edge was in the middle. Then she started screaming bloody murder. We all came running. It looked like she had buried the blade deep. I was just about to call 9-1-1 when I saw the ketchup bottle on the counter and realized it was all a scam. But the kids panicked. They were running around screaming their bloody heads off. She had to show them the knife was already broken before they calmed down. We laughed about that for years."

Wow. That sounded like child abuse to me, but what do I know about raising kids? I was about to ask about his kids when he continued.

"Yeah, she was a real storyteller. She was going to write a book about me and the ruby. And the brand, of course. She was taking writing classes and everything. We were going to use it as part of our marketing re-launch."

"What a great idea. By the way, how many kids do you have?"

"We've got one of each. Eric is twenty-two, and Mia just turned nineteen. Shame they lost their mum when they're just getting started in life." Ray looked over the pictures on his desk until he found the right one. He picked it up and handed it to me. "That's the family right there. Gooduns, every one of um."

The picture showed a smiling family of four hugging each other as they posed for the camera. "How are they taking it?"

"Well, Eric went walkabout from college this last year. He's always been a bit of a partier and about as useful as an ashtray on a motorbike. I've been telling him he needs to finish school if he wants to take over the business. Maybe losing his mom will get him to take life more seriously."

"What's he been up to lately?"

"As far as I know, he's been spending too much time, and probably way too much of my money, at the one-armed bandits. I thought it was a passing fancy like everything else. He'll hit something hard for a while and then lose interest. Not with this business. He used to hang out at Mystic Lake and Treasure Island. But that's not good enough anymore. He's graduated to the big time." Ray used air quotes on the word 'graduated.' Eric dropping out of school was clearly a trigger issue for him. "Now he spends all of his time in Vegas or Atlantic City so he can pay for fancy hotel rooms on top of his gambling debts. It seems like he's been in Vegas every other week for the past six months. This is why I may have to sell the business. My kids don't care about running it."

Ray didn't seem to mind sharing his thoughts, and I didn't want to interrupt the stream of consciousness, so I didn't say anything.

"Mia's my girl, though. She's in the business school at the University of Minnesota and works part-time at a school bookstore. She's got a lot of grit. Maybe she'll change her mind and take over for me when I retire, so I don't have to sell out to some stranger. Her boyfriend is Josh, who used to be Eric's best mate...still is, I guess."

Ray paused, and I was about to ask him a question, but he continued. "There's a bloke you should talk to—Josh Donohue. He's been trying to marry Mia for over a year, but Sheila said no. She said we would cut Mia out of our will if she went off without our consent."

Family drama. Interesting. "Good idea. I'll add him to the list. But I'd like to talk to Mia first. Can you tell me how to reach her?"

"Righto." He grabbed a pad of Post-it notes, wrote something on the top, then handed it to me. "Here's her cell number. I'll let her know you'll be texting her."

"Thanks, Ray." Another thought occurred to me. "With how things stand now, will you still oppose Mia and Josh getting married?"

"Nah. Sheila wasn't too wild about Josh, but he's all right. Reminds me of me at that age. He'll straighten out soon enough." Ray suddenly seemed pensive, like he wanted to say more but couldn't decide how much. I stayed quiet, and he soon spoke up while looking out the window so he didn't have to catch my eye. "This may not be related, but Sheila was acting odd lately. A bit cold, if I'm honest. Like maybe she was having a fling with some bugger."

I had no idea how to respond, so I said, "Sorry to hear that, Ray. I don't mean to be disrespectful, but do you have any theories on who she might have been having an affair with? I only ask because it could affect the direction of the investigation."

"Nah, you're grand. I get it. You need to know. Sheila was spending a lot of time with one of my friends lately. I'd rather not say which one 'cause I don't have any proof there was any hanky-panky."

As much as I wanted to pressure him for the name, I had questions about his other acquaintances, so I decided to let it go and move on. "What about your friends or business associates? Anything untoward with them?"

"Un-what?"

Now Dean's got me saying it. "Sorry. Troublesome, you know, is there anyone holding a grudge?"

"There's always a few cockroaches out there who think you've taken advantage of them when they're just lazy. But no one would kill because of it. Detective Copeland asked me the same thing, and I sent him a list. Hang on a sec. I've got it here somewhere." Ray turned to his computer, and in a couple of minutes, the printer cranked out a page he handed me.

"Thanks, Ray." I scanned the names for a moment. Along with the aforementioned cockroaches, several local notables immediately stood out, including the bishop, some famous politicians, and some very successful businesspeople from all over Minnesota. I couldn't see how any of these people would have taken more than a cursory interest in Ray or his businesses, so it looked like he was signaling to Copeland that he was someone with substantial influence who shouldn't be pushed around. Then, I spotted a particularly interesting listing.

"I see that a person named Nigel Lawson is listed as a minority owner of RRE."

"Righto. Nigel owns a small portion of the business. He's known Sheila and me since we all lived in Australia together. He's been a big help over the years. But he's more of a silent partner nowadays. Takes a lot of holidays. You'll probably want to talk to him, but he's in the Outback right now. Not reachable."

"When is he expected back stateside?"

"Hmm, not sure. Hard to tell with Nigel. He's a bit of a free spirit. Tell you what, I'll find out and let Kate know. She can pass it along to you."

"Do you mind if I ask how much of the business he owns? It might affect—"

"The investigation." He finished the sentence for me. "I get it. He owns twenty percent." He paused for a moment and suddenly looked serious. I got the feeling he was going to warn me about something. But he must have changed his mind at the last second and fell silent.

Then I saw Chadrick Chabot's name, and my heart skipped a beat. "Chadrick Chabot, how do I know that name." Pause for effect. "Wait, isn't he the motivational speaker?" I asked innocently.

"Yep, that's my buddy." Ray smiled, apparently pleased that I noticed someone on the list he actually could claim as an actual friend. "We started our companies about the same time. I was one of his first customers. Used to bring him in to rev up the troops. He was good at it, too. He introduced me to Kate a few months ago. Said something about them having a fling at one point. But I'm sure that's all over by now." I felt like making that smile disappear and didn't acknowledge his joke.

He continued, apparently oblivious to my discomfort. "We still get together from time to time. I hardly saw him during his heyday, but things have slowed down a bit for him, too. Hey, just had a thought. I'm taking Chadrick to dinner in a few weeks to thank him for sending Kate my way. You should join us. Whaddya say?"

Wow. Didn't see that coming. My first reaction was to say not only 'no,' but 'hell no.' Then I realized it would be interesting to meet him to see what all the fuss was about. "Sure, Ray. That sounds great."

"Great. I'll let you know when we set it up."

I went back to the list. "I see Scott Dimond's name on here. You said he was your finance guy, and I met him at the Supper Club." Scott had already told me about his role working for Ray, but it's always good to hear the story from another source, just in case things don't align. "How long have you been working together?"

"Scott is a private equity man who's been renting space from us for a couple of weeks. He's been a trusted partner for years."

You'd think a successful entrepreneur would have his own space or at least a home office. "Why is he renting space from you?"

"He was going to be in the area anyway, looking into some commercial deals nearby, so I offered him a local workplace. He's a good man, and I wouldn't say no to the extra income. But I can't see him playing into this. He's been helping me assess the business. You know, spiff things up, so if I ever decide to sell, it will be for top dollar. Your lovely lady benefited from him, too. He's the one who suggested we create the position of interim CFO to get the books in order."

That was interesting, and it made him less of a suspect. Why would he want another set of eyes looking over the books if he was trying to siphon money from the operation somehow? I decided it was better not to admit I knew about the pending offer so Ray didn't clam up on me.

"Of course, now that Kate's onboard, he's been trying to get her working for some of his other clients. Getting a little too cozy with her if you ask me." Ray gave me an obvious wink as he said it. Was that a warning, or was he trying to make me jealous? Either way, he certainly liked to stir the pot. "You might want to keep a closer eye on those two."

"Thanks for the tip, Ray. I will be sure to do that." I made a mental note to revisit this topic later.

We got up, and he showed me to the main entrance. "Thanks for stopping by, Grayson."

"Oh, one more question. DeeDee said you asked her to do the cremation as quickly as possible. Why was that?"

Thankfully, Ray didn't seem bothered that she'd shared this with me. "Very simple. It's a family tradition."

* * *

I got into my car and sat in the parking lot for a few minutes, wondering about Ray and the ruby. Did he really find the stone? Was it truly worth over a million U.S. dollars at auction? Or was that just part of the Ruby Ray legend? What if he never found a stone to build a legend on? He was a natural-born promoter, and I could see someone like him wanting to appear larger than life, but he would need some hook to set himself apart from the rest of the restaurateurs and businesspeople. What if he had commissioned some gemstone lab to fabricate a ruby so he would have something to build a brand upon and to put into a museum? And what difference did it make either way?

Then I realized it did matter. Someone killed Sheila and stole the ruby all within a few minutes. They must have made a public display of the murder as a misdirection to give them time to steal the stone. They obviously thought it was real, or why bother? Unless they wanted to kill Sheila and stole what they knew to be a fake stone to draw the police's attention in the opposite direction? Knowing if the stone was real or not would help inform the direction of my investigation, but I didn't know anyone who dealt with precious stones. This would be an excellent time to change that.

Maybe Dean could help. He always had an eclectic assortment of friends. I texted him, but, for once, he couldn't think of anyone either. A quick Google search pointed me to the Gemological Institute of America, whose website said their gemologists are trained professionals who specialize in identifying, grading, and valuing gemstones. Better still, a qualified gemologist was just north of me in St. Paul. A lesson I learned from my friend, Detective Copeland, was that you'd get much better results from interrogating someone in person instead of over the phone. So, I used Google Maps for directions to Sally's Gem Emporium and drove off. I was glad Dean still had the stone so I wouldn't be tempted to take it out during my first visit. With all of the recent press around Sheila's murder, most gem industry people would probably realize I was holding Ray's infamous ruby, and who knew what Sally would do from there?

Sally turned out to be a thirty-year-old male named Robert with shoulder-length brown hair and a goatee. Actually, no, that was Sally's son. She was out running an errand, and he was minding the store. That was bad news for me as there was no way to charm this guy, not that it would have been that much different with Sally herself.

After a brief introduction, I said, "It sounds like you'd be able to evaluate pretty much any gems I bring in, right?"

Robert nodded with a pleasant smile. "Yep, that's right. We do that all day long. What kind of stones are they?"

I wasn't ready to reveal that and had to go with a hastily conceived cover story. "My father passed a little over a year ago, and my mother has a few pieces that he'd bought her. She's getting up in years and needs a bit of cash to have some work done at her house. She doesn't wear them anymore, so she asked me to have them valued so she could decide which ones to sell. Some of them are loose stones, and some are in settings." That sounded pretty good, and Robert seemed to be buying it. "I don't really know that much about gems, so I thought I'd stop at a gem shop to learn more."

"Well, we can certainly help you out. Depending on the stone, we use microscopes and refractometers to assess each piece's color, clarity, cut, and carat weight. Then we compare that with the market value of similar items to tell you what we'd be willing to pay for them."

It sounded like he'd said that many, many times before. "That's exactly what I'm looking for." Now came the tricky part. "Does it matter if I don't know where the items were originally sourced?"

Robert squinted at me as if trying to understand what I was really asking. "I'm getting the impression that you may not know the provenance of some of the pieces?"

I thought I knew what he was asking, and I didn't have it, but double-checking made sense. "The provenance is a record of the chain of ownership to establish authenticity, right? Including some proof of ownership?"

"Ideally, yes."

"Unfortunately, I don't have that for some of the pieces. My dad was quite a character, and we never really knew some of his drinking buddies all that well." Sorry, Dad, if you're out there somewhere listening to this.

Robert crossed his arms and suddenly seemed less interested in my mother's collection. "I may not be able to help you after all. Trust is everything in this business, and any reputable dealer is obliged to report suspicious or potentially missing merchandise to the police."

Missing as in stolen, I thought. I was about to argue but quickly realized there was no point hanging around waiting for Sally to return. If he was that concerned about potentially hot stones without seeing them, just imagine his reaction if I brought out an infamous ruby. "Well, thanks for your time."

As I returned to the car, the Gemological Institute of America crowd seemed like a dead end. While there may be some less-than-forthright dealers in this group who might be willing to do a valuation on the ruby for a substantially inflated fee, it could take weeks to find them, and then could I really trust someone like that to give me an honest estimate? Worse still, I'd probably have to leave it with them for a few days, and who knew if I'd ever see it again. What would I do if they refused to return it, call the cops?

Maybe I should tell Copeland I have the stone. Then, I came to the same conclusion as before. There was no way he would believe that DeeDee just handed it to me, and I didn't want to involve her in this anyway. He would conclude that Kate had taken it and that I was trying to cover for her.

I texted Dean to let him know I hit another dead end. To my surprise and great relief, he texted back, saying he realized we might know the perfect person to appraise it, but he wouldn't give me any more intel. I couldn't wait to find out who that might be.

Chapter Eight

Thursday, May 18

Mia agreed to meet me at the Aussie House for lunch, so two days later, I found myself heading back there. I'd checked her Facebook page that morning to find, like most nineteen-year-olds, it was sparsely populated with pictures of her and her mom and a few of her and her dad. Her profile picture included a guy who looked roughly the same age, and I assumed it was Josh. I figured she was an Instagram or TikTok user, but at least I now knew what she looked like.

When I got to the restaurant, it was fairly crowded, so Mia had already grabbed a table. She had dark hair with a simple crop top and red flats. We introduced ourselves, and Mia said she'd already ordered, but I should let them know that I was with her and the meal would be on the house. That worked for me. I selected the green chicken curry pie while avoiding the temptation to order dessert and run up the bill. I soon picked up our food and drinks and dodged a few fellow patrons while bringing them to our table.

"Thanks for meeting with me, Mia." I took a bite of the pie, which was filled with spinach, green beans, and chicken inside a puff pastry shell. It was still hot, and I almost burned my tongue. "This is my second time here, and the food is great."

"Thanks. My dad puts a lot of time into the menus. He wants the food to be authentically Australian, but not so much that Minnesotans won't like it."

"He's got a real knack for it. When I met with him last week, he said you're in the Business Program at the U and work part-time at one of their bookstores. That must keep you busy."

"I guess. The classes aren't that bad, and I work the late shift at the store, so I get to study when it's not too crowded." It looked like she was enjoying her vegemite sammie. Maybe I should give it a try one of these days.

"Did your dad tell you why I wanted to meet you?"

"He did, and so did Kate. She told me how you solved the murders in your family when the cops were clueless. I think she likes you." Mia smiled to let me know she was kidding. She had a lot of poise for a teenager.

"Then you know I just want to clear Kate's name, and I have a few questions to ask you. Ray told me you've been seeing a guy named Josh, and it sounds like it's getting pretty serious."

"You could say that. We've been talking about getting engaged for a while now, but Mom, er, Sheila, didn't approve. She had some hang-ups about Josh because he always used to party with Eric. Eric's my brother. I kept telling her he wasn't like that anymore, but she wouldn't listen. I guess she was still scared from finding them passed out in our basement rec room so many times. All they ever did was drink Foster's lager, though. It's not like they were crackheads."

I knew I had to ask her an uncomfortable question that was straight from the detective shows. "So, you were mad at her but not enough to kill her?"

The tears that suddenly formed in her eyes told me I had gone too far. "Too right!" she blurted out. For a minute, I thought she was going to bolt from the restaurant, but then she seemed to calm down. I had to remind myself that she'd just lost her mother two weeks ago and to go easy on her.

"Sorry, Mia. I didn't mean anything by that. This might seem like another crazy question, but I have to ask. Could Josh have been involved somehow?"

"Josh? No way. He's way too laid-back for something like that."

"I got the impression that your dad likes Josh, and he won't try to stop you from getting engaged."

She wiped her tears away and smiled again. "I know. He's the best."

I was sure he was the best, but that also meant Mia and Josh had strong motivations to get Sheila out of the way. "Do you mind if I ask where you both were on the night of the murder?"

"No worries. I figured you were gonna ask me that. We were having dinner at the Supper Club. A lot of people saw us there, including most of the wait staff."

Hmm, that was interesting. I didn't recall seeing her there. I wonder what else I missed.

Mia suddenly looked down at her food. "I spoke with my Mom a while before the show started, but that doesn't help you much, does it?"

"Did she say anything out of the ordinary?"

"No. Everything seemed perfectly fine."

"Did you see anything suspicious at any time while you were talking to your mom or when she was heading upstairs to get to the swing?"

Mia thought for a moment. "Not really. There was a big bang in the kitchen right before Mom started swinging. It sounded like a waiter dropped a tray full of dinner dishes. That seemed odd. Most of the staff has been there for a long time, and they're way too professional to let that happen."

I'd almost forgotten about that and made a mental note to investigate it further. "Anything else?"

"Yeah, there was. Just as you and Kate left the table, I noticed Marcel got up and headed toward the kitchen. It looked like he was going to leave through the emergency door."

"Any idea where he was heading?"

"Nope. But he must have been worried about something because he kept looking around, almost like he wanted to see if anyone was watching him. He didn't see me, though. My dad wants the paying customers to have the best seats, so Josh and I always sit in the back."

This wasn't helping, and I was running out of questions for her. I thought about asking if I could speak with Josh, but I figured I'd get the same answers as the ones she had given me, so there was no point. "Who else should I talk to about your mom's death?"

"Mom used to warn me about Patter. She said he would sometimes get handsy, and not just with the piano. She had to tell him off several times and even told my Dad he should fire the guy for getting out of line. I don't know why Dad never fired him. Something about being a crowd-pleaser. Course, it could be that he worked cheap, too. Dad was always looking for a bargain."

I thought there was nothing wrong with getting a good deal as long it's not because you can't afford the real thing.

"I always stayed away from him or made sure we weren't alone. Other than that, I don't know any reason to suspect him, but you may want to see what he had to say."

Interesting. Seems odd to think the jazz piano guy would risk getting fired by being overly friendly with the wife of the person paying his salary, but there you go. "Sounds good. What about your brother, Eric? Is he someone I should talk with?"

"About being involved in the murder or stealing the ruby? No way. My folks, well, my Dad, wants him to finish college, but he just wants to party. He's already taking a year off from school. Why would he do anything to mess with that? Besides, he spends so much time in Vegas these days, he was probably out there on the night of the murder."

"Sounds like he likes to gamble. Is he any good at it?"

"Couldn't say for sure. He tells me he does great at the tables. He says he's got a system, but he won't tell me what it is. Besides, Vegas is too sexist for me. All those women running around in skimpy outfits—no thanks." That was funny. Ray said he did well at the slots, not the blackjack table. I made a mental note to look into that later, too. "He's there right now, so you'll have to wait until he gets back if you want to talk to him."

I couldn't think of anything else, so we parted company when Mia said she had to leave for a class. Since I was already at Ray's facility, I decided to look around. I walked across the parking lot to the Aussie Museum. A handmade sign on the main entrance said, 'Closed Until Further Notice.' Once the star attraction had gone missing, I thought there was no point in opening up. The Supper Club was closed, too, so I kept walking until I reached a sign on which the words "Galland Garden" had been painted in a lively combination of yellow and green with an arrow pointing down and to the left. I figured this would be a good time to get some intel on Marcel for Tom.

I followed the directions to find a large arbor, which must have been ten feet tall and eight feet wide, with the name "Galland Garden" elaborately carved into a wooden sign hanging from the top and from which several climbing plants were suspended. The arch was at the corner of the garden area, providing a clean break from the offices and parking lot. I recalled Kate telling me there were about fifty beds on an undeveloped field, which made it sound like it was still prairie land. As I passed through the arch, I realized this was far from it.

There were five rows of raised beds, each higher than the last. The rows were about four feet apart, and the ground between them was covered in mulch. The gardens in the first row were about a foot off the ground. A wooden frame surrounded each section of dirt and mulch, and each had two trellises along the back on which flower or vegetable vines could grow. The beds in the middle row were about two and a half feet off the ground, while the beds in the fifth row were about three feet high. It was a warm day, and the scent of organic fertilizer was in the air, which was not unpleasant. All the plantings looked well-tended and healthy. The flowered beds were spilling over with blooms of all colors, and the veggies looked like they would produce a bumper crop. I had to admit, it was impressive.

"Raising the beds helps keep the weeds out and creates proper drainage. They also provide easy access to our members who are wheelchair-bound or who have trouble bending low for long periods."

I turned to see Marcel standing behind me. "Reverend, I didn't hear you come up." We shook hands. He wore a black shirt and slacks, just like at the Supper Club. It must be his thing.

"Please call me Marcel. So, how do you like our little operation?"

"The design gives me the impression that your gardeners don't just love to grow things. They appreciate the aesthetic, too."

"Nicely put. I can tell you're a design guy. Would you like the tour?"

I couldn't say no to that, so Marcel walked me up and down each row, pointing out the various kinds of flowers or vegetables in each bed and the hidden sprinkler and drainage systems. He was very proud of his group's work.

"Very nicely done. How did you get into the gardening business?"

"After a few years in the Church following the rules, it felt like I was just going through the motions, you know? Not really making a difference. So, about three years ago, I spun out of the church and started gardening. It took a while for word to spread, but we now have over one hundred members from all walks of life. And a lot of millennials and Gen Zers have joined our group, too. They say the traditional church just doesn't speak to them." He stopped to adjust a sprinkler nozzle, which must have been clogged because the veggies in this area were looking a bit peaked.

I sent him a quizzical look so he would continue with his story.

"One of the most commonly cited reasons for not attending church is feeling inadequate, judged, or unsupported by other congregation members or feeling like you're not living up to the expectations of the community. We don't have that here because we take extra precautions to make sure everyone feels accepted. I spend time during each service reading headlines from the Minneapolis or St. Paul papers and then relating how the average person can bring God into these situations instead of just ignoring them. Afterward, we go outside and tend to the garden. It lets the congregation feel like they're giving back and not just by dropping a few bucks into a basket as it passes by. I must admit that I finally feel like I'm having an impact, too."

It helps that your members choose to be part of the group, I thought. I wondered how well this model would scale to people who would rather open their wallets than take the time to grow things. As we finished the tour and walked back to where we started, I recalled what Tom said about Marcel potentially using psychological manipulation and undue influence to control his group members. Maybe convincing or coercing congregants to work the soil was part of the cult-like nature of a group like this.

This seemed like a good time to broach the subject. "I've heard the bishop is concerned about your group."

Marcel looked at me and shook his head slightly, undoubtedly resigned to living in the church's shadow. "I don't doubt it. Anything that upsets the status quo is always suspected. I've invited Bishop Brennen to visit us and meet our parishioners, but he hasn't accepted my invitation yet. I'm sure he would say this is not for everyone, and I agree that it's not. A lot of people would rather attend a traditional service. Nothing wrong with that, but that doesn't make this way wrong either."

Interesting. That didn't sound very manipulative to me. Then again, a truly charismatic cult leader would have a pat answer like that available whenever he might need it. It made me wonder what conditions or activities would have to occur to change the categorization of his group from church to cult and who would make that call anyway.

I thought this distinction might come up when I Googled the good Reverend Galland, so I also researched non-traditional churches. I knew that traditional congregations were shrinking, but I was shocked that groups similar to Marcel's were popping up nationwide as new ways and places to worship proliferated. One group of entrepreneurs developed a church franchise model and offered funding and training to aspiring church founders. They emphasized the use of technology and offered engaging online sermons, mobile apps, and even a Bible app that has been downloaded millions of times.

Another approach taken by so-called 'churches' was using psychoactive substances that are generally illegal under federal law to connect with the divine. Their body-jolting, mind-altering rituals included a detoxification protocol in which poisonous secretions of an Amazon frog were dabbed on tiny burn marks on a person's skin, often inducing nausea and projectile vomiting, ingesting a potent dose of Psilocybin mushrooms, then smoking toxins from the Sonoran Desert toad. When it was done, many described a feeling of bliss while others flailed about, screaming and sobbing. It made me realize the trust that most participants put in these group leaders and the degree to which they were in harm's way if that trust was misplaced.

It seemed as if the distinctions between the traditional and non-traditional churches were being blurred like never before. Despite this, one thing seemed clear. Any group that espoused violence or used it to keep its members in line would always be a cult.

After a lengthy pause, it was clear he wouldn't volunteer any incriminating evidence, so I shifted gears back to the investigation.

"Marcel, I have to ask you, did you see anything unusual at the Supper Club on the night Sheila was murdered?"

"No, of course not. You were with me the whole time. Well, except for a bathroom break. But I didn't notice anything out of place."

"You were seen leaving the table after the murder and heading out of the club through the back door in the kitchen. Why did you do that?"

"Because I have unfinished business with the police. Or I should say they have unfinished business with me. You see, some rumors got started that I was turning this group into a cult and wanted the people to worship me, so the police have been stopping by a lot more than they used to. It's all just routine, or so they say."

I was stumped. "Wait a minute. It might be unpopular for you to run a cult out of a supper club, but it's not against the law."

"No, it's not. But you know how rumors start for no reason at all. And they tend to get uglier the more they spread. Pretty soon, someone was saying I was running drugs out of the club. It made no sense. I've never touched drugs in my life. You can talk to any parishioners, and they will tell you I'm as law-abiding as they come these days."

It didn't seem like a rumor would get police attention without some substantiation, so I figured he was holding something else back. But I didn't want to make any accusations until I had more information, so I agreed with him. "Yeah, there are always haters out there."

He took the opportunity to ask his questions. "It sounds like you're planning to solve this murder just like the others. Are you doing the bishop a favor, or do you just consider the cops to be bumbling idiots?"

Nice false dilemma, I thought. "Neither one. You may know that the Bishop is my Uncle, but that doesn't mean I'm out working the field for him. I'm more interested in clearing Kate's name right now."

"Sounds like the cops have moved on to other suspects."

"Ray might have moved on, but, in my experience, the cops don't move on until they have someone more interesting to pursue."

Marcel folded his arms across his chest and glared at me. I suddenly realized he had about three inches on me, and considering the two of us were alone out here, I started feeling a bit exposed. "And that someone might be me? So, you're going to throw me under the bus to get the police off your girlfriend's back?"

How did we go from having a cordial discussion to me being grilled in under ten seconds? "Why would I do that? I don't suspect anyone right now, and it wouldn't matter if I did—it's not like the police are asking for my opinion. I'm just checking into things in case the police are too busy to spend enough time on this case."

"Sure, you are. Just be careful you don't misstep. Ray's business has been lousy for a few years, and there aren't many people around to ensure everyone stays safe."

Did he just threaten me or Kate? This conversation was going nowhere, and I thought it best to leave.

"I'd best be going. Thanks for the tour." I offered to shake hands, but he had already turned to walk away. I headed back to my car, wondering what had really caught the interest of the police.

Just then, my phone pinged with a new text message. I almost dropped the phone when I saw it was from Bishop Tom's Fixer, Monsignor Frank Scarpello.

After we'd discovered we'd been adopted, but before we'd realized that the bishop was our birth father, Dean had been doing some research into our birth records in Rochester, MN, and he'd looked into the Reverends Tom and Frank, too. He figured out they'd both attended the same seminary school, so they'd known each other for over forty years.

As Tom moved up the church hierarchy, he naturally wanted to bring his friend with him. But Frank wasn't considered management material, so Tom submitted him to the church authorities in Rome for the role of Monsignor, a title granted to individuals who have rendered valuable services to the church. Frank had to spend time in Rome and be approved by the Vatican to carry that title, but he was a very resourceful individual, and he soon had their full endorsement. This distinction didn't include any additional authority. Still, Frank acted like his title and the connections he'd made within the church's senior hierarchy conferred a special status upon him, almost like he was one of the infamous sheriffs of the Old West who strutted around town. At the same time, the bad guys hid away in fear.

What have you found out about Marcel? The text message read.

Was he watching me? I scanned the parking lot, wondering if I'd spot Frank skulking behind the wheel of the black Crown Victoria he always drove, but I saw nothing. Could his extended network report in so quickly? I wondered. On the other hand, it was almost three weeks since Tom asked Kate and me to look into the Supper Club Church. He probably just got lucky.

Who wants to know, you or Tom? I texted back. Saying Frank and I didn't get along is like saying the St. Paul crowd didn't appreciate the residents of Minneapolis very much and vice versa. He needed to know that while I might be Tom's lackey, I certainly wasn't his, and I wasn't about to kowtow to him. It also gave me great pleasure to remind him that my being a birth son trumped his being a Fixer.

The Bishop would like to know if you've made any progress

I'd bet he would. The clock on my phone said one-thirty. As a bishop who covered the entire St. Paul Diocese, Tom wasn't assigned to any particular parish, but Frank was assigned to St. Celestine Church, and I knew they both had offices there. They must have been talking, and that prompted the first text.

St. Celestine's was just north on Sibley Memorial Highway, next to Cherokee Regional Park. I was only a short drive away, so I figured I might as well eliminate the middleman and talk to Tom directly. **I'm in the neighborhood and will be there in a few minutes.** Since he didn't respond, I figured my guess that they were at the church was correct.

Within a few minutes, I'd parked by the main entrance of the rectory. It was a large stone structure with small windows that were made even smaller by the cross-hatched pattern of wood trim over them, giving the exterior a formal look. It also made the interior seem dark, even on a bright and sunny afternoon.

After I knocked, the Monsignor opened the door. "Grayson, how good of you to stop by." We shook hands. Frank was a short, stocky priest with a full face, graying hair, watery gray eyes, a ski jump nose, and full lips. He was not an attractive man. He was dressed in a long black cassock with purple buttons down the front, signifying his special status. He seemed to wear it every chance he got.

He was playing nice, so I assumed Tom was within earshot, and I would have to play nice, too. "Monsignor, nice to see you again."

As I entered, we passed a small reception desk where the day's mail was stacked. It also held a leather writing pad and blotter set that could easily have been as old as the building. The dark paneling of the edifice instilled a reverential feeling, where speaking in hushed tones seemed oddly appropriate.

Frank ushered me to the bishop's office, a large, well-appointed room at the end of the hall. It had a thick Persian-style rug on the floor and an imposing picture of the bishop shaking hands with the current Pope on the wall. Tom's desk was massive, with wooden panels that went to the floor on three sides, finished in what would probably be called artisanal black with antique brass drawer pulls. It was solid oak—no simple veneers for our leading man. Behind the desk was a worn leather desk chair, and on it was a relatively new appointment book, a well-worn address book, and a stack of papers. Was I surprised not to see a picture of Tom and his sons prominently displayed there? Not really.

"The Bishop will join you shortly. Please have a seat." Frank indicated one of the two visitors' chairs.

"I'm fine. Thanks." I decided to remain standing for no good reason other than to avoid cooperating with Frank. He suddenly came over and stood uncomfortably close, and I realized he was about four inches shorter than me. Then, he whispered in my ear. "I texted you because I saw your car in Ray's lot." After which, he glared at me and left the office. Crazy much, Frank?

A few minutes later, while I was still wondering what the bloody hell Frank had been talking about, Tom came in, wearing the traditional black shirt and slacks, and we shook hands. Apparently, this was a fashion trend that I had somehow missed.

"Grayson, good to see you. Thanks for coming in. Sit down, please." He motioned towards the same visitors' chairs, and I gladly took one.

"No worries. I was just down the road at Ruby Ray's."

"Really? Did you speak with Marcel?"

I liked how he got right down to business. "Yes, I did. For the most part, his operation seemed legit. And he said he was reaching millennials and Gen Zers who prefer a more open approach to worship, which sounded—"

"I know how it sounds, Gray. These schemes always sound that way. They find a niche group of people, set up an operation, and declare victory. But they eventually fail, and then we have to pick up the pieces. You have to understand there are cycles in people's lives. Have you ever heard of the Amish custom of Rumspringa?"

"Isn't that where young Amish people are given free rein to experience life without having to dress a certain way or avoid technology?"

"That's right. Not all of their young people go through this process. Of the ones that do, some choose to remain Amish, while others decide to join mainstream society. The point is that's essentially what Marcel's group is experiencing. Some of his followers will eventually become disillusioned and return to the church, where they will be committed churchgoers because it was their decision to return. But the ones that don't could spiral into crime or drug use, and we can't risk that."

Tom's analogy didn't seem to work, and the implication that only church attendance can stop people from committing crimes or doing drugs seemed seriously overblown. But I thought it best to hold my tongue.

"And, if the church stepped in every time one of these groups popped up, we would seem heavy-handed, driving more people away. And those people would never come back."

"I see where you're coming from. Marcel said something interesting, though. He said some rumors were floating around that he was running drugs out of the club. Have you heard anything like that?"

"I'm afraid I have, yes. That's one of the reasons I asked you and Kate to look into this situation. I didn't tell you that in advance as I didn't want to spread any unfounded rumors. Grayson, I want you to know that despite our differences of opinion, Marcel is a good man who is trying to do the right thing. But sometimes, good intentions aren't enough to overcome human nature. I can't see him selling illegal substances out of that garden or the club. But, there may be even more worrisome activities of a financial nature happening there that could put everything he is trying to do in jeopardy. If that were the case, I would be forced to take action."

"Tom, can you clue us in a bit more here? What financial activities do you mean? And what actions would you be considering?" That might have sounded brazen, but I didn't care.

He paused as if considering how much to say. I didn't want to discourage him from sharing more, so I stayed silent. Finally, he spoke. "Let's just say that the town's current administration is not as cooperative toward our organization as we would like. However, the sentiment of the local population is trending against them, and they are likely to be replaced soon. I'm confident that the new administration will be more open to taking actions that we deem to be appropriate. As far as the activities, I'm sure you have the wherewithal to figure that out on your own."

All I could do was stare at my father in wonder. What the bloody hell did that mean, and why was he suddenly using the 'royal we' like an eighteenth-century potentate? He was already buddies with Ray and could probably get him to kick Marcel out of the Supper Club if need be. But this sounded like Tom was planning to place his own people into local government positions in case he needed to influence Marcel's activities further. Frank was undoubtedly busy pulling the strings to make that happen as we spoke. It must be nice to have a backup plan and a Fixer to implement it for you.

Tom soon filled the silence with more opaqueness. "Did Marcel say anything about originally being from Chicago?"

"No, that didn't come up. Should it have?"

"As I said, I don't like to spread unfounded rumors."

It sounded like he wanted me to look into Marcel's past before he lived in Minnesota, specifically in the Chicago area. That shouldn't be too difficult, and I could always deploy my secret research weapon, Dean, if necessary.

"Please let me know what you find out."

"I will, Tom. You have my word on it." Was it just me, or was I starting to talk like him?

Chapter Nine

Monday, May 22

A s I got off the elevator and unlocked the door to Design By Dyle early Monday morning, I strongly desired to learn more about my new friend Scott Dimond, Ray's new tenant. As usual, I arrived first, so I made the coffee, poured myself a cup, and went to my office to fire up the laptop. I Googled Scott's name, then spent the next thirty minutes going through numerous websites about him and his business. He seemed to be exactly what Ray said he was—a business partner and private equity investor. Was anyone really that squeaky clean? I tried channeling Dean to figure out how he searched the dark web, but nothing popped. So I ran a new search about how to find dirty little secrets at that scariest of online places, The Dark Web.

I clicked on the link to a video that was basically a tour of the dark web. It described the incredible amount of illicit goods or services available online. Buying or selling illegal weapons, drugs, and cars or jewelry. Enlisting the services of thieves or murderers. Not to mention images and videos that were definitely not safe for work. There seemed to be no end to the depravity of it all.

The next video described how to download The Onion Router, otherwise known as TOR, which was the dark web browser of choice. It provided anonymity by encrypting your online activity and using multiple layers to mask your IP address, which is why the onion analogy was used. It also included multiple warnings about hackers one might encounter in the dark. You could be their next victim if you didn't protect your computer. The message was clear—don't try this at home. Maybe I'd take Dean up on his offer to check out Scott after all.

I didn't see how Scott could have committed the murder since we were sitting at the same table while it was being committed. But I still wanted to talk to him, if for no other reason than to cross him off the list. I found his business card and texted him about potentially investing in our business as a pretext for a meeting. He texted back that he'd be happy to meet, and we set up a lunch meeting for Thursday.

I looked at my phone and realized it was long past time for me to stop investigating my girlfriend's murder accusation and start getting some work done at my day job. Then, I remembered the lunch with Kate and her mother was scheduled for today. I checked my emails to see if I could use some work conflict as an excuse to beg off, but no such luck. I texted Kate, saying I was looking forward to seeing her for lunch, and that part was the absolute truth. When Paul arrived and got a cup of coffee, we sat in our main conference room to brainstorm the café table design idea.

The individual offices and conference rooms had floor-to-ceiling, electro-transparent windows, which meant the glass could be switched from clear to frosted using an iPhone or Amazon Alexa. A motion sensor with a timer would switch the windows to clear after fifteen minutes if no movement was detected in the room. It was an unwritten but well-established rule that we respected the privacy of anyone in a conference room with the glass frosted. Unless someone else needed that room for a business meeting, in which case the single person could be kicked out on their butt. Hey, we were trying to run a business here. I frosted the glass to indicate we should only be disturbed in an emergency and got to work.

We usually started exactly as you might imagine: defining the problem, researching online to see what others were doing, brainstorming new approaches, and designing something brilliant. Okay, those last two steps could be tricky, and we weren't always successful, but when we were, the results were usually pretty good—at least, that's what our clients told us.

This problem was easy to state: Design a café table that can be easily leveled despite uneven flooring and will remain stable after years of use without the need to shim one of the legs using a stack of napkins or coasters.

Many tables have adjustable glides on the bottom, which can be screwed in or out to make them stick out less or more. This idea sounds good, but have you ever tried to do this in a pub? The glides are the most disgusting things in the building and probably the most contaminated. Adjustable glides were definitely ruled out.

One online website offered a 'Wobbly Table Theorem,' which suggested rotating the table until you found a stable position. It wasn't a bad idea, but it wasn't reliable. It depended on the variations in the floor lining up with the height requirements for each lag, which wasn't likely. If it did work, someone would probably have a table corner protruding uncomfortably into their gut, so that was out.

After more analysis, we realized we needed to know how variable a typical floor would be. And what better place to take a few measurements than Ray's Supper Club? I volunteered for the mission immediately and planned to go right after lunch with Kate and Elizabeth. At least I would have something fun to do later that afternoon. I texted Ray to see if he would let me into the club at about one-thirty or two, and he texted me back that he would be around and that I could stop by anytime.

I was heading back to my office to pack up when a delivery person knocked on the office door. I'd almost forgotten I'd ordered a lovely flower arrangement from a higher-end florist in a preemptive strike to get on Elizabeth's good side. I signed the delivery slip, put the package on the front counter, and opened it up to be sure it met my expectations, which it most certainly did not. The flowers were fresh, but the roses were different heights, and they were all squished together. The supporting flowers weren't working either, as they had been squashed down during the packing process. I took out my trusty Swiss Army pocketknife and started hacking at the roses to get them to the same length.

Paul stopped by to see who the delivery was for, and when he saw the arrangement and my sorry attempt at a remedy, he had to stifle a laugh.

"You're never going to fix it with that. But don't worry about it, Grayson. Kate is so smitten with you she won't even notice anything's wrong."

The pocketknife was too small to cut the thick stems properly, so I abandoned that idea and started picking at the accent flowers to perk them up. "That might be true, but these are for Kate's mother. Kate told me she used to be a highly successful real estate agent who had a real flare for staging homes. I feel she will immediately notice this thing is a disaster, and I will look like a chump. How can any self-respecting design guy give someone an arrangement like this?"

Paul sensed my frustration and pushed me aside. "Oh, get out of the way. Let me do this."

He laid the flowers out individually on top of the packaging material. Then he took a pair of full-sized scissors from the drawer under the counter and started cutting the stems to the proper heights. "You didn't tell me you were having lunch with your future mother-in-law." That's Paul, always the kidder.

He shot me a sideways glance. "So, are you nervous?"

"Is it that obvious?"

"Maybe a little. Look, you'll be fine. Just—"

"Just be myself, I know."

He placed each item back in one by one, and when he was done, the overall effect was stunning and worthy of representing our firm, not to mention me in particular.

"Thanks, Paul. That's quite a hidden talent you have."

"I didn't work my way through college at a florist shop without learning a thing or two." He wrapped the packaging around the revitalized arrangement and handed it to me. "Now, go impress the hell out of her."

* * *

As I drove to the restaurant, I couldn't help wondering about the Larson family. I'd finally done some research, and based on various websites, I found that Elizabeth's listings were all in the seven-figure range and located in the high-end suburbs west of the Twin Cities. Her Facebook page was exactly what you'd expect, and the entries fell into two categories. The first was photo after photo of her holding a large "SOLD" sign and standing next to an affluent individual or couple, all of whom were grinning incessantly. The second was her posing with a group of female friends at some exotic resort, either at a beach on a windjammer, or at a bar, living their best lives. It was amazing how no one ever had a bad hair day online.

It was interesting that Kate hardly ever spoke about her father, Brett Larson. She'd mentioned that he'd been a financial advisor and that he had died when she was in her teens, and that was about it. There was no mention of him on any of her social media accounts, or her mother's either. It took some digging to find him online since he had such a common name. Once I did, I realized why she had been so tight-lipped. Brett had been accused, tried, and convicted of mismanaging client funds for his business and personal gain. He was spared prison time because he'd confessed, but he'd been barred from ever working in the financial services industry. I'd also found his obit, which was dated only a few months after his being sentenced. The timing was suspect, but I supposed the stress of getting caught cheating your clients in a highly public manner would have taken its toll. It made me wonder how deeply this had affected Kate. So much for having topics to bring up if there were a lull in the conversation.

* * *

Not without a small amount of trepidation, I drove into the parking lot of the restaurant where Kate had made reservations for the three of us. She had purchased a new flip phone to use temporarily while the police were still holding her regular cell phone. As she had read off the number, I'd entered it into my phone and labeled it 'Burner.' She didn't say anything, but I think she had secretly got a kick out of that. I know I had.

I sent a text to Burner before leaving the car. **Arrived.**

A few seconds later, my phone dinged. **We're here. Come on in.**

Despite the smiley face emoji, I was uncomfortable for several reasons.

84

First, it was in Edina, an affluent suburb of Minneapolis. As recently as 2019, the Minneapolis Star Tribune, the largest Twin Cities newspaper, ran an article titled '*Why does everyone love to hate Edina?*' As the article pointed out, Twin Citians who didn't live there sometimes refer to people who do live there as cake-eaters. Don't get me started on the local athletics community resenting Edina's success in the State high school hockey tournament. My only time in Edina was at the Southdale Center, the first fully enclosed, climate-controlled shopping mall in the United States. It was pleasant enough. I didn't live here, so it didn't matter to me, yet I knew plenty of people who thought Edina was 'overly bougie,' as the phrase goes. Coming from a modest home in the working-class area of the relatively small town of Rochester, Minnesota, its reputation for being too concerned about upward mobility was enough for me to question how well I would fit in.

Second, we were having lunch at a restaurant in the Galleria in Edina, whose website home page featured a handsome, well-coifed lady wearing expensive-looking clothes and earrings, who appeared to be eating pearls from fancy dinnerware using a golden fork. If you can't fight it, flaunt it, right? Here, I thought they were supposed to be eating cake.

Third, the venue of choice was the Cove Restaurant in the Galleria in Edina, Minnesota. The website said it combined Midwest hospitality with the unmistakable allure of Nantucket, which was fine, but wasn't that a summer retreat for the uber-wealthy on an East Coast island? Oh boy. This was not going to go well. My flower bouquet suddenly seemed two sizes too small, and I wondered what the other guys would be sporting. Probably some nautical-themed outfits with white Oxford shirts, short white pants, bow ties, and snappy seersucker jackets instead of the light blue polo shirt and black jeans I had selected. If I wanted to match this style, I would have had to run out and buy the shirt, tie, and jacket, as nothing like that existed in my closet. Fortunately, the Galleria was jam-packed with stores that could cover these requirements.

I checked in with the cheerful young lady at the hostess stand, who told me the other two members of my party had already been seated and asked me to follow her to our table. A minute later, I was shaking hands with

Elizabeth Larson, who was elegantly dressed in a white silk blouse and a large pendant in gold and mother of pearl with matching earrings. She was shorter than her daughter, but the family resemblance was distinctive. Kate was fetching as always in a light pink silk blouse and caramel pants. Why had I never seen this outfit, I wondered. Was Kate dressing down for me or up for her Mother? And where was the advance notice that I needed to up my wardrobe game for this event? Then again, it probably should have been obvious.

"Elizabeth, so nice to meet you," I gushed, perhaps a bit too enthusiastically. "Here, I brought these for you." I handed her the bouquet.

"Very nice to meet you, Grayson," she said with an imposing voice that must have come in handy when she convinced her clients to sign multi-million dollar real estate contracts. "Kathryn has shared a lot about you." She admired the flowers for a moment, then raised them to her nose and sniffed. "And thank you for the flowers. They are lovely." She put the bouquet on the open seat next to her.

This seemed a bit dismissive, as there was plenty of room on the tabletop, and I could tell that Kate was a bit miffed, too. "Here, let me handle that for you, Mother." With that, she flagged down one of the wait staff, handed them the flowers, and asked to have them put into a vase with water. The busboy was more than happy to oblige. Obviously, if I had known Nantucket-themed restaurants had vases in the backroom that could be summoned upon request, I would have done so with a flourish. I'll bet Chadrick knew that one, and he'd probably have some witty James Bond-like quip to make everyone titter while he was doing it. I was starting to hate that guy.

"Thank you, dear." Elizabeth turned towards me. "So, you own a product design firm. How interesting. You must be very creative."

She seemed sincere, so I answered accordingly. "Thanks. I'm a co-owner, actually. My business partner does a lot of product design work, and I focus on engineering. We've been fortunate enough to build a small business between the two of us. I understand you've been quite successful in real estate."

"Yes. I've been fortunate, too."

The busboy returned and placed a vase containing the flowers on the open corner of the café table. I reached out to hold the tabletop steady as he did, then realized it was completely unnecessary as it was quite sturdy. Mental note: after we finish designing and building them, don't bother trying to sell new and improved café tables to the Cove. Elizabeth sent Kate a quizzical look, and my face started getting warm. As I stifled a sudden desire to glance at my smartwatch to calculate how much longer I'd have to endure this, another busboy placed three iced teas on the table.

"I ordered these before you arrived," Elizabeth explained. Without waiting to see what we wanted, I thought.

Kate, ever the gracious one, jumped in. "Let's look at the menu, shall we?"

An upbeat young waitress stopped by a few minutes later to take our lunch order. Elizabeth selected Lobster Guac from the Shareable menu for the three of us. Also, without checking with us, I might add. Then she ordered a Fig and Walnut Salad. Kate went with the safe and sensible Poke Bowl. I love sushi, and the options sounded great, but I could never remember the difference between sushi and sashimi, and I didn't want to seem unrefined, so I decided on the Crab and Shrimp Pasta instead.

As we chatted about the current conditions in the Twin Cities real estate market, the appetizer arrived, and I must admit, it was delicious. The conversation turned to Kate's new job, Sheila's gruesome murder, and Ray's being quite the character. It was obvious that Elizabeth knew what was happening in her daughter's life, which was good to hear. It brought her down to earth as an ordinary parent concerned about her only child.

Soon, we had finished our excellent lunches, and the plates had been cleared. Our iced teas had been refilled, and the bouquet had been removed from the vase and placed on the table in its' original packaging, ready to be taken home. I insisted on paying the check, and neither of my guests objected too strongly. After a bit more chit-chat, it seemed we would be wrapping things up, and I just might have escaped without any truly embarrassing gaffes. Only, this fairy tale ending was not to be.

"Well, Grayson, Kathryn tells me she was questioned by Detective Copeland again about her potential involvement in Sheila's death and the theft of the Poona Ruby. I have to say I was very disappointed and surprised that you didn't do anything to stop it. I thought you knew the Detective and would exert your influence to get him to stand down."

What in the bloody hell was she talking about? I certainly couldn't get the police to call off the dogs when a murder was involved. I doubted even The Bishop could do that, especially when Copeland was involved. "That's not how that works, Eliz—"

"Well, Chadrick would have done it." She cut me off and looked at her daughter. "Wouldn't he, Kathryn? He was very influential."

Hello, I'm sitting right here, I thought.

Then she turned to me. "Kathryn may have informed you, Grayson, that she and Chadrick Chabot, the famous motivational speaker, were quite an item until recently. The paparazzi loved photographing them together because my daughter is so photogenic." She said it in such an off-hand manner that it sounded like she was simply being matter-of-fact and not trying to brag or be obnoxious at all.

Paul's joke about Elizabeth being my future mother-in-law flashed in my head, and I could feel my heart racing. My face was getting warm again, which I mentally fought, as I didn't want to give her the satisfaction of embarrassing me. I had no idea if it worked. I considered telling them as snarky as possible that I would soon be having dinner with Chadrick at Ray's invitation but decided against it. Springing this information on Kate in front of her mother was the last thing I wanted to do.

I looked at Kate, who was turning white and struggling to find a way to reply to her mom's comment, and I realized I was not the only one in shock. She opened her mouth for a moment, but nothing came out.

Where was Elizabeth coming from? I wondered. Is this what happens to someone when their spouse is caught with his hand in the cookie jar, and they are publicly shamed and humiliated? They became immune to normal social conventions and just blurted out the first thing that popped into their heads. It would be difficult to sell high-end real estate if that were your approach to life.

I was about to open up with both barrels about the rude nature of her comments and how insensitive she was being, not to me but to Kate, when a new thought occurred to me. If I were to act in an undignified manner, it would simply reinforce the message that I was uncouth and not worthy of associating with her daughter. 'You see what I mean, Kathryn, my dear. Chadrick Chabot would never have acted that way,' would be her next comment. No, I needed to out-maneuver her on her home battleground—the field of civility. I assumed a calm demeanor and spoke.

"I'm sure you're right, Elizabeth. I've never met Chadrick, but I've heard that he is quite influential. Far beyond anything I could ever hope to muster. But here's the thing about relationships. You never really know who any one person is going to be attracted to. Kate shared with me that she was in a relationship with Chadrick at one point, but she broke it off, which must have disappointed you greatly. While Kate hasn't shared anything else about Chadrick, I believe she had the good sense to look beyond his influence and surface-level charm to the person he really is. Apparently, she didn't like what she found.

"I don't know if our relationship will turn into a long-term one, but I can tell you this: Kate and I have something that she and Chadrick never had: mutual respect and trust. I hope I can one day live up to your expectations for her. In the meantime, you'll just have to put up with me because as long as Kate wants to be with me, I'm not going anywhere."

With that, I stood up, pecked Kate on the back of the head, and left, mentally congratulating myself for not threatening to kill anyone. I got in my car, no longer in awe of being in Edina, and texted Ray that I would be in front of the club in twenty minutes. He confirmed, and I left the parking lot without looking back.

As I drove, my car told me I had texts from Kate. She was very touched by my outburst and wanted to come over to tell me in person that evening. While I had a pretty good idea of what she was implying, it seemed like we should consider what had happened for a bit first. Her Mother was trying to throw a wrench into our relationship, and it wasn't clear why. I thought it had less to do with Chadrick and more to do with me. Apparently, the scandal rags' lack of interest in my life meant I wasn't suitable marriage material for her only daughter. But Kate would have to sort that out with her mother, not me. I was going to be on the sidelines for that discussion. I used the voice commands to text Kate back, saying I needed time to think, and I hoped she understood. She didn't respond to that.

I soon realized I was fairly sure of one thing—if Elizabeth forced Kate to choose between an ongoing relationship with her mother and a long-term relationship with me, I would not be the one in second place.

* * *

I arrived at the Supper Club and met Ray at the door. I explained I was there for two reasons. First, to take a few measurements of the Supper Club floor to help us design a non-wobbly café table, and second, to inspect the swing that Sheila had been wired to on the night of the murder.

"If you can design a solid café table, I'll buy about a hundred," Ray said as he turned the lights on in the club's main room.

"Careful, I might take you up that." I set up a self-leveling green laser level in the middle of the room. As I plugged it in and turned it on, it sent a harmless green light across the room. I held a long ruler vertically at various places to measure the height of the beam from the floor. I found it had less than one-quarter inch of variation across each ten-foot section, which seemed reasonable to me.

Next, I asked Ray to show me the swing and explain how it worked.

He showed me to the area by the stage. "The stage, backstage, and swing area are separate from the kitchen and the rest of the dining hall," Ray explained. "When the performers enter this area, they close the doors so the noise from the kitchen doesn't bother the diners. However, the backstage door is in full view of the kitchen, so no one can enter or exit this area without the kitchen staff seeing them. Before you ask, we have a large staff doing the food prep, so yes, someone is always in the kitchen when we serve dinner. I was here when Detective Copeland questioned the staff, and no one in the kitchen noticed anyone or anything unusual before the murder was discovered."

"I appreciate you making this easy for me, Ray."

"No worries. Let's go up the ship's ladder next."

He led me to the bottom of a very steep set of stairs that looked like a hybrid between a stairway and a ladder. As we climbed up, I noticed this design minimized the footprint on the ground, which was perfect for the tight quarters backstage. We soon arrived at the top of a small platform where the swing was tethered when not in use. "When we first started the swing shows back in the sixties, a kid climbed up here and tried to swing. Sheila grabbed him just in time. They nearly gave me a heart attack. So, we've had a lock on the swing release panel ever since."

"Who has keys to the lock?"

"Me and Sheila are...were...the only people with keys. I gave the third key to Nigel Lawson long ago, but he lost it, so we shouldn't have to worry about that."

Ray opened the access panel with his key and showed me the release mechanism that allowed the swing to start moving. "The person sitting in the swing seat pushes off a bar on the floor, which raises the swing and allows them to unhook the seat. As soon as they lift their legs off the bar, they start moving forward like a kid on a playground swing.

It looked like there was no good way to work the release mechanism remotely, so the killer must have been up here when Sheila started swinging.

I noticed a small platform about twenty feet away that the performer could swing over to and pause as part of the performance. It was a miniature version of a circus act. I spent a few minutes inspecting the swing. The seat was suspended by two thick wire cables that ran through large eyelet hooks that were screwed into a thick beam running across the ceiling of the dance floor. The cables ran across the ceiling to the stage area so the performer could be raised or lowered for dramatic effect. The design and implementation seemed reasonable to me.

Ray must have noticed the wheels were turning in my head and wanted to know more. "So, what've you got?"

I didn't have a good theory at the moment and wouldn't have shared it with him anyway, as he was still on the suspect list. "Sorry, Ray. I'm still trying to work it out. It doesn't seem to add up."

Ray seemed both disappointed and relieved. "That's what I thought, too."

It was time to head out. "Is there anything else I should know?"

"Not that I can think of. It's a straightforward setup."

I looked around one more time, but I couldn't come up with any other questions. "Thanks for your time, Ray. I appreciate it."

"Come back anytime."

Chapter Ten

Monday Afternoon, May 22

I t was definitely time to get some design work done, so I returned to the office. I put the laser level back in the storage closet, then stopped by Paul's office so he would know I was back. I provided an update on the floor variation, and we agreed it was about what we'd expected. We discussed the table design, and he said he would mock up a prototype. He seemed to be satisfied, so I made a graceful exit.

I returned to my office and found an email from Kate letting me know that Eric Dixon had just returned from Vegas, and she was sweet enough to provide his mobile number, too. I texted him and explained who I was and that I wanted to discuss his mother's demise. He agreed to meet me for coffee as long as the location was near his home in Roseville, a first-tier suburb bordering the north side of Minneapolis and St. Paul. I was happy to oblige, and we set up a time on Wednesday morning at one of the coffee shops on Snelling Ave. near Rosedale Center.

While doing so, I noticed I had a couple of hours before the next meeting, so I frosted the glass and fired up the browser on my laptop. I Googled his name and ' Chicago,' based on Tom's not-too-subtle hint to investigate Marcel's past. The first results page had the usual links to websites that wanted to sell you access to Marcel's contact information and life history. Intermixed with this were links to news stories about suspicious deaths that had occurred on the north side of Chicago over ten years ago. I clicked on the link for one of the suburban news outlets. It brought up an article titled 'A Cult in Our Midst.'

The story described a fundamentalist Christian group called 'Institute for a Better Life' that their neighbors suspected was more than just an organized religion. Strict, sometimes draconian, moral codes were being imposed. This was not news by itself – the same can be said for many fundamentalist groups. The real story was the death of the group's founder, Bill Goddard, and the rumors that young females were being groomed to become part of his personal harem. The article included a picture underscoring their suspicions based on its extreme creepiness.

In it, Bill was sitting on a large chair that could easily be called a throne and sporting a triumphant grin. Two sets of group members surrounded him. Four men of various ages stood in a small ring around Bill, looking at the camera. The second group included twelve young ladies who looked to be in their late teens and who stood on a raised platform in a semi-circle behind the group of five. They were gazing at Bill with dreamy expressions. The caption described Bill as the founder and listed the other men, one of whom was Marcel Galland, as group leaders. I increased the resolution of the picture, and even though he wore his hair much longer then, it confirmed that a younger version of Marcel was in it. This group would have been an excellent training ground for someone who eventually wanted to run their cult in another city...like St. Paul, for example.

I scanned through a dozen more articles. Bill Goddard's death was ruled a homicide, and the police and reporters began investigating. Stories emerged of divisions forming within the group over the role of men and women in society. A large faction formed under the founder, who believed in male superiority and female obedience, reminiscent of the society in *The Handmaid's Tale*. In marriage, they believed the husband was the undisputed leader of the family, whose word was final. Even in the workplace, women were expected to defer to men in almost every circumstance. A smaller splinter group lobbied for a more open and accepting approach, but they were soon squashed.

'Cult-like' elements were forming, including a charismatic leader who demanded absolute and blind loyalty, authoritarian control, isolation of problematic members, and severe punishments. None of the articles quoted or even mentioned Marcel, so it was impossible to tell where his loyalties lay.

A reporter had secretly infiltrated the group and confirmed the rumors that Bill had been grooming young, impressionable females, first by getting them to join the group and then by convincing them to worship him. But it was Bill's brother who had been having sexual relations with several of the young female acolytes, and the rest of the group had squelched the story.

If a girl's parents complained, they were directed to Bill, who would remind them how lucky they were that he had personally selected their daughter for his group. The implication was that he would only save their collective souls if they looked the other way. He assured them that he would personally investigate the rumors about his brother and prevent any improprieties from happening again. In some cases, hush money had been paid to silence grief-stricken. In no cases did Bill apologize for or even admit to any wrongdoing by his brother or express regret for the incidents, which he continued to insist had not occurred.

When the scandal broke, numerous girls came forward with similar stories of abuse, and Bill was found brutally murdered immediately after that. The police suspected a disgruntled follower, an aggrieved parent, or possibly both. The group floundered without their enigmatic leader despite the efforts of a few minor characters to fill that role. With mounting pressure to own up to the scandals from the police, the media, and the local community, the group officially disbanded within a few months. The property was soon sold to a developer.

As the police investigated every aspect of the group's activities, they discovered the property had been sold at a substantial premium in a deal that had been in the works for over a year, well before the scandals broke. Marcel was heavily investigated since he was the group's Treasurer and Bill's right-hand man. After witnesses came forward alleging Marcel was the killer, he was arrested and charged with murder and fraud.

But, since this was Chicagoland, the witnesses recanted their stories one by one, and he was eventually released. The money was never recovered, which led one reporter to speculate that it had been used to bribe the witnesses and police. Upon regaining his freedom, Marcel had left the area. No additional suspects were ever identified, and the murder was never solved.

I had to give Tom credit for keeping tabs on his flock, and having Monsignor 'The Fixer' Frank perform background checks was a great way to do it. But could his intel about Marcel's potential involvement in inappropriate and possibly illegal financial activities stem from the charges in Chicago and not be relevant today?

I knew I would have to confront Marcel about this. I figured he would claim he had joined the group before it turned into a cult and got swept up in the process. He would also state that he had learned from his mistakes and took great pains not to repeat them.

I realized that contacting former cult members would be a great way to learn more, and Dean was the perfect person to do it. The cult's code of secrecy would undoubtedly still apply, so he'd have to develop some deep cover story to penetrate their defenses. He'd love it. As I thought about approaching my brother, there was a knock at the door. "Come in," I said without looking up to see who it was.

Paul walked in and started to ask about the table design when he noticed the contents of my screen. "Grayson, we have to talk." Uh-oh. I knew that tone, and it was not good.

He pulled out one of my guest chairs and sat down with his head up, back erect, legs together, hands balled into fists in his lap, and his jaw set forward. It looked like he was gearing up for battle.

"After everything we went through last time…I cannot believe that you are investigating another murder." Paul doesn't handle pressure well, and I tried not to interrupt him as he stammered. "We almost had to…lay off…our entire staff. We were days away…from declaring bankruptcy. Days…away…"

Okay, that was not true. "Wait a minute, Paul. That's not—"

He looked down and raised his hand as if to say 'stop.' So, I shut up. Melodramatic much, Paul?

"We almost lost our business," he said. Then he paused. "You know what, just forget it." With that, he stormed out of my office.

I knew it wouldn't do any good to remind him that I'd actually solved multiple murders while simultaneously winning some new work for our business. Or that my girlfriend was currently the police's number one suspect for Sheila's murder and the theft of the ruby, and I couldn't just ignore that. Besides, just for the record, we did not almost lose our business. We were a good two to three weeks away from that.

I also knew I just had to wait him out, and he would give me the silent treatment for a while, but he would eventually come around, especially if I solved the murder again.

* * *

The next day, I struggled to maintain a positive work environment while tiptoeing around Paul. Over time, I'd learned it was best to concentrate on the work in these situations. First, it took one's mind off the doomsday scenarios running through one's head, and second, it meant we got some work done.

Working also took my mind off the dinner with Chadrick that Ray had set up for that evening at a fashionable restaurant in St. Paul. I felt guilty about not having told Kate about this, but it seemed rude to cancel at the last minute. Plus, I secretly wanted to meet this famous motivational speaker to see what he was made of. So, I stuffed down the guilt and focused on the job, knowing I would do whatever was necessary to make it up to her later.

* * *

The Concord opened in 1935 and had been an icon of the St. Paul crowd for many years. It closed a couple of years ago for a much-needed face lift and quickly regained popularity upon reopening. The three of us met in the lobby and checked in. The Maître D recognized Ray and Chadrick immediately and warmly welcomed them back. He led us past large stained-glass windows facing Grand Avenue to the Chef's Dining Room. It was gray with large mirrors on one side and had windows looking into the kitchen on the other, as he showed us to the best table in the house.

The last time I'd had dinner here was the night our uncle, James Brennan, had been killed. I'd connected with James through DeeDee and her vast family tree on an ancestry website and invited him to meet at the Concord with Dean and me. As we dined, James claimed to be our birth father, but instead of welcoming us to the family, his main concern was keeping Dean's and my existence hidden from his wife and daughter. He flippantly revealed that our birth mother was a young girl named Maggie Fitzgerald, who had died right after I was born, and I could stand it no longer. I flew into a rage and loudly threatened to kill him in front of the packed restaurant. To make matters worse, later that night, James had been shot to death in his law office. The police, with Detective Copeland heading the charge, soon descended on the office, The Concord, and me. Okay, it was much worse for James than for me, but still.

Even though it had been over a year, I could tell the Maître D remembered me by the stern look he shot me when my dining companions weren't looking. It was a clear warning not to mess things up again. Boy, you inadvertently threaten someone with death one time, and they never forget. I figured there was a wanted poster of me in the kitchen with the caption 'Do not serve this man.' The fact that I eventually discovered the bishop was our birth father and then solved the mysteries of who killed James and our birth mother and a couple of other poor souls who were collateral damage was probably lost on him. I acknowledged the message with a brief nod, wondering if Chadrick would say anything about Kate that would make me give an encore to my previous performance.

Ray recommended a particularly fine red wine, which sounded good to us. Chadrick dove right in after we ordered dinner.

"Kate tells me the two of you are dating now."

"That's right. We've been seeing each other for over a year. I understand you two were an item at one point as well."

"Yes, we were." Chadrick seemed to be truly forlorn about their relationship not working out. Either that or he was one hell of an actor. "She broke it off, and I have to say, I can't blame her. Even though I've written a dozen self-help books, held countless motivational seminars, and have over a million followers, she made me realize I needed to work on myself just like the people I was helping."

While I wondered if there was a difference between shameless plugs and humble bragging, Chadrick went on. "Are you living up to your true potential as a product designer, Grayson?"

I didn't know if he couldn't help himself or was bent on playing some weird mind game. Either way, I had to admit he had done his homework. But I wasn't about to get dragged down that rat hole. "Well, Kate seems to think so." I was mentally adding points to my side of the scoreboard while trying not to grin. At least not too much.

Chadrick shifted uncomfortably, then quickly changed the subject. "Have they found the ruby yet, Ray?"

Ray frowned slightly, which I took to mean one of two things. On the one hand, he may not have known that Chadrick was aware of the theft. It hadn't been in the news, which meant he had insiders who were feeding him information. On the other hand, he could have been unhappy that Chadrick asked that in front of me, admitting that he told Chadrick something that was supposed to be secret. "No, they haven't. I don't have much faith in the coppers on this one. Not the full quid, if you know what I mean."

Chadrick just blundered on. "What I can't believe is that Sheila was killed by cone snail venom. It must have been a slow, torturous death. Who would do that to someone? Sorry if this is a sensitive subject, Ray." Ray just looked down at his plate and didn't answer. Okay, this was getting out of hand. 'Read the room,' I wanted to scream. 'Your inability to control your showing off disrespects Ray's wife and makes him uncomfortable.'

Someone was doing some severe oversharing with Chadrick. I hated to think it was Ray or Kate, but who else could it be? Either that or Chadrick was the perpetrator. That was something worth considering, but what motive would he have had? I changed the subject by asking Chadrick about his favorite topic—himself. "So, your latest book is called 'Beat Yourself.' That's an intriguing idea. I see it's already a Times bestseller. What's it about?"

Other than masochism or self-flagellation, I thought. He had used a risqué title just to attract attention, which would probably work by increasing interest and, therefore, book sales. Authors. You had to hate the cheap tricks they used.

"It's about being your best self and living your best life by increasing your capabilities and expanding your horizons a little each day." He obnoxiously raised the empty wine bottle as our waiter walked by and shook it to indicate it was empty and he wanted another one. "Most people tend to set lofty goals for themselves, like running five miles a day or losing thirty pounds, but have no idea how to get there. So, they take on too much too soon, become frustrated with their lack of progress, and give up. My new book talks about setting small, incremental targets that are attainable so you will stay the course and achieve your ultimate goals over time. I'll gladly sign a copy for you if you like."

I didn't know how to respond, but fortunately, I didn't have to as Chadrick rambled on about how he'd personally used this process to improve his focus on writing. He was now writing two thousand words a day when his previous personal best had been only one thousand. He paused to take a breath, then suddenly blurted out, "Damn you, Grayson Dyle. Kate was supposed to be mine." It sounded like the ranting of a privileged person who couldn't understand why he wasn't getting his way. The weird thing was, as self-centered as he sounded, I had to admit the plan in his new book seemed to make sense. I thought I'd pick up a copy and take him up on his offer to sign it.

Chadrick became melancholy and stared into the bottom of his almost empty wine glass. Even though they'd broken up long ago, he seemed genuinely lost without Kate. I felt sorry for him.

"Well, I would be devastated if I lost Kate, too." It was all I could muster. I looked at Ray, who didn't know what to say either. Ray looked at me. I opened my eyes wide and tipped my head twice in Chadrick's direction, a classic move that meant 'say or do something.' Ray must have gotten the message and changed the subject back to the book, asking when the tour would start. Chadrick perked up a bit and launched into a rundown of the tour scheduled to start at a famous New York bookshop in a couple of weeks.

As he prattled on, I considered the comment that Kate was supposed to be his. 'His,' which implied ownership. What an odd way to phrase it. What would Kate say to that? I wondered. A wave of self-doubt suddenly came over me. What would Kate do if Chadrick, riding a resurgence of success with his charm and wit fully restored and recharged, swooped in and tried to take her back? Would they ride off into the sunset in Chadrick's brand-spankin'-new convertible Mercedes while he grinned at me through the rearview mirror? The thought made me want to throw a glass of water in Chadrick's smug, book-peddling face, and he hadn't even done anything yet. I didn't recall ever being this insecure. Of course, I didn't recall ever being this attached either. The ecstasy love brings and the price we pay for it.

Then again, maybe these feelings were the result of being adopted. The certainty of knowing who I was and where my roots were grounded had been ripped away on the day that Dean and I discovered that we were not Ben and Lynda Dyle's biological children and that they'd been hiding this fact from us for over forty years. Was this a symptom of abandonment syndrome caused by our birth parents casting us aside?

We eventually figured out who our birth parents were and learned of their reasons for not being able to raise their offspring, but did that make it any easier to take? True, our father was a catholic priest, and our mother was a young girl working at the church, and it seemed like they really were in love. But they could have made different decisions. Yes, it would have completely disrupted their lives. The priest would have been defrocked, and the girl would have been run out of town on a rail for having sex at such a young age, but so what? Wasn't making difficult choices what you did when you loved each other and your children that much, even if they involved extreme sacrifices? Didn't they take the easy way out by giving us up?

I realized I had put all of these thoughts in a box and stuck it on a high mental shelf so I didn't have to deal with them, and this was not the time to open it up. Besides, they were nothing that ten years of in-depth psychotherapy wouldn't fix.

I snapped out of my reverie to find Ray pretending to be interested while

Chadrick was still blathering on about some famous bookstore in L.A. that he was looking forward to visiting again because he'd hooked up with the store's sexy young manager on his last tour. And here I was, feeling sorry for him. We soon parted ways, and Ray made sure to get an Uber for Chadrick. I nodded at the matre 'd on the way out, hoping he would treat me like a normal human being and let me dine here again in the future, but he just looked the other way. I guess you don't get credit for not terrorizing people.

On the way home, I realized I could see why other people would get caught up in Chadrick's charisma, especially when they didn't know him. I patted myself on the back for not falling for his schtick. But then I thought about Elizabeth's comments over lunch and wondered if maybe I needed to work on my charm after all.

Chapter Eleven

Wednesday Morning, May 24

I had looked Eric up on Facebook, so I recognized him as he entered the coffee shop and introduced myself. We shook hands and got into the line. I ordered my usual medium light roast, and he ordered a large White Chocolate Espresso Shaker and a Raspberry Flavor Shot, which sounded good but was not inexpensive. I paid, and we grabbed our drinks and found a seat at a café table for two, which was surprisingly sturdy. I wondered if it was new and leaned down to see if it had any telltale labels underneath. Eric looked at me oddly, so I sat up and got down to business.

"Your dad said you were in Vegas. How was your trip?"

"It was fine. Grayson, I'm still not sure what I'm doing here. My dad told me that you are looking into Mom's murder and also the theft of the ruby. I have to ask you why. Why not just leave it to the police?"

"Well, it's a bit complicated. Have you met Kate, Ray's new finance person?"

"Not yet. I hear she's a real hottie, though."

"Kate and I have been dating for over a year now." I thought he might be embarrassed for commenting on my girlfriend's appearance, but he was showing no sign of it. "Anyway, Kate and I were at the Supper Club on the night in question. When we realized Sheila was deceased, Kate became concerned about the ruby. She ran to the office to safeguard it, and I ran after her, but we were too late. The safe was open, and the ruby was gone. Your dad initially thought she might have been involved, and he told the police about that. Kate became their main person of interest, and they are still fixating on her since they can't come up with any other suspects. While they are busy trying to prove she's guilty, I'm trying to find the real killer so I can clear her name."

Eric was sipping his drink and nodding, so I thought I was making progress, although maybe not that much. "I understand you're taking a skip year from college right now. If you don't mind me asking, what have you been up to?"

"I've been working as a freelancer." Could he be much vaguer than that?

"What kind of work do you do?"

"I've been working for small companies without an in-house marketing team creating digital marketing campaigns for Instagram and TikTok. It's not glamorous, but it pays the bills."

I wondered why Ray didn't ask his son for help marketing the business to millennials. Unless he thought Eric would tell him that no amount of marketing would get young people interested in an Aussie Museum. "Is that why you're frequently in Vegas, creating ads for hotels and casinos?"

"Something like that, yeah."

It sounded like he had a way of making money, but was it going out as fast as it was coming in? "Speaking of which, how'd you do in Vegas? Do you have a system for beating the house?"

Eric just laughed. "Everyone in Vegas has a system for beating the house."

Since Ray said Eric plays the slots, and Mia said he likes blackjack, I thought it would be interesting to see what he claims to play. "What game do you normally play?"

"Look, I know you have this whole 'amateur detective/save the innocent girl from the big bad cops' schtick going, but I don't need to be a part of it."

Eric got up and left, leaving most of his expensive coffee drink behind. I found myself wondering if fighting with your parents so you could stay out of school to help casinos attract more gamblers was enough of a motive for murdering your mother.

* * *

104

Our road trip to Rochester started with Dean's text on Monday night. I had just taken the stairs up to my condo after work when it arrived.

Have to cancel our meeting — something came up at work

That's too bad, I replied.

Yeah, they seem to think I can get things done at the push of a button

Maybe Thursday or Friday?

Sounds good. I'll get back to you

It took a few minutes for me to realize that Dean's use of the term 'button' was a hidden message. Years ago, he'd read that when they have a warrant for your phone, police investigators will tear through it looking for any and all communication tools because most bad actors will not just text each other even if they are using burner phones. Based on this and his obsession with never doing anything untoward, or at least his obsession with never *being caught* doing anything untoward, my brother created a small communication app called Button, which allowed us to text each other securely and privately. He encrypted the messages, so you had to have the app on your phone to read them, and they were immediately deleted when they were read, so there was no trail to be discovered later. He'd sent this to me years ago, but we never seemed to have a real reason to use it. Until now, of course.

I scrolled through the apps on my phone and finally found the Button icon on the last menu screen. Even the icon was innocuous, and access to the app itself was obscured as you had to get through a whole bunch of screens saying the app was no longer in service, all designed to throw off investigators. I finally figured out how to open it up and found two messages from the last ten minutes waiting for me.

Grayson, are you there?

Button is the keyword, remember?

I wondered if he realized that texting me to use Button through Button would not work.

Yeah, just figured that out. I texted back

About time. I know someone who can appraise the stone

Awesome, who is it?

You know them too, but I'm not going to tell you until later

When?

On our road trip to Rochester

Wait, what? What road trip? Okay, this Button thing was fun, but it was also getting annoying. Why didn't we talk? It's not like anyone was going to record that.

I called Dean, and the next thing I knew, he had convinced me to buzz down to Rochester on Thursday. He pointed out that it wasn't just to have the stone appraised. It was an opportunity to see Mom and visit our adoptive father's grave, which we hadn't done since the funeral over a year ago. It's fair to say he guilted me into it.

Normally, Dean liked to drive separately in case one of his clients had an outage in their home automation systems. God forbid they should have to get up off the couch to turn the lights on instead of yelling a command at a Google Assistant or Amazon Alexa. But, in this case, he was willing to drive together as long as he could return to the Cities immediately if an emergency call came through, either with me or without me. I wondered what an Uber for the ninety-mile trip from Rochester to Minneapolis would cost.

After my semi-disastrous meeting with Eric, I drove down to Dean's home in Eagan and parked in front of his second garage door. As I did, the first garage door opened, so I got in Dean's car, and we headed out.

"So, who is this mystery precious stone appraiser, and how do I know him?" I asked from the passenger seat of his Genesis G80 Electrified Vehicle. I noticed the plush leather seats and appealing dashboard—I have to consider getting one of these.

I was trapped in his car going 75 on Highway 52, so Dean had no problem disclosing the name. "Lindsey Brazzer."

I hadn't heard that name in years, and I couldn't place it. "Lindsey Brazzer. Wow. I recognize the name, but I'm drawing a blank about how I knew him. Did he go to our school?"

"Yes," Dean says with a smile.

Then, it hit me, and I was incredulous. "Wait a minute. Do you mean the burnout that was always smoking dope and selling it on the side to support his habit? That Lindsey Brazzer?"

"That's the guy."

"No way. I would have thought he'd be locked up by now."

"I know, right? But get this: our former schoolmate now owns a chain of jewelry stores in malls across southern Minnesota. His main store is in the downtown Rochester area, which is where we're meeting him. He offered to assess the stone with no questions asked and was even willing to waive the fee just to become part of the 'legend of the ruby,' even though he can't brag about it because I've sworn him to secrecy. Just wait until you see his store. I Googled it, and it's unbelievable."

"He probably has a few felonies under his belt. How do we know we can trust him?"

"I know he doesn't have a criminal record because I ran a background check, and he was the one who suggested it. Besides, he was in my grade, remember? I know things about Lindsey that no one else knows from when we hung out together. There's no way he'd double-cross me."

I was still in shock, but it was too late to turn back. No wonder my brother hadn't told me until we were underway. "Whatever you say, Dean, it's not as if there's a fortune in jewelry and Kate's future hanging in the balance."

We drove in silence for a while. We were getting out of range of the Twin Cities radio station we'd been listening to, so I cruised the dial but couldn't find anything I liked. So, I cranked up some alternative rock tunes on Spotify instead.

"So, what else have you been up to?" I asked as we passed the Flint Hills Oil Refinery, which we used to call the stinky plant when we were kids.

"I've got a new project from X."

Here we go, I thought. X was Dean's largest client and apparently had money to burn. He'd been an average IT guy from a modest working-class background when he had become very wealthy through a series of shrewd investments in high-tech start-ups. He acquired a five-acre property on Lake Minnetonka in one of the ritziest neighborhoods in the state, with a fourteen thousand square foot mansion, three outbuildings, two pools, and over four hundred feet of shoreline. As a home automation specialist, Dean's company sent him to X's estate on a regular basis to install expensive electronics, such as a system that simultaneously flew a fleet of over five hundred drones over the lake in various formations, including 3D animations. It was a big hit, especially on national holidays like the Fourth of July. He had also installed a system that automatically recalculated the value of the mansion's wine collection when X added or removed a bottle from the cellar. Since we had time to kill while we drove, I dove in. "Remind me why you call him X again. Is that short for Xavier?"

"No, it's not. I can't tell you his real name due to our nondisclosure agreement. When we started working for him, I told my team to call him X so no one would accidentally say his name publicly. He overheard us and insisted we call him that all the time. Okay, it might be a little pretentious, but we're now his go-to company anytime he gets the slightest whim for a new project, so we just roll with it.

"Anyway, he's got this trophy wife who bought a Persian cat she wants to enter in the next Cat Fanciers Show. She wants to take Best of Breed, maybe even Best of Show. But the house is so freaking big that she can never find the damn thing. They have to organize a search party to flush it out for every grooming appointment. They tried using a collar with an embedded GPS tracker, but the cat always wriggled out. The vet implanted an ID chip, so Mr. X wants me to set up motion detectors, chip scanners, and thermal imagers throughout the house and hook them to an iPad app so the groomer can track it down."

I just shook my head like always when Dean told me about X's extravagances. "Talk about your first-world problem."

"It's a living. The show is only a few weeks out, and Mr. X wants the system up by Monday, so it's been keeping me busy."

A question that I'd been meaning to ask my brother for a while now popped into my head, and since we were trapped in the car for the next hour, this seemed like the perfect time. "So, what's the deal with X?"

Dean shot me a frown. "What do you mean? He's alright. He pays his bills on time, and the work has been steady. He's fine."

"Doesn't it seem odd that X has all this money and doesn't know what to do with it, so he spends it on all this extravagant gear?"

He seemed to get my point finally. "This is why I don't tell you everything about X. Sure, he can be a little out there. But…"

"Okay, wait a minute. You can't just leave me hanging like that. What do you mean a little out there?"

My brother hesitated for a minute. He's always been a bit defensive of X, which made it seem like he knew too much. He glanced at me, then launched into a story. I felt he'd been dying to talk about this for a long time but never had the right venue. "It's funny. X blows through money like water in some areas but struggles to spend it elsewhere. He can't stand paying for things he used to do himself and could still do if he wanted to. Simple things like paying someone to mow the lawn really seem to bug him, even though it takes two full-time employees to maintain his estate.

"One day, I was drilling a hole to install a motion sensor in the Calacatta Gold marble of his expansive master bath and noticed he had a small jar next to the shower with nubs of soap bars in it. They were too small to use, but he couldn't stand throwing them out, so he collected them in a jar. After he has enough of them, he must have someone melt them back into one bar so he can use them up."

"Wow, that's…interesting." I stopped myself from saying 'weird.' Based on Dean's previous descriptions, X had always seemed shallow and self-centered. Maybe I shouldn't have rushed to judge him.

"On the other hand, X was driving one of his luxury SUVs, the Land Rover Defender, when the MIL became illuminated." He pronounced MIL as 'mil,' like the first syllable of the word million. "This was the third time in a month—"

"Wait a minute, what's a MIL?"

"Other than a Mother-In-Law? MIL stands for Malfunction Indicator Lamp."

"So, the 'MIL becoming illuminated' is Land Rover-speak for saying the Check Engine Light turned on."

"Pretty much, yeah. Anyway, it was the third time that month that the MIL became illuminated, which bugged the crap out of him. Since it already had over twenty thousand miles on it, he drove it to the dealership and traded it in on the spot. The new car manager was so happy to see him that he simply handed him the keys to the latest model, which they had just rolled onto the showroom floor, and told him they would charge it to his AmEx Centurion card along with a generous credit for the trade-in. The whole thing took less than ten minutes, and he was out of there."

Stories like that always seemed funny. I knew there were people out there with money to burn, and that seemed like a good thing—a thing that many of us mere mortals aspired to. But then you found out how they actually lived their lives, and you discovered you didn't want to be like that after all.

While contemplating the lives of the rich and famous, we passed a sign for a small town called Cannon Falls, and I suddenly realized a pit stop would be a good idea. I suggested we stop at the gas station right off the highway to refill our coffee and snacks, and Dean agreed.

I always had a soft spot in my heart for Cannon Falls because it was the home of Pachyderm Studio. Most people knew Prince was originally from Minnesota, but hardly anyone seemed to know about this infamous landmark of our State's music scene. Many famous musicians recorded at Pachyderm, including Nirvana, which used the studio to record its 1993 album *In Utero*, Soul Asylum, They Might Be Giants, and Trampled by Turtles. I'd driven by the studio just for fun in the past, only to find that the parking lot and any buildings on the property were set back behind a wide expanse of trees so as not to be visible from the road. There wasn't even a sign marking the entrance. It reminded me of the island of Tortuga in the Pirates of the Caribbean movie—you can only find it if you've been there before. We soon got back in the car and were making good time for Rochester.

"How's Kate doing?" Dean asked in between bites of a chocolate-frosted mini donut.

"Kate's doing great, for the most part."

"Uh-oh. That doesn't sound good."

I grabbed another mini donut for comfort and told Dean that lunch with Kate and Elizabeth wasn't the big hit I had hoped for. "She didn't even seem to notice the flowers. She just tossed them aside like they were nothing."

"Sucking up to Kate's mom with flowers, huh? Wow, you really are smitten."

I ignored the dig. "Despite her mom's crass comments at lunch, Kate wants us to have dinner with her."

Dean seemed sympathetic, but I got the impression he was trying not to laugh at my plight. "Hmm, on the one hand, it's a good sign that she wants the two of you to get along. It makes it so much easier to have her approval before you pop the question."

"Wait, what?"

"On the other hand, there's no escaping from a dinner if it's not going well."

"I just can't imagine why she wants to get back together so soon. We really should give it more time. Like a year or two, for example."

Dean's laugh finally escaped. "Gray, she's been trolling you like a walleye. A few more visits with her mom to smooth things over, and she'll try to set the hook."

I looked out the window thoughtfully. "I know. I don't mind that part. It's just that she's made some weird comments about her mother being a ruthless real estate agent after we started getting serious. I don't know if that was an advance warning or if she was saying maybe I'd be more successful if I was more ruthless."

Dean just shook his head. "You might be overanalyzing this just a little. Why don't you ask her?"

And take relationship advice from my brother? No way. "Wait until you hear about the dinner with her ex-boyfriend." Even though I knew he would give me grief for months, I told him the whole story.

After I finished, Dean produced a low whistle. "You, my friend, are a glutton for punishment."

I found it hard to disagree. "The thing is, Chadrick knows too much about the night of the murder and the theft. Either someone is feeding him a lot of intel, or he was there. And, if he was there, it must have been because he was the murderer. Or an accomplice. We need to figure out which one it is so we can continue the investigation."

"I'd be happy to check out Chadrick. See what he's really been up to."

"Nah, I'm good. I'd rather do this one myself. You might be able to do some digging on some other suspects, though."

"Why, what's up with them?"

"Kate told me that Ray's businesses have been slowly declining for years. The Aussie House had been holding its own because there weren't too many other options for lunch in that area, and Ray had really built some interesting menu options. But the Supper Club had been losing customers for years. People didn't seem interested in the ruby anymore, so they went to weekend hours only for a while and eventually shut it down. No one wants to see Ray's old prospecting gear without the main attraction. He's been looking into selling the business, maybe even closing it down, and selling off the property. He even has an offer on the table. But now they're suddenly doing better due to the notoriety that the murder brought. She's worried that Ray will think his business has been saved, but then it will end as fast as it started when the press moves on to other scandals. Anyway, here's how you can help me."

I walked Dean through the discussions I'd had with Tom, Frank, Ray, and Marcel and the history I'd discovered about Marcel's involvement in what was basically a cult in the Chicagoland area.

"You've been busy, too," said Dean.

"Tell me about it. Paul is driving me crazy because he's worried I'm spending too much time away from work. But Kate can't do it, she's the main suspect. And Tom must not have wanted to sully Marcel's reputation by saying anything to Copeland, so who else is going to do it?"

"How about Frank the Fixer?" The way Dean scoffed as he said the name confirmed he had about as much respect for Monsignor Frank as I did.

"I asked Tom about that, and he said Frank was too well-known in this community to make any progress. Anyone he spoke with would think their comments would go back to him or the police, and they would clam up. People in Chicago would probably make him for a clergy member, just like they would make undercover cops."

"So, that leaves me?" Dean asked innocently.

I smiled. "Exactly. You're the perfect guy, and besides, you love this stuff. You could pose as a reporter revisiting the story or maybe a former cult member trying to track down an ex-girlfriend who had also been in the group."

The grin forming on Dean's face told me he was in.

"I have to get this project for X done first."

"Of course." Just like the Blues Brothers, Dean always claimed to be on a top-secret, critically important mission from God to help X with some lame project or another. But I knew he would find a way to multitask and immediately start the investigation. Having an actual reason to delve into someone's deep, dark secrets versus just exploring out of curiosity would be too tempting for him to put off.

"While we're on the subject, have you ever heard the names Nigel Lawson or Scott Dimond?"

Dean thought for a minute, then shook his head. "Nope, why do you ask?"

"Ray told me that Nigel owns twenty percent of the company, but he's a silent partner and spends a lot of time taking vacations to Australia. I'd like to talk to him, but he's supposedly in the Outback now, so he's unreachable. Scott has been their financial advisor for years and recently rented an office in their HQ building. Ray told me Scott promised to hook him up with a marketing company to market his enterprise to millennials. But a new ad campaign like that is going to be expensive. You don't just create a bunch of marketing collateral and wait for the customers to roll in. You have to buy ads across the main social media platforms and newspapers and maybe erect billboards across the city for a long time to get the message across. And that's just the start. The list goes on and on.

"I know Scott is a venture capitalist, so he's probably sitting on big piles of cash. But I can't see him investing that kind of money in the Ruby Ray story. I mean, what's the outcome going to be? More traffic to the museum and the restaurants? Plus, it would be too risky. There's no good way to predict the results, which is not how VC guys operate. It would be cheaper and easier to just start with a new restaurant theme."

Dean got the message. "So why is he hanging out with Ray?"

"Good question. Ray said he's renting the space to Scott because he's looking into commercial opportunities in the area."

"Okay. So, he dabbles in retail, too. So what?"

"It just seems odd. Ray also said he wouldn't turn down the extra income, so maybe it was all about the money as usual." I took a breath for a minute, considering if I should press my brother further, and then decided to go for it. "How'd you like to look into them, too?"

Dean looked down while shaking his head, apparently in disbelief. "Sure, why not? I suppose you've got to get back to running your business."

"There is that. But I'll hold up my end of things while you do that." I told him about my meeting with Ray's daughter, Mia, and his son, Eric, my plan to meet with the entertainer, Patter, and my decision not to meet with Mia's boyfriend, Josh. "Paul is going to kill me, but I've got to keep working on this. While investigating, can you run a quick check into Ruby Ray's financials?" I said it quickly, hoping to sneak it in. Dean didn't react.

"Wouldn't it be easier just to ask Kate?"

"Nah. She won't tell me anything specific. Something about a confidentiality agreement."

"Hmm, not sure about that one. Let's see how far I get with the cultists and the other two guys first."

Chapter Twelve

Thursday, May 25

We arrived in Rochester at about nine-thirty a.m., parked the car in the ramp of The Grand, which Dean assured me was the swankiest hotel in town and entered the lobby, which was big enough to include a small mall. It was almost impossible to miss the name 'Brazzer Jewelers' prominently but tastefully mounted above two display cases, one on either side of the main entrance to the store. We caught up with Lindsey, who was just opening the doors.

"Dean, Grayson, so good to see you again." We shook hands. "Please, come in."

I had to admit the shop truly was spectacular. Bright white lights highlighted numerous display cases, which contained every form of precious stone I'd ever heard of. A large sign proclaiming the name 'Brazzer' in brushed aluminum and backlit with blue lighting was mounted on the marble tiles of the back wall. A nicely appointed office with glass walls and a glass door was in the corner between the signs. It felt luxurious, and I could hardly believe the kid we knew from high school was behind it.

I'll bet he couldn't change the office glass from clear to frosted using his phone like we can, which would be handy when his clientele brought in their briefcases full of cash. Then, I wondered why I needed to be petty about his apparent success.

He showed us into the office and offered coffee, which we politely refused.

"Good to see you're doing well, Lindsey," said Dean.

Our host suddenly got very serious. "Thanks, Dean. As you know, I used to party quite a bit in high school. What you may not know is that I got busted dealing pot during our senior year, but the judge offered me another chance. He said he would drop the charges if I could stay clean for one year. So, I got religion and turned my life around."

Dean and I started stammering about how awesome that was when he burst out laughing. "Sorry, guys. Just kidding. I can't say things like that with a straight face anymore."

Dean and I looked at each other, wondering what he was talking about.

"No, my Father sat me down one day when I was twenty-five and showed me the books. I realized there was way more money to be made in the jewelry business than selling pot, and it was all legal. He told me a few secrets about the business. If you're visiting Rochester and staying at the Grand Hotel, we know a few things about you. First, you have enough disposable income to stay at the most expensive hotel in town. Second, you're probably here to visit your Aunt Martha at the Mayo Clinic. Third, the only reason she's at Mayo is that she has some weird condition no one's ever heard of, which means she may not be long for this world. Fourth, rich people who are worried about Aunt Martha suddenly dropping dead will happily splurge on gifts to make themselves feel less guilty about the way they've treated her all these years." Lindsey laughed again. "So, we provide a valuable public service in the guilt erasure business!"

Dean and I chuckled mainly at the absurdity of that statement.

"From your website, it looks like you've got other locations, too," Dean said.

"That's true. You know what's weird? I seem to have a knack for running the business. Maybe it was from all those years of dealing pot. We only had the downtown store back then, and I realized we didn't get much trade from the townies. So, I convinced my dad to open another store in the Apache Mall. The locals don't buy as many big-ticket items, but the business in Mother's Day gifts, engagement rings, and wedding sets are steady, and the store is doing great. Once that worked, we opened up other locations, too."

Lindsey seemed to think he had spent enough time on his background. "So, what have the two of you been up to since high school?"

I jumped in with a quick summary as I didn't want to spend much time reminiscing. "Well, Dean is an automation engineer, and I'm co-owner of a small product design firm."

We talked for a few minutes about what automation engineers actually did and the types of products Paul and I designed. "Hey, my business partner is quite a talented design guy. If you ever need help designing new jewelry products, he would be happy to send you a few ideas."

"Wow, that sounds good, Grayson. We're always looking for innovative designs. If he is truly talented, I'd love to work with him. Here's my card. Ask him to get in touch." That justified the trip to Rochester right there, I thought as I put the card in my wallet.

"So, I'd like to see this ruby. But wait a minute." He took out a remote and frosted the office glass. Talk about a cruel irony.

Dean took the ruby out of his pocket and handed it to Lindsey, who examined it for a minute. "Hmmm, Interesting. Can you leave this with me? I want to do an in-depth analysis for you. It shouldn't take more than an hour or two."

"Um, can we get a receipt?" I still couldn't believe Lindsey had left his dodgy past behind, so this seemed risky to me without proof we'd handed over the stone.

"No worries, Grayson. We can do better than that. Dean, take a picture of us." He posed beside me, holding up the stone with a big smile, and my brother snapped a pic.

We told Lindsey we planned to visit our mother, and she'd probably want us to stay for lunch, so we'd see him after one, which he said was fine.

Dean said to me in a low voice as we headed out, "Remind me to delete that once we leave here with the stone."

* * *

We'd driven around a bit just to see what had become of our old haunts.

Lindsey had given us a heads-up about some of the area's new stores, restaurants, and festivals. Rochester was substantially bigger and had changed so much that it was hard to believe this was the same town we'd grown up in. While we cruised about, I texted Paul to let him know I had an exciting new opportunity for him to put his design skills to work. I didn't expect him to text me back, and he didn't, but I was sure the message had been received and he would want to learn more.

Dean and I soon pulled into the driveway of our childhood home right before lunchtime. It was a classic, single-story rambler with tan stucco and light brown trim. The yard looked much better than the last time we were here. The landscaping company I'd hired was well worth the money.

We greeted Mom at the door with big hugs. Her white sweater and light blue slacks didn't hang from her frame quite so loosely, which was a good sign. Dean asked Mom if she still wanted to visit Dad's grave. I must have missed the memo where he told me we were going on this side quest, but that was okay. It seemed like a good idea. Mom said she was ready, so Dean drove us to the cemetery. It had been over a year since the funeral, and we took a few wrong turns, but we soon found the right section. Dean parked, and we walked over to the gravesite. I offered Mom my arm just to be safe, and she graciously accepted.

Mom took a small bouquet of lilies from her handbag and placed them on Dad's grave. She seemed a bit unsteady as she got up, so I put my arm around her again for support. We stood there side-by-side, each of us lost in our thoughts. I wondered why Dad never told us we'd been adopted. He would have had plenty of opportunities to do so. But it never happened, and I was still struggling to come to terms with it. Maybe he didn't want there to be any doubt that we were his kids. I laughed to myself at that. Who would take an eight-year-old golfing and then let him drive the golf cart, sending the other golfers running for cover, but his own father? Soon, it was time for lunch, so we drove back to Mom's house.

We walked down the hall to the kitchen, where all good family reunions are consummated. I knew there was no point asking if she wanted to take a break from cooking and order out as soon as I spotted the pot of her famous chicken soup with the homemade, hand-cut noodles on the stove and the fixings for turkey sandwiches already laid out.

"Why don't you boys sit down? I've got lunch all ready."

Dean and I sat in our usual places. It was just like old times, yet it was completely different without Dad. Mom seemed lighter on her feet as she served up the soup. It was just the way I remembered. The three of us made small talk about Rochester, the neighbors, how the relatives were doing, and which of Mom's friends had recently passed. It felt like we'd driven through a black hole and landed in a Norman Rockwell painting, which was fine by me.

We were just finishing lunch when the inquisition started, right on cue. "So, how do you feel about being adopted now that the shock has worn off?" Mom was never one to avoid the elephant in the room.

I was going to ask her the same thing about dealing with the loss of her husband of over fifty years. It was just like her to be more concerned about her boys than herself.

"It's really not much different than not being adopted because we never knew, and no one seemed to make a big deal about it," Dean replied.

"What about Aunt Phyllis?" I asked in as polite a manner as possible. "Remember all those family parties where she was making chitchat while her perfect little angels terrorized us behind your back?"

Mom laughed. "That was just kids being kids." That was not at all how I remembered it, but I decided to let it go.

"And how is Kate doing?" I got the sense she'd wanted to ask the question the moment we arrived and could hold out no longer.

"She's doing great, Mom. Thanks for asking." I knew that wouldn't be enough to satisfy her curiosity. "I had lunch with Kate and her mom on Monday."

"Oh, Grayson, that's wonderful. She wouldn't ask you to meet her mom if she wasn't getting serious. Most girls want their mother to approve of their future husband no matter how old they are."

I had a feeling this would be a frequent topic of discussion in future conversations with Mom and started wondering if maybe I had overshared.

"That's good to know, Mom."

Now, it was my brother's turn. "Have you been seeing any nice young ladies, Dean?" Mom said it with such a sweet smile it would be difficult to take offense.

"Unfortunately, no. I've been too busy at work."

Yeah, installing a fancy cat finder for some rich guy, I thought to myself.

"Well, okay, but I'm not getting any younger."

Dean and I volunteered to clean up the dishes as we finished lunch while Mom made a quick phone call. About ten minutes later, there was a knock at the front door. "Dean and Grayson, I have a surprise for you. Aunt Phyllis is here for a visit!" Mom said as she went to the door and opened it. To my shock and awe, Mom's sister, Aunt Phyllis, walked in. Yes, it was the woman whose two kids terrorized Dean and me at every party since we were old enough to walk around while she did nothing but pretend to look the other way and snigger. Phyllis looked about the same, only older, just like the rest of us. She was always a bit taller than Mom but, in my opinion, nowhere near as pretty.

Things got wrapped around the axle pretty quickly. I rarely became rattled, but I was feeling anxious. When we were standing at Dad's grave just a couple of hours ago, I started thinking I could forgive my adoptive parents for withholding the news about our birth status. After all, they took us in, provided a good home, and raised us in the best way they could. It just didn't seem like a big enough issue to cloud whatever time Dean and I had left with our adoptive mother. Now that the mother of our childhood antagonists was in the room, it was completely different. The feeling of forgiveness was being replaced by shame. And, if I was honest, anger at not being shielded from her offspring.

Because our cousins were two years older than us, they had an advantage all through our childhood, which they took every opportunity to milk. Nothing unusual there. Like when we were at a family birthday party, my oldest cousin taught me the S-word and then told me to show it off to my mother. So, I trotted down, interrupted her conversation, and blurted out my new word with a big smile on my face, and most of the relatives watching. I'll never forget her look of horror and embarrassment, the look of contempt on my aunt's face, and my cousin sniggering in the background. To my mother's credit, she quickly read the room and, instead of scolding me, just laughed and made some wisecrack about kids being kids and then went on talking as if nothing had happened.

But, being adopted introduced a whole new level of complexity. Would my aunt have let her kids mistreat us if we had been wrought from the family's flesh and blood? There was no way to know. And yet Dean and I had identified our birth parents, and I could say with complete certainty that we came from good stock. At that moment, I wanted to tell her who our birth father really was just to see the look on her face. Of course, the backstory of a catholic bishop fathering two children was a bit problematic, but still.

I looked over at Dean. I didn't know if I was projecting, but watching him fold his arms across his chest and breathe heavily made it seem like he was having similar thoughts. There was no way we were going to subject ourselves to this kind of torture, and since we were fully grown adults, we didn't have to.

"Aunt Phyllis, what a surprise. It's so nice to see you," I said from across the room without moving a muscle to shake her hand or hug her. I turned toward our mother. "Mom, I wish you told us you were expecting company." I also wish you would explain the thought process wherein you concluded that inviting this person to meet with us was a good idea, I thought. "The thing is, Dean and I have an appointment downtown in fifteen minutes that we really can't miss."

I looked back at Dean. His face was relaxing, and the look of relief was palpable. He followed my lead. "Yes, we're meeting with a friend of ours about a potential business opportunity, and we really can't be late."

Mom looked a bit crestfallen, but did she really expect us to play happy families and just let the past go? "Oh, okay. Sorry, Phyllis, I didn't know about their meeting. Why don't you sit down, and we can chat, okay? Would you like some coffee?"

Phyllis had a bewildered look on her face, which was trending toward resentment, so it was definitely time to bail. "Well, we'd better run. I'll call you soon, Mom." Dean and I hugged our mom, sidestepped any contact with her sister, and got the hell out of there. Dean and I got in his car and immediately fist-bumped while grinning like we were hopped up on Adderall.

"Nice job, Grayson. I wouldn't have lasted five minutes without lashing out irrationally at that woman."

"You and me both, brother." Every once in a while, given the right circumstances, being petty felt pretty damn good.

* * *

By the time we returned to the jewelry store, Lindsey had finished his inspection of the ruby. He showed us into his office and frosted the glass again.

"I had my doubts about the stone's authenticity when you first handed it to me because the color didn't seem quite right. So, I decided to run some in-depth tests to confirm my suspicions. Do you want to know more about them, or should I get to the bottom line?"

Dean and I both said we wanted to know more, so Lindsey continued with his assessment as he turned the ruby over and over in his hands.

"I used a refractometer to measure how light bends as it passes through the stone, then compared the refractive index with known values for natural and synthetic rubies. Then, I examined the stone under ultraviolet light, which shows fluorescence patterns, and under a microscope, which shows gas bubbles and flux inclusions. In this stone, even with the naked eye, you can see the grain boundaries of the crystals are way too uniform." He held the stone up to the light as if to take one last look before passing judgment. He must have confirmed his findings because he carried on. "Based on all that, I am convinced this stone is synthetic. It's a fake. It never touched the earth unless someone dropped it. They did a nice job of sculpting it, though. My guess is it was created in a lab somewhere in Eastern Europe, probably through a process called 'flux growth' or 'flame fusion.' It's pretty simple, really. You start by melting corundum in a high-temperature furnace, then slowly add small amounts of chromium oxide, which gives it the red color, then you add a seed crystal..."

Lindsey looked up to see that his audience had lost interest in the monologue and were getting ready to bolt from the theater. "Well, you get the idea. I wish I had better news for you, but I'm afraid someone is trying to pull a fast one on you." Lindsey suddenly leaned forward and gave us a serious look. "Guys. It's none of my damn business how this item came into your possession, and I would never try to tell you want to do with it, but this stone sure looks a lot like the pictures on Ruby Ray Dixon's website. Just be extremely careful. Trust me when I say you do not want to end up in prison."

Dean finally found his voice. "Good advice—we'll do our best to stay on this side of the fence. As a matter of fact, that's why we wanted to meet with you in the first place. We're trying to help Ray figure out if he's been charging people to walk by a worthless lump of red rock all these years or if someone swapped stones on him. Is there any way to tell how long ago it was made?"

"Unfortunately not. There is no 'signature style' of the stone maker either, if that was going to be your next question. And it's not exactly worthless. I'd guesstimate its worth about ten percent of the actual ruby itself."

This begged the next question, "If Ray really did find a ruby like that, what would it be worth?" I asked.

"Well, the Big Kahuna Ruby was over forty-five hundred carats, and it was valued at over seven million U.S. dollars when it was found in 2007. It would be over ten million today. Of course, it was pretty rough, and they had to cut it up quite a bit to get the goods.

"This stone is over three thousand carats. If it was real, it wouldn't need to be cut much. Given current market conditions and the provenance of a real stone like this one, especially considering the latest notoriety of the owner and the fact it was stolen while his wife was being murdered, I'd put the value somewhere between three and four million U.S. dollars at auction. If you're interested, I know some great auctioneers who would jump at the opportunity to sell this piece. But you're probably better off taking it to one of the big New York houses. That's where you'll get the best price. Of course, you'd probably be arrested if you just showed up with it."

I have to say I was impressed. This thing really did belong in a museum. I wondered why Ray told me it was only worth a million at auction. He must have had a better idea of its true value. Maybe he was downplaying it so the loss wouldn't seem so great. "But the range you just provided is based on the auction house receiving the stone on a legitimate basis, right? What if someone wanted to sell it without a proper provenance? On the dark web, for example."

"Well, I'm not interested if that's what you're thinking. I've got too much at stake in the real world." Lindsey thought about it for a minute. "You probably could sell this on the dark web if you knew what you were doing. How much would it fetch there? That's really hard to say, but it would definitely be in the seven figures."

Over a million dollars. Dean and I looked at each other. We were each probably wondering if the other would want to try to sell this thing.

"You'd have to use cryptocurrency to do the deal," Dean volunteered quietly.

I looked back at Lindsey, who was displaying a slight grin. Was he waiting for us to ask him for some kind of verification of authenticity that we could use to sell the stone online illicitly? I was pretty sure Dean was not serious, but he may have thought differently. It was time to move on from this awkward situation. Then I remembered the story DeeDee told me about the crematorium. "Here's a weird question for you. How well would a synthetic ruby stand up to high temperatures after it's been made? Would it melt down again?"

"Just about everything will melt if the sun goes supernova. How hot are we talking?"

"Hang on a second." I didn't want to let on that a crematorium worker had found the stone in Sheila's ashes, so I quickly did an AI search to find the temperature at which bodies are cremated. "As high as eighteen hundred degrees Fahrenheit."

Lindsey looked at me funny. I'm sure he was wondering why I was asking, but as a former drug dealer, he knew not to get involved.

"This is a high-quality reproduction. I'd say it could handle eighteen hundred degrees with no issues."

We chatted for another hour about Lindsey's family, what some of our old classmates were doing these days, and how much Rochester had changed since high school. Then, we thanked him for his expertise and opinions and departed.

"So, did Ray know the stone was fake the whole time or did someone con him after he got to the States?" I asked Dean as we headed out of town. "If you buy the story that Ray spent all those years mining the field, he should have been able to tell a real ruby from a synthetic one. Look at the way Lindsey noticed the color didn't seem quite right as soon as he handled the stone. So, maybe he had it made to create a persona that he could build a brand around, and he's been selling the dream all these years."

Dean thought about it for a minute, then agreed. "I can't see it going any other way. It would be a shame if Ruby Ray's whole business was built around a fabrication, but it's not a crime. Big companies do it all the time."

Chapter Thirteen

Friday, May 26

Dean and I had stopped for a quick dinner on the way back from Rochester, so I didn't return to the office until after everyone had left for the day. The next morning, I wanted to continue investigating, but first, I needed to spend some time actually running the business.

I got to the office before nine a.m. and saw the lights on in Paul's office as I walked in. It looked like the text had drawn him out of hiding. It was kind of like dealing with a wounded deer. I decided not to approach him too quickly so as not to make a big deal about the situation or spook him into running across the road through traffic. I made sure he could see me talking to the staff about several different projects during the course of the morning. I even asked for his opinion on the finer points of a particular product's design, although it wasn't really necessary.

Right before lunch, I noticed Paul heading toward my office. The scowl on his face told me I was in trouble. He must have heard I'd been AWOL yesterday. I quickly stood up, took Lindsey's business card out of my wallet, walked out of the office, and called Paul over, pretending I didn't know he was coming. "Paul, come on in. I have a surprise for you." The squint in his eyes as he came in and sat in one of my visitors' chairs told me he was skeptical at best. "You've often told me how you'd like to use your design skills for things other than manufactured products. Yesterday, I was talking to a former classmate who owns a series of jewelry stores in southern Minnesota. He said they are always looking for innovative designs, but he's been having trouble finding the right talent. I told him all about you, and he is anxious to see what you can do. Here's his card."

"This isn't one of your diversions, is it? I know you were out all day yesterday."

While that hurt, I suppose I had it coming. "It's real, Paul. I met with Lindsey yesterday, and he is truly interested in working with you. The merchandise they sell out of their main downtown Rochester store is high-end and very fashionable. It could be a nice sideline business for our company."

I'd seen someone's face go from crabby to overjoyed that fast before.

"So, that's why you were gone yesterday?"

"I didn't want to put you in touch with him if it wouldn't pan out. So, a quick trip to Rochester seemed worthwhile."

"Thanks, Grayson. I don't know why I ever doubted you."

Probably because I lucked into this opportunity, I thought. Paul got up to leave, and I figured he would call Lindsey as soon as he returned to his office when he suddenly stopped and sat back down. "I didn't want to trouble you with this, but the team is having some issues with the café table support post design. I can see why these damn things are so hard to build without them wobbling."

We discussed the issues for a few minutes, which came down to the post not being strong enough to support the tabletop when someone leaned on the table edge unless we made the metal much thicker, which would increase the weight and costs to unacceptable levels. Since this was an engineering issue, it fell into my bailiwick. "Have you seen some of the latest Artificial Intelligence design tools launched in the past few months? I'll bet we can use one of them to design the support while keeping the weight down."

You would have thought I'd suggested we touch up the Mona Lisa to make it more modern-looking. "Oh my god, Grayson. We can't do that! That's cheating. Our clients are paying for our expertise, not some computer program. They can hire anyone off the street to do that."

"We don't even have any clients for this yet – we're doing this on spec, remember?

"Still, I'm not going to associate my design skills with a project engineered by some bot somewhere."

"Why not? The car companies do it all the time. They save money on design work, and the planet benefits from stronger, lighter cars that save gas. I don't see…"

"Just forget it, Grayson. Do whatever you want. I don't want to talk about this anymore." He got up to go and then sat back down again. The look of regret on his face suggested he felt like he had overreacted. "I meant to ask. You probably stopped by to see your mother when you were down there. How is she doing?"

"Well, Dean came with us, and we had some good quality time in the car. It was great to see Mom again, of course. It was a bit painful when we visited my dad's gravesite." I knew he would appreciate the story about Aunt Phyllis, and I proceeded to tell it as dramatically as possible.

"Oh my god, that's too funny," he said.

"Thanks. Do you want to hear a weird memory that popped into my head when we were at my mom's house?"

"Sure."

"You know that the bishop brokered the adoption back when he was still a priest, right? Well, Father Tom used to drop by occasionally to see how we were doing. My folks didn't know he was our biological father at that point, and they were always glad to see him. I suddenly remembered all five of us sitting in our living room when I was about ten. He wore a small smile, almost like he had a secret, and of course, he did. But it was also a weird look of satisfaction. Like he had done something he was proud of and was sitting back and enjoying the results. Imagine how different life would have been if he had just admitted what he'd done. I got shivers just thinking about it."

"I know just what you mean, Grayson. That happened to me, too, once. I know I've told you that I came out to my parents when I was in my early twenties, and my mother accepted it, but my father took it very hard. He wanted a sturdy young lad to follow in his footsteps, marry some local girl, and settle down to buy a house and start a family. Once he realized that wouldn't happen, our relationship was never the same again. Later, after he was diagnosed with cancer, he called me over to his deathbed and said he forgave me for being the way I was. I knew he was trying to make amends, but implying that it was my fault that I was gay certainly wasn't the right way to do it. Then he said he had a confession to make, too."

Paul was choking up a bit, and I started to regret that telling him the story about Father Tom had made him relive this event and feel bad. But he soon continued.

"Then, he leaned forward in his bed and whispered that his famous bar-b-que sauce recipe was a fake. He never had one. He would shoo everyone out of the kitchen and then use an off-brand product that no one would recognize. He even cooked it a bit to get an authentic smell going. After he told me, he fell back onto the bed and died a few minutes later with a look of relief on his face. I guess he'd been waiting to unburden himself of that lie for years. But to equate his trivial secret with my coming out—"

"Wow, that does seem really insensitive. I'm sorry you had to go through that."

Paul and I usually kept our relationship on a mostly business basis, and this was the most we shared about our personal lives. We fell into an awkward silence after that. To our relief, there was a knock on the front door of the office. As I went to answer it, I could see it was Detective Aaron Copeland. The day just went from frustrating to worse. He flashed his badge through the glass, which must have been out of habit because I certainly knew him.

"Hi, Grayson. I have a few questions for you. Do you mind if I come in?"

"Not at all." The detective was fashionably dressed as always in a grey suit, white shirt, and light-yellow tie. "Can I offer you some coffee? I was just going to pour myself a cup."

"Sounds good, thanks." He followed me to the break room.

I poured cups for both of us and motioned toward the cream and sugar, but he passed. I led him to my office, which provided the best home-field advantage in case I needed it. I frosted the glass as we entered and sat down.

"Grayson, I need to ask you again about the night of the murder. Did you see anything suspicious? Anything I should be aware of?"

"No, Detective. I didn't."

"So why have you been snooping around my investigation?"

This must've been the real reason he's here. He's probably stuck and wants to see if I have any leads he is unaware of. I thought maybe he'd open up before I shared anything just to get me talking. "The last thing I heard was that Kate was your main suspect. Since I obviously have a vested interest in clearing her name, it seemed to make sense to work some of the angles you might not be working. Besides, the last time we worked together, didn't you tell me that people will share things with friends or colleagues that they won't tell the police?"

The Detective thought about that momentarily but left the 'last time we worked together' comment alone. "Truth be told, at this point, our evidence against Kate is circumstantial. We don't have a smoking gun, and frankly, I don't think we're going to find one. She doesn't have a motive for killing Sheila, at least not one that I can see. And stealing the ruby doesn't seem to make sense, either. She'd have to sell it in the private market, and I doubt she has those kinds of connections. I'm having a hard time putting her in the frame for either crime."

Well, that was refreshingly transparent for a change. He really did have nothing. For what seemed like the first time in all of my dealings with Copeland, I felt like I could relax when speaking with him.

"So, who do you suspect?" he asked me at last.

"I haven't uncovered anyone new lurking about on the night of the murder or any other time, so I have to believe my list of suspects is the same as yours."

Copeland didn't respond to that but went off in a new direction. "I know you've spoken with Rev. Marcel Galland, and so have I, multiple times. What I don't get about him is his true status with the local community. Is he an extension of the Catholic Church, or is he going to splinter his group off one day? I know the bishop is not ecstatic about him running a place of worship out of a supper club. But I wonder if it goes beyond that. At what point does a leader like Marcel become a cult figure when they don't have an organized religion behind them to keep them on the straight and narrow?"

Why was he asking me that and not the bishop? I wondered. "That is a really good question. I've been wondering the same thing, but I'm afraid I don't have a good answer for you."

Was he implying that Dean or I do some additional digging with the local MN crowd? Did the cult reference mean he knew about Marcel's history in Chicago?

"Well, as you know, there are things people won't tell police about, but they might tell a guy trying to clear his girlfriend's name." I wondered if Dean had been making any progress in interviewing the other Institute for A Better Life members. I almost told Copeland he was doing this but then realized it was best not to say anything. We didn't have anything concrete yet, and if Copeland didn't already know about it, he would only start mucking around and get everyone to clam up, making it that much harder for Dean. I made a mental note to check with him the next time we connected.

"Well, if I do find out anything worthwhile, I'll be sure to let you know. Can I expect you to do the same for me?"

Copeland just smiled as he got up to leave. "Sure thing, Grayson, sure thing."

We seem to have formed an uneasy alliance, which put me in a very difficult situation. We both knew he wasn't going to tell me anything. Maybe he just wanted to be the first to know if I solved the murder so he could take the credit. One thing was clear—I couldn't say anything to Dean about this. After spending all of our high school years dodging the cops while drinking beer or staying out late, he'd give me grief for the rest of my life.

I was about to see him out when I glanced at my phone and realized I needed to head out, too. I followed the Detective to the front door, where we shook hands and left together.

Twenty minutes later, I was shaking hands with Scott Dimond, the private equity investor who was Ray's new tenant, in front of the Red Steer Restaurant on Selby in St. Paul. I'd made a reservation for us, so we were seated immediately. The space took advantage of the building's brick façade, but the only windows were along the street, so the room seemed a bit dark for a sunny day in May. I figured this would play to my advantage as it would make our meeting seem more personal.

The Red Steer was known for its handcrafted gourmet burgers. We both ordered the sixty/forty, which was made with sixty percent Certified Angus Beef and forty percent ground bacon. I asked him a few questions to break the ice.

"Thanks for taking the time to meet with me, Scott. You mentioned over dinner that you do private equity investing. How does that work exactly?"

"Good question. PE investing is just a fancy name for a person or small group of people who buy into a business. It's just like buying shares of Apple from an online stockbroker, except the transactions are not open to the public. The big difference is that Apple investors are passive while some PE investors stay involved in the business to help them spend the money they've just received wisely."

"Got it. How long have you been doing this kind of investing?"

"It's only been about ten years or so. I attended the University of Miami, and if it wasn't for a financial aid scholarship, I would never have been able to afford it. My degree was in aquaculture, and I didn't know it at the time, but my timing was perfect. After graduating, I got into the farming business as an engineer, just as the industry took off. I did pretty well but eventually realized the investors made the lion's share of the money. So, I started dabbling in real estate and eventually got into private equity to fund people like Ray. How about you, Grayson?"

The waiter stopped by with our burgers, and we dug in. As we ate, I told Scott that I'd worked for a large product design firm where I met my current business partner, and we left to start up our own business. "It ran into a tough time when our biggest client, Carson Company, moved their design work offshore, and there were times when I wondered if we were crazy for leaving corporate America. But we recovered nicely, and now we're doing well. In fact, it seems like this would be a good time for a cash infusion so we can hire a salesperson and some additional staff. Are we the kind of company you'd consider for an investment?"

"To be honest, I usually target companies in industries I'm familiar with, but I'd make an exception in your case. You seem like a sharp guy, and you've successfully navigated a major disruption, which says a lot about your resiliency. I'd have to know more about your financials, but I assume they are solid, especially with Kate around." Scott smiled to show he was joking, but it reminded me I still needed to be wary about his interest in her.

"Okay, but before we go much further, I'll need to discuss this with my business partner to make sure he's on board." It was time to get to my real purpose for the meeting. "So, it sounds like you've been investing in Ray's business?"

"Not yet. I've only been an advisor up to this point. As you may know, his enterprise has been fading recently, and we're discussing ways to get it back on track. Once we agree on the company's future direction, I may invest at that time."

"Interesting. Do you mind if I ask what options you are looking at? I might learn something from your approach."

"I can see that you're a lifelong learner, which is an important trait for a business owner, but we're not ready to reveal the details yet. Let's just say Ray believes there is an opportunity to revive the Ruby Ray brand with younger people."

Could Ray think that millennials or Gen Zers were suddenly going to become interested in an old stone in a dilapidated museum? Maybe he could market it as a roadside attraction, like the world's biggest ball of twine or the statue of Lawrence Welk? Weirder things have gone viral with that crowd, but I thought he would have to hire a truly talented marketing guru to pull it off. I noticed that Scott didn't say he agreed with Ray about the possibilities here.

"Isn't a new marketing campaign going to take a large investment? Wouldn't you need to inject some cash first?"

"You're a shrewd operator, Grayson. I can see why you solved some murders that the police couldn't. Unfortunately, we're not ready to talk about this yet."

Something wasn't adding up here, but he obviously wouldn't disclose anything. "No worries."

Scott had finished his burger and got a bit wistful. "I must tell you, Grayson, Kate has been a godsend. She has a way of explaining new ideas to Ray in plain English that gets him to go along. You're a lucky man to be dating her."

That was the second time in a week that someone had told me how lucky I was, which I was well aware of. I made a mental note to buy Kate a bouquet of flowers that wouldn't need refurbishing. I wondered if Scott's actual interest in investing in my company was to create a ready-made excuse for hanging around with her a lot more.

I remembered Ray saying Sheila had been acting cold toward him lately. Maybe Scott and Sheila had been having an affair, and now that she was gone, he was turning his attention toward a new conquest named Kate. I'd never met Sheila, so I couldn't make a call about a potential relationship with Scott. But, if they had been sleeping together, could that lead to murder? Maybe she wanted to call it off, but he refused to accept it. That seemed like a stretch, but it could have been possible.

It didn't seem like there was much more to learn from Scott, so it was time to move on. We agreed that I would talk to Paul about the possibility of Scott investing in our company and let him know what we decided. I paid the bill, and we headed out.

Chapter Fourteen

Monday, May 27

I'd spent a solid day in the office on Friday focusing on design work, so when I found myself on the St. Paul side of the Mississippi River to visit a client on Monday, I didn't feel too guilty sneaking over to Ruby Ray's office complex. I wanted to connect with Patter, the piano player at the Supper Club on the night of the murder, to see if he had seen anything suspicious. Cheryl greeted me at the main desk, and I asked where I could find him.

Cheryl looked at the clock on her desk. "Patter usually rolls in after lunch and practices two to four hours a day. He's probably in there right now," she said, motioning toward the Supper Club with her pen.

"Wouldn't we hear him if he was playing the piano?"

She just smiled. "It's hard to explain. Just follow the sounds, and you can see for yourself."

As I approached the club, I heard some tapping and clicking noises and soon found the man himself in one of the back rooms. Patter was sitting at an old baby grand piano that looked as ancient as he was, if not more so. A lit cigar lay on the edge of an old, beaten-up marble ashtray, sending smoke curling toward the ceiling. He was tapping on the fallboard and banging it against the body of the piano while simultaneously playing the keys. The odd thing was that no music was coming out. He finally realized I was there, stopped playing, and took a drag off his stogie with one eye closed while the other eyed me up suspiciously.

"Hi, Patter. I'm Grayson Dyle. Cheryl said I'd find you here." I grabbed a seat at one of the nearby café tables, which wobbled badly.

"Grayson Dyle. Where have I heard that name?" He tilted his head back, almost for effect. "Oh yeah, Kate talks about you. Aren't you two an item?"

"You could say that, yeah." Even though I tried to make it a neutral statement, a certain amount of pride must have come through because Patter smiled.

"Okay, I have to ask you: How can you play without sound coming out?"

He smiled again. "It's not that hard." He lifted the cover of the baby grand to reveal a blanket had been spread over the strings to stop them from reverberating. "This old building isn't as soundproof as the ones they got today, and the worker bees used to complain if I played too much. So, I made a deal with Ray. I can practice as much as I want as long as I don't make too much noise. Sides, sometimes I want to hear the percussion, but my ears don't work so good no more. So, it works for everyone."

Pretty smart if you ask me. I was about to ask him why he didn't use an electronic keyboard, then figured an old blues guy like him wouldn't be caught dead playing one. "So, where does the name Patter come from?"

"It's from a song my friends used to sing about me, you know?" He took the blanket off the strings, closed the lid, and started playing a blues tune with a classic eight-bar chord progression, similar to Elvis's "Heartbreak Hotel."

"Oh, Patter is a banger. He don't need no strings.

He just pats down the piano, and he makes it sing.

He's the king of the keys, the maestro of the night,

With each stroke, he paints a tale filled with soul and might."

The song was intriguing. It would have sounded bragging if he hadn't told me someone else had written the lines. He must have realized it, too, as he soon stopped taking a drag off his cigar as an excuse to do so.

I had to admit I was fascinated by this guy. He had to be at least 80, and he seemed to be a tortured soul when he wasn't playing. As soon as the music started, though, he smiled, and his fingers flew across the keys like a teenager's. There was obviously more to him than met the eye. It was sad to hear he may have alienated some of the ladies by being overly friendly.

"Wow—that's awesome. Kate and I enjoyed your show a few weeks ago."

"Much obliged."

It was time to get to the business at hand. "How well did you know Sheila?"

"I saw her around the office a bit, you know."

I was expecting a longer answer and was prepared to wait him out. Patter stared off into the distance as if he longed for her. In a few minutes, he got a bit wistful and started up again. "Sheila was a mighty fine woman. I would've snatched her up if she ever gave Ray the bum's rush, you know? But she never did, and I never even touched her. She ignored me, and I always dealt directly with Ray. It was better that way."

Then he looked down and frowned while balling his hands into fists. "I know she was telling the other ladies that I was bad news and they should watch out. That wasn't right, you know? I'm not *inappropriate*, you know?" He spat the word out. "I never did nothing to nobody."

If Sheila was spreading unfounded rumors about him, was that enough motive for murder? I thought it best to change the subject before he punched the piano...or me, you know?

"Did you see anything unusual on the night of the murder?"

Patter thought about it for a minute. "Nope, can't say I did 'cause I didn't."

"You had just left the stage before Sheila's body was discovered. Did you see anyone suspicious leaving the area?"

"Didn't see a thing."

He was holding back, but I couldn't think of a way to get him to talk. Patter turned back to his keyboard and started hitting a few notes, which was probably his way of saying the meeting was over.

I got up to leave. "Well, thanks for talking."

"Anytime," he said over his shoulder.

I got as far as my car when I heard someone shouting my name behind me. I turned to see Ray flagging me down in a panic.

"Grayson...you've got to...help me." Ray was out of breath and panting when he reached me, even though he'd only run a few yards.

"Take it easy, Ray. I'm right here. What's wrong?"

"Let's go to my office. I want you to hear something."

Ray regained his composure as we reentered the building and walked back to his office.

"I'm so glad I caught you. Please sit down." He closed the door to his office, and as we sat, Ray leaned forward and lowered his voice so he could be sure no one else could hear him. "Eric is in trouble, Grayson. I just got a threatening message from someone at a Vegas Casino. It must be one of their 'debt collectors.'"

Ray picked up his mobile phone and played the voicemail he had just received.

"Ruby Ray. We're looking for Eric. We know you're his father. I want you to help us locate him." The voice was deep–perfect for a mob boss. "We need to discuss a financial arrangement. It will be to his benefit if he contacts us right away. We can send someone to find him if necessary. But it will be best if you have him call Victor within two days at 725-555-2368."

Okay, I had to admit, the message had me concerned about Eric's well-being, and I didn't even like him that much after he stormed out of our meeting.

Ray was clearly panicked. "They must be extorting him to do something he doesn't want to do to pay off his gambling debts. I'd like to go to the police, but what if Eric has been involved in something illegal out there? He needs to have a clean record if he ever wants to get a business loan." Good thing you have your priorities sorted there, Ray.

"I don't know who else to turn to. Can you help me, Grayson?"

"This isn't really my thing, Ray. What do you want me to do?"

"I don't know. Call this guy back and talk some sense into him. Tell him that Eric is a good kid and that I will pay off his debts, but they need to leave him alone."

Ray was so distraught that I couldn't say no. "I'll look into it and see what I can find out." That seemed pretty safe, and it was all I was going to commit to at the moment. To demonstrate my sincerity, I decided to make a copy of the message and took out my phone. "Play that again, will you? There might be a clue we haven't noticed yet, and I'd like to replay it later."

Ray hit the play button, and I captured the message on my phone. I didn't have any other ideas, so I got up and shook Ray's hand to his profuse thanks. As I left, I wondered if Eric stole the ruby and replaced it with a fake so he could sell it and pay off his gambling debts without getting his family involved. I also wondered if he was so desperate that he would kill his mother as a diversion.

* * *

I returned to the office and actually worked on a new product design for a change. Paul stopped by a few times with innocuous questions. I got the impression he wanted to make sure I was working on the business, and it was fine by me. I probably would have done the same thing to him if our roles were reversed.

I wanted to engage Paul about some business issue or another to show him I was really focused on our mutual success, and this seemed like a good time to mention Scott Dimond. I stopped by Paul's office and provided a recap of my recent discussion with a potential investor and a brief explanation of the concept of private equity and how we could use the money to expand our business.

I thought Paul would be receptive to the idea and maybe say he would want to meet Scott before offering his opinion, or the timing for a cash infusion wasn't right. But no, his response was immediate and unequivocal. I believe the term 'no freaking way' came up a few times in the verbal tirade that followed, along with the notion that we already had assumed too much business risk by me gallivanting all over town and pretending to be a P.I. instead of finding new clients. I would have reminded him that the café table idea would likely be a lucrative new business line for us if I could have gotten a word in edgewise. It was good to know we had an open and honest business partnership in which we could share our thoughts and ideas in a nonjudgmental manner. I decided not to tell Scott we weren't interested in his help until after the investigation was over, just in case I needed a reason to talk to him again.

Paul left for the day at about five-thirty, and I felt good about the progress I'd made on a few of our projects despite our altercation, so I decided to do some digging on our friend Chadrick. A quick search showed the usual fan-based sites. I learned a lot about his business dealings and net worth, both of which were impressive. Celebrityselfworth.com said his estate was worth over three hundred and fifty million dollars, and he owned twenty-three companies in various industries. The part of his story that stood out the most was his creation of a pseudoscientific approach to personal development that he claimed could cure phobias, depression, and learning disorders, which would allow its practitioners to focus on and achieve larger life goals. What a bunch of hooey.

Call me petty, but I noticed his teeth had become unnaturally perfect and preternaturally white about ten years ago. He must have had veneers installed. While it somehow made him more human, he also seemed more vain. At least, it was what I wanted him to be.

I was about to give up for the night when I realized quite a few of the news articles referred to 'Beat Yourself' as his comeback book. I checked the dates and discovered that most of his other big successes were older, and the newer ones were less spectacular. Sure, his businesses were doing just fine, and he was still worth a fortune, but Ray was right about Chadrick's empire. It was waning, just like his. No wonder they were such good friends. Great. Now, I felt a small bit of superiority and pity for him at the same time.

Suddenly, all manner of bizarre questions occurred to me. Some were simple, such as, did Chadrick steal the ruby to sell it and prop up his sagging business? But there were more sinister ones, too. Chadrick was obviously still very interested in Kate. What if he blamed her for breaking up because he had become a B-list celebrity? If he assumed he was going to an A-lister again soon, would he also assume she would come running back to him? Did he introduce Kate to Ray to bring her back into his sphere of influence? But, to me, the million-dollar question was, what had really happened between Kate and this guy to cause their breakup?

Chapter Fifteen

Tuesday, May 28

I got a text from 'Burner,' which was Kate telling me she would arrive early for dinner at my condo on Wednesday night. It was an inadvertent reminder that being a suspect in a police investigation was massively inconvenient and even more frustrating that the police had not cleared her by now. Twenty minutes later, she let herself into my place with her key and wrapped me up in a big hug.

I told her I'd ordered food from the 'farm-fresh fast-casual organic restaurant' on the first floor of my building. It was convenient, and the food was good, even if the menu was a bit limited. "The order should be up shortly."

"Thanks, Grayson." Kate smiled and walked over to the large windows along Lake Street. The unit's description listed a partially obstructed view of the lake. It was technically true, but I didn't mind. The convenience of living and working in the same building made it an easy choice. Besides, I liked to think of the view as partially unobstructed. I walked up behind her and put my arms around her. She melted into me as we were entertained by the walkers, joggers, bikers, paddleboarders, and sailors for a few minutes. I was seriously considering kissing her again when the doorbell rang. I hit the buzzer and gave the delivery guy directions to the unit. I grabbed the food when he arrived, slipped him a decent tip, and we sat at the island counter to eat.

"So, what's new at Ruby Ray's?" I asked in between bites.

"Mia announced that she and Josh just got engaged," Kate said. "Now that her mother's funeral has been over for a few weeks, she saw no reason to wait any longer. Isn't that great?"

"Absolutely." Mia seemed nice, but I'd only met her once and was having a hard time coming up with much enthusiasm other than wondering what impact this would have on the investigation. "Do you know if Ray approved?"

"Well, I'm not one to gossip…" Was that really true? I wondered. I knew that Kate liked to know things, and there was a fine line between knowing and sharing. But she always seemed to know exactly how much could be shared without divulging personal information, even with me. "…and I have to admit, I didn't hear this from Ray directly, but the rumor mill says Josh asked Ray for his permission prior to proposing, and Ray gave them his blessing. It sounded very romantic."

We'd been acting like a serious couple for over a year now, and I couldn't help but wonder if there might be a subtle hint aimed at me in all of this. Kate's sudden desire to establish a relationship between me and her mother seemed to confirm this idea. And, as my mother pointed out, none of us were getting any younger.

Kate continued. "And why wouldn't he approve? Josh is a good catch. He comes from a very wealthy family, and I'll bet his father has a place lined up for him in the family business whenever he wants it. Besides, he's cute."

"I thought he was a party boy. Wait, don't tell me that Mia plans to get him to change his ways. Because that always works out well."

"Okay, yes, Josh likes to party. But Mia brought him around to show off her ring, which was huge, by the way, and I got the sense he is more serious than people give him credit for."

"That sounds like a buddy of mine from college who hid the fact that his parents were quite well off. When I found out and asked him about it, he said he wanted to give his friends the impression he was a party boy so they would treat him like they did everyone else." I had been sneaking peaks at Kate's dinner and finally couldn't help myself. I reached over and grabbed a small piece of her focaccia, ran it through the hummus, and popped it into my mouth.

"Exactly. That's what I'm talking about. He's the kind of person who will settle down when he graduates college."

"Wait a sec. If Josh's family is wealthy, he wouldn't need to marry Mia for her family's money, right? So, his only motive for getting rid of Sheila would have been to remove her objection to their marriage."

Kate laughed. "Yeah, no one is marrying into the Dixon family for money."

That was an interesting comment. "What do you mean?"

Kate looked down. Even when she was trying to hide a blush, she was good-looking. What was she doing with me again? "Nothing." That was all she would say. It must have been that confidentiality clause again. I didn't want her to betray her position of trust with her employer, so I let it go. But it sounded like Ray might be hurting financially more than anyone was letting on, despite all of his bravado. No wonder he was so anxious for a marketing effort to start rebuilding his brand.

"Not to pry, but would Ray want Josh's family to invest in his business?"

She wouldn't say another word on the topic. But, as long as we were discussing clues, this seemed like a good time to ask her about the ruby. "Kate, did you know that Ray's ruby is fake? He must have found someone to fabricate a synthetic stone and then made up the whole story about his big find in Poona."

She frowned. "No. That's not possible. We just had the stone revalued a couple of months ago when the insurance came due. The appraisal came back right where we thought it would. What makes you think the ruby is fake?"

It was time for true confessions. I told her the story about the road trip Dean and I took to Rochester, our meeting with Lindsey Brazzer, and the extensive process he had used to authenticate the stone, which only proved it was manmade. We both sat in silence for a few minutes, trying to figure out how this piece fits into the puzzle. Then, a question occurred to me. "Who assessed the ruby?"

"It was one of the big auction houses in New York. The stone's true value goes beyond its commercial value as a jewel. A big chunk of the value is tied up in the provenance or the backstory, starting with Ray's original discovery of the stone and the fact that it is the largest ruby ever found in Australia. The auction houses are the only ones who can consider that part of the value."

She sounded like a tour guide at the Ruby Ray Museum for a minute. "Okay, that makes sense, but how did it get to them?"

"Nigel Lawson personally took it to them. The New York folks are not about to come here, and we didn't want to trust something so valuable to a courier we didn't know."

"What happens once he gets there? Is there any chance they could have swapped out a fake ruby for the real one?"

"I don't see how. Nigel stays with the ruby throughout their entire valuation process. It's a common practice with a piece that is so valuable."

At that particular moment, I thought it best not to mention that Dean and I had left Linsdey alone with the stone so we could go off for a nice leisurely lunch with our mother. "And how did they deliver the appraisal?"

"They produce a signed and notarized document and give it to Nigel at the end of the assessment. Then he brings the ruby and the appraisal back with him and turns them both over to Sheila, who returns them to the safe."

Hmm, on the surface, that must have seemed like a reasonable process, but it seemed fraught with potential issues to me. Nigel could have swapped out a fake for the real stone on his way back, for example. Or he could have colluded with someone at the auction house to certify the results, make the change, sell the real one, and split the proceeds.

Just then, Kate's face scrunched up. "Wait a minute. How did you even get the stone in the first place? I thought it was stolen."

This put me on the spot. I knew she would keep anything I told her confidential if I asked her to, but sometimes people slip up, and I couldn't take the chance that DeeDee's involvement would be exposed. "It had been stolen. Kate, I'm really not at liberty to say how I got it."

She wasn't buying it. "Now that I think about it, why don't we give it to the police right now? Once they have it back, I'll be off the hook for the theft and probably look less guilty of the murder, too. I thought you were trying to help me here."

"Kate, I would like nothing better than for one of us to turn it in, but I don't see how we can." I walked her through the same thought process that Dean and I had used, and she soon hit the same impasse, especially because the stone we had was a fake, and the police would think we'd swapped it out. I didn't like playing the relationship card here, but it was the only thing I could think of. "Can you just trust me until we solve the murder and the theft? I will explain everything afterward."

Kate seemed wary but agreed anyway. "Fine. I do trust you, Grayson."

That was nice to hear. After finishing dinner but having made no progress on the case, we broke open a bottle of wine and retired to the couch for the rest of the evening.

* * *

I was in my office the following day, minding my own business, when Paul burst in.

"Grayson, are you planning any new projects with a thug?"

"Umm, not that I recall. Why do you ask?"

"Because we have a big one contaminating the lobby, and he is asking for you."

I figured it must be a guy from the Vegas mob, and my mind immediately jumped to Ray's voicemail. The person who left the message yesterday demanded a response within two days. Since I didn't have a good answer, I had planned to delay as much as possible before calling him back. Now that he was here, I felt Ray had gotten nervous and pointed them in my direction to take the pressure off him and Eric.

The prospect of meeting with the mob was scary, but I put my fears aside and strode briskly out of my office, ready to face this creature head-on. I turned the corner to see Paul had not been exaggerating. There stood a giant of a man who must tip the scales at over three hundred pounds and be at least six-six. It wasn't so much the size as the packaging. It was obvious he was no stranger to gym equipment.

I considered how I'd mount a defense if one because necessary, then realized that Detective Copeland never returned the 22-caliber Ruger that he confiscated over a year ago when he suspected me of James Brennan's murder. I really needed to get that gun back. My adoptive father gave me it, along with an attached scope, when I turned twenty-one, so it had sentimental value. But, just like John Wayne's single-action Colt revolver, each round had to be loaded separately, which meant you'd have to call for a timeout in the middle of a firefight to reload. Not that I had ever been in the middle of a firefight, but still. Maybe I should ask Kate for a semi-automatic handgun for Christmas. Nothing says Happy Holidays, and I love you like the gift of a shiny, new firearm.

Still, I had no quarrel with him and wouldn't be intimidated. I marched over and extended my hand. "Hi, I'm Grayson Dyle. I understand you're looking for me."

"Hi, Grayson." We shook hands. I half expected a bone-crushing experience, but he was actually quite pleasant. "Is there somewhere we can talk?" Given the circumstances, I noticed he didn't say his name, but I figured I'd let that go. I was going to offer him coffee but decided against it, at least until I figured out what the hell was going on.

"Sure, right this way." I showed him to the main conference room in case I needed to get someone's attention by waving because this guy's hands were around my throat. "Please have a seat."

As he sat, my guest leaned forward and looked directly at me, saying sternly, "I'm looking for Eric Dixon. I've been all over the Twin Cities and need to return to Vegas soon. Ruby Ray said you are the best private investigator he knows and that you can help me find his son. I believe you recently met him for coffee, so you must have his mobile number. Will you give that to me, please?"

I recalled that Kate had given me Eric's number, and I had to stifle an involuntary twitch to grab my cell phone. "I don't have it, I'm afraid."

He folded his arms over his chest, and I could tell he thought I was lying. But he couldn't really call me on it, so he tried a different tack.

"Did he say anything about his whereabouts or if he had plans to leave

146

town?"

He certainly was a well-informed thug, and he confirmed my theory about Ray spilling his guts. "As much as I appreciate the endorsement, I don't know who you are or why you want to find Eric. I'm afraid I can't help you."

He thought about it for a moment, then leaned back and smiled. "You are right, of course. Forgive me. Sometimes, I get too focused on the mission and forget the niceties. You can call me 'Victor.' I represent a Las Vegas concern. I only want to talk to Eric about a business venture."

Was that what the kids were calling extortion nowadays? I wondered. This was getting really annoying. "I'm not actually a P.I. You may have noticed my name on the sign when you came in. This company is my full-time job. I really…"

"Ah, but you have not heard my offer yet. I can provide you with a substantial finder's fee of fifty thousand dollars for your assistance. And I am willing to give you half up front. You have to admit that is very generous for something that may not be a lot of work for someone like you."

"Look, Victor. I really don't do P.I. work. My pesky day job keeps getting in the way."

He leaned forward again with another cold stare. After a minute of that, I was seriously reconsidering my options.

"Perhaps you should think about it before you say no to this kind of money. I will return tomorrow for another discussion." With that, he got up and showed himself out.

I wondered what had just happened when my mind started racing. How much money would someone have to owe the Vegas mob to justify an enforcer offering fifty G's to help nab them? Maybe the mob killed Sheila in an extreme way to intimidate Eric so he'd start paying them back. You can't kill the guy who owes you the money, or you'll never get paid back, right? And did anyone break kneecaps anymore? That was so cliché. Then again, maybe Eric killed Sheila to create a diversion so he could steal the ruby and sell it to pay off the mob.

I was at a loss about what to do next, so I went to my usual backup plan and texted Dean, who said he would meet me at our usual spot shortly.

* * *

Almost exactly one hour later, I was in line at the coffee shop when Dean arrived and grabbed a table by the window. As we sipped our drinks, I updated him on the thug.

"So, I may leave town for a bit. It's been a while since I've taken a vacation. Maybe I'll surprise Kate with a trip to Cabo or the Bahamas."

"In May? Doesn't that kind of defeat the purpose of going somewhere warm?"

"Not to me, it doesn't."

Dean just laughed. "Going into hiding will just put you in harm's way. The mobsters love it when their targets run because they are used to chasing people, and you're not used to being chased. It makes you an easy hit."

That sounded right, but how did he know this, and was it really true? I wondered.

"You can't outrun him, so you might as well meet him again. The best place to meet is a highly public place, but you may not want to be seen with him. So, I suggest meeting at your office because he will not harm you or anyone else with all those witnesses present."

"But we'll be holed up in a conference room. I suppose if I asked people to walk back and forth frequently, that would keep him straight."

Dean just smiled. "I've got something even better."

"Great—what is it?"

"There is a secret skunkworks project we've been working on for X, and we need to do some field testing with it. It's perfect for this situation."

"So, what is it?"

"Grayson, you have to commit to absolute secrecy. No word of this can get out, or our first-mover advantage in the marketplace will be lost, and our relationship with X will be ruined."

Geez, what the hell was this thing? "Okay, okay. You've sworn me to secrecy about fifty times already. We should be covered by now. What have you got?"

"We are developing a small video recorder with a wireless camera and a mic that fits into a ring. We're also planning to develop a version that fits in a pendant. It'll be perfect for your meeting with this guy."

Dean seemed as if he expected me to go crazy over the brilliance of his idea, but I wasn't seeing it. "How does that help?"

"Oh, come on." Dean threw up his hands as if to say the application was obvious, and why was I suddenly being so thick-headed? I just raised my eyebrows to let him know he would have to enlighten me. "Okay, wait a minute. Do you remember that TV show from the early seventies called *Search*? We always watched it when we were kids. Burgess Meredith was known as the Director and ran a team of spies that wore cameras just like this. The original device had a Comsat relay, infrared light, ultraviolet light, and EKG capability in addition to the camera and mic. I can neither confirm nor deny that we have plans to add those features to this device in the future. I'll give you a ring you can insert it into, and I'll be able to monitor and record everything from the next room." At least one of us was excited.

"What do you call this thing?"

"Good question. We can't call it a ring camera because that name is taken, so the code name we're using is STING, which stands for Stealthy Tactical INtelligence Gathering."

"Someone came up with the name, and then you worked backward for the words, didn't you? You can tell because you have to initialize two letters in the word intelligence to spell it right. Besides, that describes what it does, not what it is."

"Okay, nobody will know we worked backward. I suppose you've got a better idea?"

I thought for a minute and said, 'Sneaky Telecorder Insect-like Nondescript Gizmo.'

Dean laughed. "No way."

"Okay, here's a good one. 'Super Tiny Inconspicuous Ninja Gadget.'

Dean seems to actually consider this one. Then said, "It's too bad you weren't around a few months ago when we named the thing. But it's too late now. X has already approved it."

I just shook my head. "This is why you leave the creative work to the design guys, not the engineers. Why does X want this thing anyway? Aren't there a bunch of devices just like this already out there?"

"No one is really sure why he wants it. It could be that X just liked the TV show, that he is going into the international espionage business, or that he has way too much money and doesn't know how to spend it all."

"That last one seems the most likely to me."

Dean agreed and went on. "Our Dev Team wants to do more field trials, and I can check the device out and bring it by this afternoon as long as you promise not to muck it up.'

"Me? Not in a million."

"Great. Once we get you outfitted, all you have to do is meet with…what was this guy's name again?"

"Victor."

"Victor? He will definitely not be the victor in this transaction. Anyway, all you have to do is meet with him and accept the payment. I'll record the whole thing, and we'll have him dead to rights."

"How so?"

"This will be proof that he is paying you for illicit services, and you can use the recording as leverage to get him to back off of you and Eric, too."

"Sounds like a plan. He showed up at nine this morning. Can you be at the office from seven to seven-thirty to make sure we have time to set up?"

"Absolutely."

I figured we were done, and I started to get up when Dean stopped me.

"Hang on, Grayson. You're going to want to hear this. I looked at Ray's businesses and discovered some interesting facts about the property they sat on. It's quite long and runs almost a quarter of a mile along Highway 13. Most of it is undeveloped for three main reasons.

"First, it consists of a fairly narrow tract of land between the road and the river. The city's covenants require that buildings be significantly setback from the road in order to be aesthetically pleasing, and most of Ray's property is nowhere near wide enough to include both the setback space and the building space.

"Second, the area is zoned for single-family residential use only. Sure, you could build a few small homes there, and they would have great views of both cities, but the lots would be long and narrow, which is not very desirable. The speed limit on Highway 13 is only forty miles per hour, but there would still be quite a bit of road noise, which would also limit their value. Building a five or ten-story condo or senior housing unit with commercial businesses on the first level would be the best way to maximize the land value. But that would require the city council to approve a zoning change and a variance on the setback requirement, neither of which is likely to happen."

"How was Ray able to build on that land? Didn't he run into the same roadblocks?"

"He must have built before this zoning was implemented, which meant he would have been grandfathered in."

"Got it. What's the third issue?"

"Ground stability studies performed over the years have shown there are variabilities in the rock formation along much of the undeveloped land tract, which would make it difficult or impossible to build on. Paving the land for a parking lot would be fine, but the weight of a building of any significant size could cause part of the cliff to shear off and drop into the river, taking the building with it."

"Interesting. Ray has owned this property for a long time, so he must have paid for the studies. Sounds like he doesn't have a lot of options here, and his personal finances are suffering. No wonder he's considering selling out and retiring. I wonder how much of this Sheila knew."

"I was wondering the same thing."

It was definitely time to go, so we headed out of the shop. On the way back to the office, I thought about our discussion about why X wanted the device and realized we'd missed one. Maybe there was trouble in paradise, and he just wanted to spy on his trophy wife. No matter the reason, there were already spy cameras of every shape and size on the market, so why build your own? Go figure.

* * *

At seven-thirty a.m. the next day, I was sitting in my office wearing a STING that had been inserted into the ring on my right hand. The face of the ring was about half an inch in diameter, and a pinhole camera was hidden in an intricate pattern that resembled a lion from an ancient coat of arms. I wouldn't have noticed it without knowing it was there. As I waited for Victor to reappear and tried not to act nervous, I wondered if X asked for a 'king of beasts' motif or if the design team came up with that themselves. Dean was in the small conference room furthest from the front door, listening in and ready to record everything the ring could see.

I had looked up some of the details from the TV show and used them to needle my brother. "Hugh Lockwood from World Securities Corporation here. I'm calling for the Director. Can you hear me?"

Of course, STING currently had no speaker, so one-way communication was all it could provide. Dean texted me back. "Loud and clear. Knock off the chatter. It's bad form."

Okay, he was taking this thing way too seriously. I still thought there were fifty other ways to record this guy without involving STING, Hugh O'Brien, or Burgess Meredith, but it was too late to change tactics.

Since we were using the business office, I felt I had to inform Paul of our plans in advance. I expected his usual pushback about not focusing on our business, etc. Instead, he jumped on board immediately and offered to meet him at the front door, just like last time. I had no issues with that.

"Richard can't believe this guy is as big as I say he is. Do you mind if I take a quick picture when he arrives?"

"Go for it, Paul. I'm sure he won't mind. Would you like me to pose with him?"

Paul wisely dropped the idea and went back to his office to wait. At precisely eight-thirty, Victor knocked on the office door, and Paul answered. I could hear him suddenly flustered, but he managed to show the guy to the conference room without incident, then came and got me.

I entered the conference room and saw Victor sitting at the same table. He had placed a thin briefcase on the table in front of him, which he patted and asked, "Have you thought about my generous offer?"

"Yes, I have. I'd like to accept your generous offer, but I'd like to confirm the payment is in order first."

Victor took a thick, heavy-duty envelope from his sports coat pocket and placed it on the table next to the briefcase. I had assumed modern-day thugs still used the tried-and-true one hundred dollar bills in their bribes and that the money would be in the briefcase, but I had neglected to calculate the size of a twenty-five thousand dollar stack. So, I tried not to act surprised when he slid the envelope over to me instead. It was over two inches thick, and as soon as I picked it up, I realized I should have worn STING on my left hand because I was having a hard time thumbing through the cash while pretending to scratch my chin with the right hand so the camera would point into the envelope. I couldn't tell if he noticed me fumbling around, but he didn't say anything, and he seemed like the kind of person who would call me on it if he did. Then he patted the briefcase again. It was either a weird nervous twitch or an implication that he had ready access to the weapon inside of it.

I put the envelope in my back pocket. "Looks like it's all in order."

As he stood, he handed me a business card with the name Victor Hawkes and a phone number printed on it.

"Call me as soon as you have a location. Don't make me come back here to get it."

I didn't know if he meant the information or his money, but he picked up the briefcase and left, and I was glad to be rid of him.

A few minutes after the elevator door in the foyer closed, Dean entered the conference room with a big smile. "Except for the operator error, I'd say this was a successful field trial of STING. I can't wait to show the video to the team."

I was glad he was having a good time blaming the field staff. "Operator error? Shouldn't the development team have anticipated the use of the device and suggested I wear it on the other hand?" I suddenly realized I should have thought of this and wondered why anyone would hire me as a P.I. Maybe I really should stick to the design business.

Chapter Sixteen

Sunday, June 3

Kate and I had set up a lunch date for the following Sunday, and I planned to take her to a fancy new restaurant in the Highland Park area of St. Paul. She needed to get a financial report ready for Monday, so we agreed I would pick her up at the parking lot of Ruby Ray's office at noon and then drop her off again afterward.

On a whim, I decided to arrive early and make a surprise visit to Galland Garden to see if Marcel was really as devoted to his cause as he claimed to be. I showed up unannounced without even letting Kate know I was coming, just to be safe. I parked by the Garden in the spot that was furthest from the Arbor at the entrance and casually strolled over to it. Marcel was halfway down the garden and working on some kind of staff. As I got closer, I realized he was holding a hammer in one hand and a wooden cross in the other. The vertical arm of the cross was about seven feet long and was made of an old, worn piece of lumber. The horizontal arm was about two feet across and made from the same lumber. It had several willow branches affixed to it that formed the shape of a pentagram or five-pointed star with a circle around it. As memory served, this was called a pentacle, a symbol widely used by Wiccans and other paganists who were associated with cult activities. It was difficult to tell what he was doing with it. Was Marcel showing his true colors? I wondered.

As I walked up, Marcel finally noticed me. "Hey, Grayson, help me with this, would you?" Was I just imagining it, or did it seem like he had just changed what he was doing?

"Sure, what do you need?"

"Hold the cross part while I pry off the branches." Within a few minutes, he'd used the claw part of a hammer to yank out the staples that held the branches in place and pulled the nails that held the cross together. Then he threw the branches into a recycling bag and tossed the parts of the cross into a burn barrel to be incinerated later.

"I don't mean to intrude, but where did that come from?"

"Someone planted this damn thing overnight, probably just wanting to create havoc and intimidate our team members. It's a good thing I got here early. Otherwise, the group would have wanted to talk about this, and we would have gotten bogged down in a pointless discussion."

It seemed like a conversation on either cult symbols or hate crimes would have been appropriate for Marcel's group, but I wasn't in charge. One thing did bug me, though. "If someone is trying to harass you or your team, shouldn't you have turned that over to the police?"

Marcel picked up a trowel and started weeding a nearby raised bed. He gave me a sorry smile. "The police don't have time for trivial things like that."

"What if the person who did this followed someone here from Chicago?"

Marcel nearly took off the stem of a flower when he heard that. He looked at me and lowered his head in what I could only interpret as a threatening manner. Then, he seemed to think better of it, looked up again, and smiled. "I suppose it would be easy enough to find the online articles about my involvement in the Institute for a Better Life in the Chicago papers. If you did, you'd see that the local cops arrested a whole bunch of us when we announced we would expand our building and offer more services. It was a blatant attempt at intimidation, but it didn't work. You also should have noticed that I was cleared of all wrongdoing, including the murder of Bill Goddard.

"You're right, I did see that. They never found Goddard's killer, though, did they?" I hoped the implication that I thought Marcel could still have been involved was clear enough.

Marcel seemed insulted and waved me off with the trowel. "That was all a long time ago and has no relevance now. Did I learn a few things from Bill about how to run a congregation? Sure, I did. You couldn't be part of a group like that and not pick up a few pointers. Does that mean I'm using that knowledge to start up a new cult? Absolutely not. I'm just trying to use what I learned to do good—to reach out and support the community as best as I possibly can. Look, the team members will start arriving soon, and I need to get back to it." He turned away and started packing up his tools. I was dismissed.

I was not having it, though, and thought this would be a good time to test his faith. "Hang on, Reverend, before you go, would you mind if I attended your service today?" I half expected him to say no, that I was not a true believer and needed to come back after I'd gotten more religion or performed some other penance to prove my worthiness.

To his credit, Marcel immediately answered. "All are welcome here, Grayson." It seemed like there was an unspoken "even you," but then maybe that was just my imagination. I followed him into the Supper Club and was surprised at the transformation. As Kate had already mentioned, drop cloths were over some of the racier pictures. But it looked like Marcel's group had spent a good chunk of their earnings and donations on creating a whole new atmosphere for the space.

As a design guy, I knew that stages could go from elegant to cheesy very quickly, but whoever designed this set knew what they were doing. Three large screens had been set up toward the back of the stage on which a series of projectors would display images. Behind them was a large black backdrop that would further hide the room's back wall to minimize the Supper Club motif. The café tables had been cleared away, and seats had been set up in rows of eight across the dance floor. Patter's piano had been pushed to one side, and a set of large speakers had been stacked in its place. A small lectern had been erected on one side of the stage, which would be used to read the good word and preach. There was even a small play area off to the side of the stage in case someone brought small children.

Conspicuous by their absence were the usual Catholic trappings, such as an altar, crucifix, signs of the cross, and so on. This seemed like a conscious choice and another way to create distance from traditional worshiping.

I didn't want to intrude and knew I was not likely to attend any future services, so it didn't seem appropriate to greet the participants. But I did want to see Marcel speak, so I returned to my car and watched as the crowd filed in. By eleven-forty, I figured the service had started, and I headed back in, where lights, music, and singing bombarded me. It was an impressive display of worship, and I had to give Marcel credit for that.

Soon, the lights softened, and the music died down as Marcel took his place on the stage. His sermon, assuming that is what he called it, was about discontentment and how it was the main root of the sin of covetousness, which was addressed by the tenth commandment. Advertising is about creating this thought, he said. It makes you believe that you need this new product or service to be fulfilled. He railed on social media as one of the key sources of images, videos, and messages about how perfect other people's lives were, which only served to further the notion that your life was incomplete and you were somehow lacking. I liked how he tied the message to things we encounter every day in our lives, which really drove the point home.

As I listened to his address, I could easily have imagined Bishop Brennen saying the exact same thing from his pulpit at St. Celestine or, for that matter, any priest in any church in the country. But if the messaging was basically the same, it must be the venue, something about the institution of the church that people were objecting to and voting with their feet to show it. Maybe Bishop Tom was right when he said many of the people in groups like these were just rebelling against their parents' way of worship, and they would eventually return to the traditional church. I was glad not to have a horse in this race.

I started getting antsy as Reverend Marcel led the congregation in more prayers. It seemed as if the service would be over soon, and, as I recalled from our discussion at the Supper Club, the group would go out and tend the gardens next. Since I wasn't a gardener and didn't want to be fussed over as a prospective new group member, I slipped out a side door unnoticed.

I was really looking forward to a nice, quiet lunch with Kate. But, as I walked down to the main office, I didn't see her car in the almost empty parking lot and knew I would have to wait. I was about to return when the door opened, and Patter stuck his head out. "Hey, Grayson. Got a minute?" he said in a strained voice. Maybe he really did practice every day.

"Sure thing." I headed toward him, expecting to go in, but he came out instead, kicking a wedge under the door to keep it from closing and locking him out.

He scanned the grounds nervously, then led me away from the door a few feet, apparently to be sure no one inside could hear us. "I got a bad feeling, Grayson. A bad feeling. Ain't had a bad feeling like this for a long time. Not since the last time the Vikings lost the Superbowl."

"Okay, you got a bad feeling. Do you know what it means?"

"No, I do not. Don't always know what it mean. Back in seventy-seven, I told everyone that would listen that the Vikings would lose, you know?"

I had to get him to focus for a minute, especially with Kate working in the building two or three days per week. "What about now? What kinds of things usually happen when you have a bad feeling now?

"No way to tell. But it ain't going to be pretty, you know? Bad things are going to happen here." Just then, the door opened, and a young girl in a dark green cleaner's uniform walked out, got into a car, and drove off. "I gotta go," Patter said, and he went back inside, leaving me to wonder what the bloody hell he'd been talking about.

I would have let it go in the past, but after helping Marcel dismantle the pentacle, I had to admit I had a bad feeling, too. Two cars remained in the lot, so I decided to see if one was Ray's. Maybe he knew something about the threats to Marcel, the garden, or its members. I grabbed the door to the main entrance just before it slammed shut and headed down the hallway to the office area. As I turned a corner, I nearly bumped into an older man in a worn, dark green jumpsuit pushing a damp mop around the faded Formica floor.

"Sorry about that," I said and turned to go around him when I realized I knew the guy. Sure enough, the nameplate embroidered on his jumpsuit read 'Karl.'

While searching for my birth parents, Karl had provided access to the records room at the John Wilkes Maternity Hospital and Home for Unwed Mothers in St. Paul, where Dean and I had been born. In exchange for a small fee, of course. Karl also provided access to the admin records room for another fee, revealing the names of the midwives who had attended our births. This information had been very helpful in unraveling the murder of my uncle, James Brennen, and the subsequent murder of the midwives, too.

"Karl! What are you doing here?" Okay, that was a dumb question. He was obviously part of the off-hours cleaning crew. "How've you been?"

Karl just half-waved and smiled. I recalled that he was a man of few words who knew how to coax the value out of each one. He slowly turned and used his mop to wheel his bucket down the hall, the keys on the ring at his waist jangling as he went.

I was about to resume my quest for Ray when I realized Karl could be useful to me again. I quickly caught up with him and said in a low voice, "Do you still have the keys to the kingdom?"

Karl smiled and patted the key ring.

"Are you willing to share?" He hardly paused for a moment, then nodded briefly. That's Karl, I thought. Anything for a buck. As glad as I was to see him, I couldn't help wondering why he was working here now. "You didn't get in trouble for giving me access to the admin room, did you?"

Karl stared at the floor and slowly nodded. "Did Kate get you the job here?"

He looked up and smiled, which was all I needed to know. "Can you take me to Sheila's office?"

With another brief nod, he turned and led me through the cubical farm to Sheila's office, which was right next to Ray's. I didn't see anyone else around, so I figured one of the cars I'd noticed earlier must be Karl's and the other must be Patter's. We were clear to rifle through as many offices as we liked.

I grabbed the handle of Sheila's office door and waited for Karl to turn the key, but he just stood there. Finally, he held up his hand and rubbed his finger and thumb together. Silly me. I almost forgot this was a pay-to-play arrangement. As I recalled from our last encounter, the going rate was two hundred dollars. I figured if I asked him, the new rate would be higher. Fortunately, I had recently visited an ATM, so I counted ten twenties from my wallet and handed them over. He put them in his jumpsuit pocket without recounting them, unlocked the door, and stepped aside to let me in.

Sheila's office was almost as big as Ray's but with way more Aussie artifacts, which created a claustrophobic feeling that Ray and Sheila seemed to revel in. She had the same oversized desk, large windows with a great view, and posters of famous Australian landmarks. I started the search with the credenza, which was covered with authentic-looking Aboriginal musical instruments such as didgeridoos and clapsticks. Next to these was a collection of well-worn books on writing and publishing, which reminded me of a library's reference section for aspiring authors. I did a double take when I saw Chadrick's latest book, Beat Yourself, in the pile. A quick search of the title page showed the author had personally dedicated it. 'Sheila, thanks for your support! Yours, Chadrick,' it read. While that was interesting, it could mean a lot of things or nothing.

Karl made a small noise behind me, which I thought was his way of telling me to hurry up. I turned around and jumped when I realized he was standing beside me, as I hadn't heard him creep over. Karl pointed to the book I was holding with a serious look. "He was here."

"Who was here, Karl? Chadrick?"

Karl nodded. "Arguing."

"Sheila and Chadrick were arguing?" Another nod.

"Do you know what it was about?" He shook his head no.

Karl must have really wanted to convey a message because he spoke again. "He came back later." Then he patted the pocket containing the money I'd just given him.

I thought I was getting his cryptical message. "So Chadrick came back after their argument and brib... I mean, provided you with a donation to let him into Sheila's office, right?" Another nod.

"Did he take anything?" Head shake.

"When was this, Karl?" He just shrugged.

"Was it within the last few months?" Head nod.

His whole economy of words schtick was getting on my nerves. It was like talking to a banana. I didn't know what to ask him next, so I decided on a general question. "Anything else I should know?"

Head shake. Okay, that was a wrap. What the hell were they arguing about, and what had Chadrick been searching for, I wondered. Whatever it was, could it have given him a motive for Sheila's untimely death?

I sat in her chair and tried the credenza doors, which she either didn't bother to lock or the police forgot to relock, only to find the usual office detritus. It was the same with her desk drawers. I leaned back in the chair to ponder things, then wondered if she and Ray had installed matching his-and-her safes. A quick scan of the floor revealed they did not, at least not in this office.

Hoping a more systematic approach would yield better results, I went through the desk drawers again, more slowly this time. When I got to the middle drawer, I reached to the back to see if I'd missed anything. As I did, my knuckles bumped something. Further investigation revealed that someone, presumably Sheila, had used painter's tape to affix a memory stick to the underside of the desktop. It couldn't be seen from the outside even if the drawer was all the way open, so the police must have missed it. I put it in my pants pocket, closed the drawer, and left the office.

Karl followed me out and went back to work, which, in his case, meant moving his mop back and forth over the same spot. I thought I'd try my luck and pointed toward Ray's office with one hand while making a key-turning motion with the other. Apparently, this whole minimal use of words thing was contagious. Karl held up his hand and rubbed his finger and thumb together again. Damn, another two hundred? Really? Talk about inflation. I remembered taking out three hundred from the ATM and knew I didn't have that much on me. "How about one hundred? It's all I've got left." I reached for my wallet to show Karl I was being honest when he shook his head, looked down, and used his mop to push his bucket down the aisle. It looked like we were at an impasse. Maybe he'd cave if I started to leave, I thought.

"Okay, well, thanks for your help, Karl."

He waved over his shoulder without looking back. I guess the memory stick would have to do for now. I could always come back next Sunday with more blood money. As I turned to leave, I saw him pat the pocket that held the two hundred dollars and resume mopping. He really should put some water in that bucket one of these days.

* * *

I waited for Kate by the main entrance, wondering what was keeping her and watching Marcel's congregants say their goodbyes and drive off. She arrived fifteen minutes later, apologized profusely for running late, and said she just wanted to grab her sunglasses off her desk. I watched the hem of her summer dress bounce as she swept through the aisles and was once again reminded of how lucky I was to have her in my life.

Just as she returned to the front door, a loud bang rang out. We both froze. Unfortunately, I'd heard this sound a few times during my previous investigation, so I knew it was gunfire immediately. My immediate reaction was to get down and yell at Kate to do the same, but I realized it wasn't loud enough to be in the same room. "Kate, I'm pretty sure that was a gunshot. We have to check it out. Someone might be hurt."

"Are you nuts? There might be a killer on the loose." Okay, that was a good point. Maybe it was a character flaw, but I couldn't let that stop me from searching for a potential victim. Or the shooter. I would just need to be extremely cautious.

"It sounded like it had come from the Garden. I'm going to move slowly in that direction to see what's going on."

"Grayson, no. We have to wait for the police. I'm calling 9-1-1." She took out her new cell phone and started dialing. Since she was currently occupied, I went outside and moved past the Supper Club, staying very close to the building. I saw no movement of any kind and soon arrived at the Garden to find Patter splayed out on the asphalt just outside the arbor. He'd been shot in the chest and was bleeding profusely. It didn't look good. I wanted to apply direct pressure to his wound but didn't want to be a sitting duck for the shooter. I scanned the area for a minute but didn't see anyone, so I returned to Patter's side, examined him for a moment, and checked for a pulse but couldn't find one. I was pretty sure Patter was dead and, not being an EMT, really had no idea how to help him without making his condition worse. I started hearing sirens in the background, and as they got louder and louder, I thought it best to leave any treatment to the professionals.

It was then that I noticed something seemed out of place. Just past the arbor, someone had posted a pentacle on a cross. It was just like the one that Marcel had dismantled. Was this somehow related to Patter's death? Maybe he caught Marcel posting the cross and demanded he take it down, which led to an argument and his brutal slaying. Or maybe it was the reverse, and Marcel caught Patter, who didn't like being disturbed while posting cult symbols. Did this have anything to do with Sheila's murder? I wondered.

While I contemplated the options, an ambulance and squad car converged on us. The EMTs sprang into action, assessing Patter's condition and determining the best course of action. The police asked me to step back so they could secure the scene, and I was fine with that. I tried to saunter away, but no luck. One of the officers asked me to stick around for questioning. By now, I knew the routine all too well.

As I waited for Copeland to show up and give me the third degree, I realized I was sad about Patter. He was a talented guy who practiced every day to keep up his skills. I had to think he was an innocent bystander who had gotten in some psycho's way and ended up as collateral damage. It only strengthened my resolve to find the bastard that was doing this and make sure they were brought to justice.

Chapter Seventeen

Monday Night, June 4

D ean texted me on Monday night, saying he had big news about Ray, but it was too big to share via text. My brother didn't normally succumb to cheap hyperbole, so we agreed to meet the next morning instead of Wednesday. I wondered what news could be so big that he couldn't text me but felt the need to foreshadow the announcement.

His text reminded me that I still hadn't explored the memory stick from Sheila's desk. I guess all the excitement of being interrogated by the police, again, and Patter's murder had gotten me distracted. I found the stick in the pocket of the pants I had worn on Sunday and opened up my home laptop. I hoped Sheila had not bothered putting password protection on it. Dean would probably be able to get into it eventually, but it would delay the whole process by at least a few days, and I didn't want to wait. I ran a security scanner app as I inserted the stick, which came back clean, and File Explorer opened immediately. I guess Sheila figured taping the memory stick to the underside of her desktop would be secure enough.

There were two folders in the file list, one named 'Financials' and another named 'Writing.' I opened the first one to find two Excel files. One was creatively named 'Payments One,' and the other was similarly named 'Payments Two.' They sounded like names Dr. Suess would use. The first spreadsheet contained a list of dollar amounts and dates. They might have been payments on a mortgage or car loan, except the size of the payments had been creeping up over the past few years. They'd started at two thousand dollars per month and were now over eight thousand. Could this have been one of those reverse mortgages?

I closed the first one and opened the second spreadsheet. It contained another list of payments totaling over one hundred thousand and the dates on which they were made, but there was no outstanding balance. That was odd. Maybe they were payments being made to her?

Then, I wondered if Sheila had been paying off Eric's gambling debts. The amount seemed about right as casinos don't offer unlimited credit lines— at some point, they cut you off until you convinced them you were good for it and started paying them back. Had these payments been made to a Minnesota-based casino? Maybe Eric owed them so much that they refused to extend his credit. Then, he moved on to Vegas and started the process over.

I recalled that casinos shared information to avoid this kind of situation. Did the Native American casino owners in Minnesota share their data with the Las Vegas-based owners? I wondered. And, would he really have let his mother pay off his debts like this?

I closed that file and backed out of the folder to get to the main file list. I clicked on the folder called 'Writing,' and a dialog box asking for a password popped up. It looked as if Sheila knew how to protect her files, after all. I knew the odds of me randomly guessing the right password were slim to none, despite what you see in the movies, so I would have to get Dean involved. Out of curiosity, I checked the Properties for that folder, which said it contained forty-three files and was over 12 MB in size. Based on these numbers, each file would have been about 280 Meg, which was large enough to hold the draft of a large book. I recalled that Ray told me Sheila was writing a book about him, the ruby, and the business they had built together. If this memory stick held Sheila's work, she must have been well on her way to telling their story. I wondered if she had been trying to publish it yet.

As I copied the unencrypted memory stick contents to my laptop, my cell buzzed with an incoming call. I looked at the phone to see who it was. There was no name, just a number, which I soon realized was owned by

Victor Hawkes. It had been almost a week since our last encounter, and I was shocked he'd waited this long to contact me. I sent it to voicemail.

A minute later, the phone indicated a text from the same number had come in. **You've had plenty of time to find Eric. Where is he?**

Okay, this was crazy. Since we weren't at the same location, or at least I didn't think we were, it was time to bring this guy back to reality. **Victor, I haven't found Eric. I don't even know where to look. As I said, I'm not a P.I. Why don't we just forget this whole thing? I'll give you the money back, and we'll go our separate ways, okay?**

It's too late for that. You can give the money back, but you will help us whether we pay you or not.

I took a deep breath and let it out slowly. What the bloody hell had Ray gotten me into? **Fine. I will keep looking.**

I don't know if he texted me again because I shut off my phone in a vain attempt to make the whole thing go away.

* * *

I had ordered and grabbed a seat at the Caribou on Lake Street by the time Dean arrived for our Tuesday morning meeting. "You are not going to believe this." He didn't bother saying 'hi,' 'thanks for the coffee,' or 'how about those Twins.' He just launched right into it. "I'm pretty sure Ray and Sheila were not married when they left Australia. At least not married to each other."

Wow, that was a shocker. No wonder Dean was grinning so smugly. "And I can't find any records of Ray and Sheila being married here either. It's possible they aren't hitched at all."

"Wait, what? How did you figure that out?"

"Well, each state and territory in Australia has its own centralized registry for recording births, deaths, and marriages, which is quite handy for researchers. I had to pay a small fee to an Australian agent I found online who had the official access to get the job done. It turns out that Ray married a woman named Halena before finding the ruby. Unfortunately, these registries don't handle divorces, so we don't know if they are still married or not. There's also no record of Halena's death either, but that doesn't prove she's still alive. She could have died elsewhere without the records in Australia being updated. And it's possible that Ray and Sheila got married in Las Vegas or somewhere else with dodgy record keeping. I could see them doing that, but it puts a whole new spin on your investigation."

I took a big gulp of light roast, trying to consume this new information. "Maybe Ray had a bad marriage, and he and Sheila were fleeing the country in the dark of night."

"I don't know anything about the quality of their marriage or their travel arrangements, but running away to America with a new woman is one way to escape whatever unfortunate situation you find yourself in."

"I wonder whatever happened to Halena. She must have figured out that Ray emigrated to the U.S. at some point. You'd think she would have reached out to him by now if for no other reason than to end their marriage."

"I know. I haven't been able to find out anything about her in any other records. It's like she just disappeared."

The thought of Ray luring his wife out to a remote part of the Outback and then coming back alone popped into my head. But that didn't seem likely. Leaving the country to escape his troubles, yes, but murdering his wife and leaving her to the vultures, no.

"In any case, this would explain why Nigel Lawson ended up owning twenty percent of the business when the three of them originally came to the US."

Dean scrunched up his forehead. "How would that work?"

I thought it was obvious. "Ray already said they didn't have a prenup agreement, but they did have a basic buy/sell agreement for the business. Let's say Ray and Sheila are married, and they own the business fifty/fifty. If things went south, they would end up in divorce court like everyone else does, no worries. But, if they weren't married, Sheila could do whatever she wanted with her half, like sell it to someone that Ray hated. If Ray has his mate Nigel as part owner, they form a voting block that can stop Sheila from selling to anyone. In fact, they could force her to sell it to them."

Dean considered this for a minute, then asked a good question. "Yeah, but couldn't Nigel and Sheila form a voting block against Ray?"

"Yes, they could. Ray must have figured his best mate would never turn on him like that. So, we—"

"...really need to talk to Nigel. I know. I will track him down even if I have to go to the Outback to do it."

"Sounds like a plan to me." The mental note I'd made the last time I spoke with Copeland finally kicked in. "Speaking of tracking people down, any luck with the Institute for a Better Life people in Chicago?"

"Yep, I was just getting to them. I could confirm that the four men surrounding Bill Goddard in the group picture you sent me were his lieutenants. Your friend Marcel was considered second in command and the heir apparent if anything ever happened to Bill. He had two main roles on the leadership team. First, he oversaw recruiting new members, which mostly meant looking for kids in their teens or twenties who were disaffected by their peers and who would be impressionable. But he also looked for people in their thirties or forties if they were struggling with their current life. It sounds like he was very good at it."

"We could have predicted that based on his work in the Twin Cities. That must have been where he learned his organizing and evangelizing skills."

"Right. His second role was to manage the books."

"I caught that from the articles I read recently. The police considered him a prime suspect for both the murder and the shady real estate deal, and they arrested him. But eventually, the charges were dropped."

"Exactly. But that doesn't really clear him. It just means they couldn't make the charges stick. The next person was in charge of group discipline, otherwise known as 'The Muscle.' I can't recall his name, but it doesn't really matter as he's dead. He was incarcerated for killing a guy in a knife fight outside a bar and then was killed in prison by that guy's brother."

"Nice crowd they run with over there in Chicagoland."

Dean scoffed. "No kidding. I spoke with the third guy for about twenty minutes a few weeks ago. He was older and moved to Florida a few years after the Institute broke up. He became an insurance adjuster and eventually retired. He said he didn't have a specific role assigned to him, but I got the impression he was in charge of developing their code of beliefs. He talked a lot about everything wrong with our political system these days. But he wasn't much help as he didn't stay in touch with any of the former members and hadn't been back to Chicago in many years. At least that's what he said. I didn't have any reason to think he was lying."

"So that leaves one other leader. Did you find him?"

"Why do you always doubt me? Of course, I found him. His name is Greg Hopkins. He and Marcel attended the same Catholic grade school as kids, and he still lives in the Chicagoland area. He immediately became suspicious when I started asking about the group and asked me if I was a reporter. I assured him I was not and told him some of the things you told me to sound like an insider. I also told him I wanted to learn more about coaching new members into the lifestyle because Marcel wanted me to help build his group in Minnesota."

"Hey, that sounds like a good angle. What did he say?"

"When he finally let his guard down, he admitted that he was in charge of 'indoctrination,' as he called it. He had some scary but very interesting things to say about the 'coercive persuasion tactics' they used to trick kids into joining and then breaking them down until they would do whatever they were told to do. He didn't know who murdered Bill, but he always assumed it was Marcel. It sounds like Bill caught him and an accomplice with their hands in the cookie jar, and Marcel killed him to shut him up. He was as surprised as everyone else that Marcel was released. But then he just seemed to disappear. They didn't talk for many years after that until Marcel called him a few years ago to reconnect. That's when he found out Marcel was living in Minnesota and running a new group. Greg assumed it was a cult, but Marcel told him he had gotten religion and gone clean."

"That makes it hard to know what to believe about Marcel. Was he a good guy running from his past, or did he have a longer-term strategy to create a group of followers that he could eventually bend to his will?" I wondered.

Dean sat back and held up his hands. "I believe that's your department. I just do the research."

It was my turn to update Dean, and I told him about my unsuccessful attempt to dig up anything meaningful on Scott Dimond and my subsequent lunch with him. "So, I was wondering if your offer to do some dark web research was still good."

"I figured this would happen. It's why you should hire IT professionals instead of designer engineers when you want the inside scoop." I had the feeling he was throwing my words back at me. I didn't care as long as he agreed to do the work.

"I already did the online research and didn't find anything you'd be interested in. The problem was that there was too little information available. No one is that clean or that below the news radar. So, I went offline. I knew X was screwed into the Twin Cities investment world in a big way, so I asked him." Dean leaned forward and lowered his voice, possibly so anyone hiding in the garbage bin next to us couldn't hear him. "Gray, you have to keep this to yourself. X doesn't know Scott personally, but they have many mutual friends who he tapped into. The word on the street is that Scott has a big real estate deal cooking that will be highly lucrative if he can close it. X doesn't have any details yet, but he's still working on it."

No wonder I couldn't find anything. It's not online, I thought. "Wow, that's impressive. He didn't mention that over lunch."

Dean scoffed again. "That's not surprising. These rich guys never let us little people in on their deals. They're worried we'll try to horn in somehow and mess it up for them."

"As if I would know how to get in the middle of a deal like that. Of course, I never thought I'd be in the middle of a mob chase, but here I am. Speaking of which, Victor Hawkes started sending me threatening texts this morning. I wonder what took him so long."

Dean shook his head. "He must have had other lowlifes to harass in the meantime."

"No doubt. Is there any chance that Victor killed Sheila as a warning to Eric that he would be next if he didn't find a way to pay them back?"

Dean looked out the window for a minute, deep in thought. "That seems like an extreme approach, but who knows? All I know is we need a plan to deal with Victor."

Talk about stating the obvious. "I couldn't agree more, but the only way we're going to get him off our back, my back, is to show some progress without ratting out Eric. Maybe we send him off somewhere with a false lead.

"So, you'd text Victor that Eric will be at a certain place at a certain time, even though he won't be, just to give him something to do?"

"It doesn't sound that good when you put it like that. If he thinks we're running him around, he's going to get pissed off, and guess whose butt is on the line?"

"Better you than me." Dean threw up his hands. "I've really got nothing, though."

"I know, me either. We probably only have a couple of days to come up with something before he starts showing up at the office again."

Dean nodded. We changed the subject to the latest update to AI tools Dean was working on and how the café table designs were progressing. As we were wrapping up our conversation, I recalled the memory stick in my pocket. I pulled it out and explained where I got it and what was on it. "There is a folder called Writing that is password protected. Can you get in?"

Dean just smiled. "My guess is that Sheila used the standard Windows file encryption program to set up the password, so it should be a piece of cake." He took the stick, and we left together.

* * *

On the way back to my office, I thought about Dean's news. I couldn't help but wonder if Copeland was doing this level of research into potential suspects. Based on what I knew of the case volume and time constraints he and his team had, it didn't seem likely. I thought maybe if he'd be willing to meet and share what he knew, I'd be willing to do the same. We'd used each other this way in the past, especially when he was running out of suspects. So, I texted him to see if he was available. He texted me back, saying he could spare a few minutes, but only if I dropped by his station. I agreed and headed for the parking garage instead of the office.

The twelve-mile trip to the St. Paul Police Station took about twenty minutes, and I was soon checking in.

"Detective Aaron Copeland, please," I said to the officer at the reception desk through a small metal voice port in the three-inch-thick bulletproof glass that separated the waiting room from the rest of the station.

"Is he expecting you?" asked the receptionist loudly enough to be heard over the police scanner in the background.

"Yes. I just texted him. My name is Grayson Dyle."

"I'll let him know you're here." She pointed her pen toward a beat-up wooden bench along the wall. I'd sat in that seat before wondering where they were going with the design of this room. Large rivets in broad metal columns held the glass in place, and the concrete block walls were painted a neutral tone of beige that looked too much like a decaying mushroom for my tastes. Paul would run screaming from the room after about five minutes in this place. You couldn't tell if they were shooting for sterile and foreboding to intimidate visitors or warm and welcoming to say relax—the police are here for you. Because right now, it accomplished neither.

"Grayson, thanks for coming." The detective opened the security door, shook my hand, and showed me in.

"Thanks for meeting on short notice."

"No worries. I was just wondering what I was going to do for entertainment today when you texted me." That's Copeland—always a kidder.

He offered me coffee, but I turned him down, so we headed back to one of the conference rooms. It was nicely appointed and well-lit, with framed pictures of famous local buildings, including the Minnesota State Capitol and the St. Paul Landmark Center. Not a single pane of one-way mirrored glass was in sight. Of course, the last time I was in this room, he had accused me of murder, but I decided not to let that bother me.

"So, what can I do you for?" The detective was cordial but also seemed to be wary that I would be wasting his time.

"I was just wondering if there was anything new on Sheila's or Patter's murder."

Copeland stared at me for a moment, and it seemed like he was trying to decide if he should share some minor news or just accuse me of one of the murders as long as I was in the building.

"As you know, we found a Satanic symbol called a pentacle near Patter's body, but the murder itself looks like a straightforward, non-Satanic killing. At this point, we don't know if the symbols were simple misdirects or if there really is a cult involved. Have you found anything regarding Marcel's background?"

"I know Marcel was involved with a group called the Institute for a Better Life that was rumored to be a cult when he lived in the Chicago area over ten years ago. The charismatic leader of the group, Bill Goddard, was murdered, and Marcel was a person of interest for a while. However, the group was never proven to be a cult by the Chicago Police or the FBI, nor was he confirmed as being involved in the murder, which has still not been solved. The group disbanded after Bill's death, and there was some controversy about Marcel's involvement in the sale of the Institute's property, but that was never proven either.

"Marcel certainly learned a thing or two about organizing and operating a religious group because he moved to Minnesota not too long after that and became a Deacon within the Catholic Church. He was assigned to St. Celestines, and..." I realized I was boring him. "But you know all of this already, don't you?"

Copeland just grunted. "Well, be sure to let me know if you learn anything new. I know you like working the family members. Have you learned anything from them?"

I assumed he must have been talking about how I found a family connection that helped solve the murder of James Brennan, so I shared what I knew. "I've already spoken with Mia and Eric, the—"

"Sheila's daughter and son. I've spoken with them, too."

"Right. Mia checked out, but Eric seems like he's hiding something."

"He was out of town at the time of both murders. We've checked."

Okay, that cleared him, but it didn't clear Victor. For a moment, I thought about mentioning the Vegas connection but decided against it. The last thing

I needed was another group of people pressuring me to find Eric. "I still think there's something Eric's not divulging. Anyway, have you connected with Mia's boyfriend, Josh? Or I suppose I should say, fiancé. Have you heard they've gotten engaged?"

Copeland shifted forward in his chair, which usually signaled that the meeting would be over soon. "Nope, hadn't heard that one. Not sure it changes anything, though."

"Well, Sheila had been blocking their engagement, and now that she's gone, Ray has given them his blessing. So maybe…"

The Detective seemed skeptical. "Josh comes from a wealthy family. Sheila would have relented after he graduated, especially if he straightened himself out. But we may take another look at him if we have time."

Copeland was better informed than I thought. I tried to come up with some juicy tidbits to share but realized I had nothing. "Thanks, Detective."

"Don't be a stranger." With that, the meeting was over.

Chapter Eighteen

Wednesday, June 6

The next day, I woke up to hear my phone ringing, which was odd because no one texted first to make sure a call was okay. At least, that's what the millennials who worked for us assured me was their standard protocol. I immediately became concerned this would be unwelcome news, but I didn't recognize the number when I looked at the screen. The screen also said five-forty-three a.m. It was on the fourth ring when I decided to chance it and answered.

"Hi, this is Grayson."

"Grayson Dyle, how are you?" It was said with such a happy tone that it sounded like the caller had a big smile on their face. "This is Nigel Lawson." Nigel Lawson...who was that again?

I was still a bit groggy and couldn't place the name, so I ad-libbed an answer. "Hi, Nigel. I'm good. How are you?" Then I realized it was Ray's silent business partner.

I must have sounded sleepy because Nigel started apologizing. "Oh my gosh, look at the time. It's not even six a.m. Sorry, Grayson. I just returned to town and'm still on Aussie time. Why don't I call you back later?"

I didn't want to take the chance he would decide not to call again. "No, it's no problem at all. My alarm is usually set for six a.m., so I would have been up shortly anyway." That was a total fib. I never set the alarm before seven, if I did set it at all. "Thanks for returning my calls. I assume you've heard about Sheila."

"I did hear about her. What a tragedy. She was a lovely person, and I enjoyed working with her. Heard about Patter, too. Ray told me he's got you looking into things on the QT. What's the latest?"

I remembered that Ray said Nigel was in Australia on the night of Sheila's death, but he was in the Outback and not reachable. I wanted to ask him when he found out and who told him, but I didn't want him to know he was a suspect on my private murder board just yet. He'd find that out soon enough. "Well, it's early days, so I don't have much to report. But, I would like to get more background on some of his team members. Would you mind if I asked you a few questions over lunch or dinner?"

There was a pause, and I thought I'd lost him, but then he perked up. "Sure, Grayson. Why not." I got the sense he'd be trying to pick my brain as much as I'd be trying to pick his. "My schedule is pretty open right now since I just got back. How about we meet at Ray's Aussie House at eleven-thirty?"

"Are you sure you don't want to go to a burger place? You must be tired of Aussie food."

"No worries, mate. See you there."

* * *

I arrived at the restaurant right on time, but Nigel was already there picking up his order. I guess we wouldn't have to fight over who would buy lunch. Even if I hadn't looked him up on social media, I could have easily picked him out because he was the only person there wearing an Outback hat, complete with mesh sides, a handy chin strap, and a weathered look that boasted its owner had recently been navigating the Outback like a native. Either that or he paid extra for the pre-worn version. Between that, his ruddy good looks, the short-sleeved shirt, and worn khakis, it looked like he was auditioning for the role of Aussie House spokesmodel. I ordered and joined him at his table. "Nigel, nice to meet you in person."

"G'day, Grayson, nice to meet you, too." We shook hands as I sat down. I noticed he was enjoying a Foster's Lager, which was pitched as the most

176

popular beer brand down under. I wondered if he knew that while Foster's originated at a brewery in Melbourne, two Americans were now running it, and his beer had actually been brewed in Fort Worth, Texas. Either way, I was hoping it would loosen him up.

"So, when did you get back in?" I asked between bites. I had to admit this was another good meal.

"Yesterday. Sorry about not getting back to you sooner. I usually don't return messages 'til I'm back Stateside. Don't have too many urgencies nowadays."

"Did you have a chance to hit the Outback?"

"Nah, not on this trip. It's not as glamorous as you see in the ads." He indicated a huge scenic shot of Mount Conner, as labeled in the sign below.

"So, tell me about RRE."

"Ruby Ray Enterprises." The way he said it made me think things were not ace as they say in Australia. "You've got to admire Ray's showmanship like that bit with the ruby museum. It was his idea to take a hunk of rock and spin up a big story. Turned a ruby into gold." Nigel laughed at his own joke.

"Was he a good businessman, too?"

"Yeah, he was alright. He knew a good idea when he heard one. That's where I came in."

"So, you were the brains behind the showman."

"You could say that, yeah. Ray would be the first to admit it if you bought him a pint or two. Course, he got himself into hot water a few years ago. Sheila and I had to talk sense into him. He would have been bankrupt a long time ago if it wasn't for the two of us."

"What happened?"

"Well, we don't talk about it much." He stopped to take another bite while he studied me, probably deciding how much he wanted to share. "Let's just say Ray had a few things to learn about running a business when we first started out. He wanted to go the whole hog and launch the entire operation all at the same time. We didn't have the cash flow to support that kind of thing. Sheila and I talked him down from the edge more than once. Things got a bit rocky, especially with his wife always taking my side. But we eventually worked it out, and now we're doing great. I'll bet he didn't tell you that part of the story, did he? Naw, I can see he didn't. That's okay, though. Look at the branding on this place. That's all Ray's handiwork. That's where he shined."

I wondered how much Ray would agree with Nigel's version of events.

"So, how did you decide to move to the U.S. and go into business together?"

"Naw, it's your turn next. What have you been finding out?"

I put the last piece of pie in my mouth to buy some time. I couldn't really share that much because I didn't know if he was somehow involved in either murder, even though he was probably out of the country when they happened. But I had to say something. Marcel seemed like a safe topic, and I could get some bragging rights from my close connection with the police. "Well, the lead person working the case is a Detective named Aaron Copeland…"

"Like the composer?"

I knew Copeland was tired of that reference, and I suddenly realized why. "Well, yes, they have the same name, but Aaron is a fairly tall African American in his mid-thirties, so no relation. Anyway, I just met with him to compare notes, and one of the people we're looking at is Reverend Marcel." I didn't want to start any rumors, but the stories about his involvement with the cult-like group in Chicago were easy to find online if you bothered to look. So, I presented a highly watered-down version of Marcel's background and the concerns that Copeland had mentioned.

"Naw, can't really see Marcel behind any of this. I mean, what motive would he have? Besides, he's got religion."

I just let that comment go and changed the subject. "You were about to tell me how you ended up in business with Ray and Sheila."

Nigel finished his meal and sat back in his seat. "Well, that story goes back a long way. Not a lot of people know this, but Ray wasn't married to Sheila when they left Australia. He was actually married to a lady named Halena. Decent girl. Well built, sturdy, if you know what I mean. Ray thought she was perfect for him, but they jumped into a wedding and never really got along. Pretty soon, he wants to quit her and marry Sheila. Halena wasn't overjoyed with Ray just then, and she probably would have agreed to cancel the whole thing, but then he finds the Poona Ruby. Big game-changer, that was. He knew he'd never be rid of her if she found out. So, he and Sheila packed their bags and got out of town on the QT. I tagged along for the ride. They decided to play happy families once they got here, but Sheila really wanted him to get a proper divorce so they could get hitched. Ray didn't want to ask Halena for one. He didn't want her or her attorneys mucking about in his finances, not with the ruby in the mix. He wasn't about to share that with her. So, he kept putting it off. Shelia eventually got tired of asking. And it's been that way ever since."

It was good that Dean had given me a heads-up about this situation. Otherwise, I might wonder if he'd make the whole thing up. "Didn't Halena ever find him? It wouldn't have been that hard."

"Too right, today. Back then, not so much. Halena wouldn't have been trying to find him back then. She was too mad. But Ray had been covering his tracks, too. None of us had two coins to rub together. Ray said he'd use the ruby as collateral. But he needed Sheila and me to be part owners, so it would be harder to track him. I agreed. Thought I was doing him a solid. Even after the ankle biters came along, we stuck to the story. Everyone thought Ray and Sheila had tied the knot before they came over."

Nigel looked around the pie shop, leaned forward in his chair, and lowered his voice as if he were going to tell me a deep, dark secret. "Then, about four or five months ago, suddenly Halena contacted him from Australia. Said she knew about the ruby and the business and wanted her share. Threatened to sue him or hurt him if he didn't go along. Ray told her the business wasn't worth anything, and the ruby was a fake—he just made the whole thing up to build his reputation as a gem hunter. He tells her to piss off. He sent me down there to talk some sense into her, but she wouldn't meet with me.

"Then, Ray decides I should sell him my minority share in the company. He claimed we had some verbal agreement that would expire as soon as Halena found out. I said no way. And nothing in the contract says I have to. What a load of rubbish. Typical Ray, though, always trying to get one-up on everyone else."

Wow, interesting stuff. I was surprised at how open Nigel had become and wondered how far I could push him. "So, who killed Sheila?"

That took him by surprise. Nigel leaned back, slowly formed the fingers on his right hand into the shape of a gun, and used it to push his hat back. He was definitely a bit larger than life, but I had to admit I liked the guy.

"Who cares what I think?"

"You've known this crew for years. You probably know where the bodies are buried, so to speak. You'd probably know if anyone has a secret motive for wanting Sheila out of the way. You may know and not even know that you know."

That seemed to throw him, so I tried again. "Let's say someone had a grudge against Sheila from something that happened a long time ago, and they finally found the right opportunity to kill her. The police wouldn't know what had happened in the past, and neither would I. Was Sheila ever involved in anything illegal? Anything someone from her past would hold against her?"

"Not Sheila. Everyone loved her."

"What about Halena? Would she come here and kill Sheila to get her rich husband back?"

"Naw. Spend all that time in the air so you can take out your man's girlfriend? I can't see it. She would have taken Ray out first so she could inherit."

I was running out of material, but another question still bothered me. "One more thing, when did you arrive back in the U.S.?"

"Crikey, you think I'm a suspect, don't you? I bet you can't wait to update your murder board." He laughed at his own joke again but didn't answer the question. I considered telling him that Ray was right and the ruby actually was a fake, then asking if he knew anything about that, but I decided not to. He didn't seem to know there was a fake floating around, and it seemed better to leave it that way. He'd just deny any involvement in swapping the stones anyway. Nigel had to run, so we shook hands, and he took off.

* * *

180

As I was driving back to the office, I couldn't help wondering if Nigel had some grudge against Sheila and Ray for how the business had turned out. He certainly had no issues taking credit for its early success and seemed to blame Ray for the recent shortcomings. I guess silent partners were like that. I called Dean from my cell phone using the car's speakers.

When he answered, I didn't bother to say hello. "You can call off the search for Nigel. I just had lunch with him."

He didn't miss a beat. "Stop searching for Nigel. Got it. What did he have to say?"

"He claims not to have visited the Outback on this trip, and I believed him. I wonder why Ray lied about that." I updated Dean on Ray's marital status, his wife's recent reappearance and threats, and their contract. I told him about the meeting with Copeland, too.

"That must be why Ray told you Nigel was unreachable—he figured you'd just let it go if you thought he was out of the country at the time of both murders, and he didn't want Nigel telling you all of that."

"That makes sense, but he doesn't know me very well, does he?"

"Not like I do. Anyway, I managed to get more intel on Ray's financial situation. I connected with a city council member who said Ray attended one of their meetings about a year ago. He had the audacity to float the idea of turning the Supper Club into a strip club, claiming it would bring substantially more tax revenue to their coffers."

"What? No way. The planning commission is way too conservative, and there are too many bedroom communities right next door. They would have tossed him out on his ear. I would have loved to have been at that meeting."

"Yeah, they shot him down pretty fast. But, it shows you how desperate he was getting."

I drove in silence for a minute and considered the pace of the investigation, which seemed to be crawling along like a cone snail. I'd interviewed just about everyone who was even remotely involved in the murders and still didn't have a credible suspect. I started feeling sorry for myself and thought this might be a good time to check in with my big brother. "You know, Dean, I don't seem to be getting anywhere on these murders. Maybe solving the last set of murders was just a one-off, just a fluke, and this whole thing is a big waste of time."

I don't know what I expected Dean to say to that, but for once in his life, he didn't give me grief about something that was bugging me.

"Ordinarily, I would agree that you are just wasting your time. But the last time wasn't just a fluke. You figured out what happened when no one else could. I was right there, and I didn't get it. And, just like the last time, the police don't know where to look, so they're not going to figure it out. Besides, you just met with Copeland, right? How much progress are they making?"

"None."

"I rest my case."

It was good to know Dean was capable of being supportive from time to time. I figured it would be interesting to see how long this mood would last. "So, what do I do next?"

"Hmm, good question. Let's think about this."

I kept quiet, not wanting to interrupt what I hoped was a brilliant train of thought.

After a few minutes, he made a suggestion. "You should talk to Ray again and let him know you've got Nigel's side of their history to see how his story changes."

"That's actually a really good idea."

"Why are you so surprised? Isn't that what professional investigators always do, bounce back and forth between potential suspects until one of them trips up?"

I couldn't argue with that.

Chapter Nineteen

Thursday, June 7

Following Dean's sage advice, which was undoubtedly honed over hundreds of hours watching TV detectives and listening to true crime podcasts, I drove to Ray's office the next day to see if he was available. I arrived right before lunch, figuring I could confront Ray and then take Kate out for a bite if she was available.

I stopped at the front desk. "Hi, Cheryl. Is Ray here?"

"Hi, Grayson. Nope, he's not here."

"How about Kate?"

Cheryl must have seen the hopeful look on my face as she gave me a sympathetic smile. "I'm afraid she's not here either." In hindsight, I should have texted first.

As I thought about what to do next, it occurred to me that TV detectives usually got a few insightful clues by questioning the murder victim's staff. Cheryl appeared to have a lot of roles in addition to Office Manager, such as receptionist and Sheila and Ray's personal assistant. No wonder she had seemed so weary. She probably knew a lot about the company scuttlebutt, and I felt she wouldn't mind sharing. I considered asking her out for lunch but then realized that was not a good idea, as a lot of people would misinterpret it. "Okay, thanks. Would you tell Kate I stopped by?"

"Will do."

As I was about to head out, I realized something was still bothering me about the swing. Would it have been possible for the murderer to release the swing remotely? A theory began to form in my mind, and this seemed like a good time to check it out. "Cheryl, would you mind if I headed over to the Supper Club for a few minutes? There's something I want to investigate."

"I suppose that would be okay. You're part of the company's extended family now, right?"

"Absolutely. Will the lights be on over there?"

"No, but they're not hard to find." She told me where to find the light panel, and I headed over, turned on the lights, and climbed up the ship's ladder to the swing station.

I immediately noticed a small shiny eyelet screw sticking out from the side of the platform that the swinger stood on. I hadn't noticed it before because I wasn't looking for it. Sure enough, there was another eyelet at the bottom of the ship's ladder and a third on the door between the hallway and the kitchen. That told me it was possible to pull the pin remotely, and I knew exactly what had happened.

The murderer poisoned Sheila to prevent her from struggling, and it eventually killed her. Then he dragged her to the dance floor, lowered the swing, bound her to it, and raised it again. He inserted the release control key and connected it to a wire so it could be pulled from a remote location. He then fed the wire through the eyelet on the swing cabinet, through another eyelet at the bottom of the ship's ladder, then ran it across the hallway to the kitchen and looped it through the last eyelet on the door to the backstage area. When this door was closed at the start of the show, it pulled the wire, which also pulled the pin and released the swing. For a brief moment, it was taut, which the killer must not have counted on, and one of the hustling wait staff tripped over it, dropping their tray and causing the commotion we'd heard that night. That action broke the wire loose and it ended up on the floor, where it would have looked like something that had come off some part of the old building they were in. The only incriminating evidence would be the key that was still attached to the wire, and the killer would have had to collect it. But that could have been done later, during the commotion caused by the discovery of Sheila's murder.

It stood to reason that only someone intimately familiar with the swing set-up and mechanism could have rigged her up in the relatively small amount of time they would have had. And they must have been fairly strong to do all the dragging and hoisting, which meant the murderer was most likely a male who had inside knowledge of the company. Even though I couldn't be sure of his motive, my money was on Ruby Ray.

As I climbed down the stairs, I considered calling my friend Detective Copeland to see if he would send out a crew to dust for fingerprints, but then I realized it was way too late for that. At the bottom, I was met by an attractive young girl in a spangled costume accompanied by the Maître D, who angrily asked me what the heck I was doing and why I was trying to ruin their dress rehearsal. Apparently, Ray had already found his new swing girl. I was about to say I'd like to stay and see the new act, but his deepening glare suggested otherwise. I just said 'sorry' and left.

* * *

As I got to work the next day, which, thank God, was Friday, I was glad to have discovered how the murder had been accomplished. I'd decided overnight not to tell Kate about my new suspicions of Ruby Ray. It would only cause friction between us as she almost certainly would have lost sight of the fact I was trying to clear her name and would insist that Ray was innocent. Dean was a different matter, and I texted him to see if he had time to talk soon. He didn't respond immediately, which was odd, but I figured he was either tied up on a new project for X, using STING to spy on some foreign nationals, or following another worthless pursuit. As luck would have it, Dean stopped by about fifteen later.

"Dean, great to see you. We have to talk."

"Yeah. That's why I'm here."

"Oh, right."

"I was on the road anyway and decided to make a pit stop when I got your text."

I led the way down to my office and frosted the glass as we took our seats.

"I figured out what happened on the night of the murder."

Dean seemed skeptical and raised his eyebrows. "Okay..."

After explaining the whole story, Dean smiled with a look of amazement and let out a low whistle. "Wow, that sounds like a plan you would have designed."

For some reason, I was expecting him to be impressed by my deductions, not the murderer's plan, but I let it go. "By the way, Ray hired a new Swing Girl for the Supper Club. We'll have to grab a dinner there one of these days."

Dean seemed surprised. "I don't see how Ray will find anyone to replace Sheila. My Ex and I used to go to the Supper Club just to see her act. God knows it wasn't for the food."

"Yeah, well, the show must go on, right?"

"Absolutely. Considering these new suspicions, you need to confront Ray as I suggested."

"Which I tried to do yesterday when I made the discovery."

Dean looked out the window for a minute. It seemed like he was getting rather pensive about the whole situation. "What if it wasn't Ray? What if the Vegas mob was sending Eric a message, and it was Victor who killed Sheila?"

I couldn't see it. "That doesn't seem likely. They would have had to figure out the swing mechanism and develop the cone snail death plan very quickly. Victor couldn't do that. He doesn't have the brain power."

"No, but we can't rule them out yet, either. They could have sent Victor to be the muscle and someone else to do the hit on Sheila."

"I suppose. Seems like a stretch, though. Speaking of Victor, he's expecting me to call him soon with some kind of update. What am I going to tell him?"

I started imagining various scenarios when one made me laugh, and I had to share it with Dean. "Can you imagine DeeDee meeting Victor and trying to reason with him? He wouldn't know whether to knock her off or accept her invitation for lunch at her house."

Dean smirked. Then, we both seemed to realize at the same time that using DeeDee just might work. When people met her for the first time, which Victor would be, they usually thought she was either eccentric, not very bright, or both, so she tended to be disarming. Dean and I knew that behind that somewhat dotty façade was a keen mind, and she would have Victor eating out of her hand.

"We'd have to be super careful not to put her in harm's way."

"Of course, that goes without saying. We can use the same approach we used with you. Hold the meeting in public with lots of potential eyewitnesses around." Dean looked out the window and went into planning mode. "I'll have to get the Dev Team manager's approval to use STING for this purpose, but I'm sure he'll let me. Good opportunities for actual field surveillance are surprisingly difficult to come by."

"Great," I said loudly enough to bring him back to reality. The thought of DeeDee trying to record the meeting with a camera on her finger while simultaneously keeping body and soul together flashed into my head. It didn't look pretty. "Wait a minute. You said there would be a pendant version of STING, right? Let's go with that one. It will probably be a lot easier for her to maneuver."

"We don't have a pendant version available at the moment, but producing one should be very simple. All we have to do is uncouple the camera from the cylindrical housing…" Dean saw the bored expression on my face and accurately read the room for once. "In short, we can make a pendant version available for this mission with two days of lead time."

"Excellent."

"You'll contact DeeDee, right? Will she go for it?"

"Yes, I'll call her. Will she go for it? Let's see. Get out of the house, go on a top-secret mission using advanced surveillance technology, sweet talk some big mug into submission, potentially have a brush with death, all while hanging out with her two favorite relatives? Yeah, she'll go for it. The only way we could make this more attractive to her would be to throw in a Bingo game or two." We really did have to figure out how we were related to DeeDee one of these days.

* * *

I contacted DeeDee to ask if I could stop by her place the next afternoon. She was happy to hear from me, as I knew she would be, and she'd been even more delighted that I suggested we meet at her home. By two, I found myself sitting at her dining room table, sipping from a steaming cup of coffee. DeeDee was sitting next to me with an expectant look, and Harry was on the table next to her in his big, shiny silver urn. I didn't know what expression he had, but I had to assume he was happy to see me, too.

"Thanks so much for coming over, Grayson."

"Thanks for meeting with me on such short notice." I paused to take a deep breath. "Dean and I have gotten ourselves into a bit of trouble." I gave DeeDee my best serious look, which included squinting my eyes and furrowing my brow to show her I meant business. "And we need your help to get us out."

Her face became an ear-to-ear grin. "How thrilling! What do you want me to do?"

First, I emphasized the importance of keeping this mission secret. She readily agreed. Then, I explained how we were still investigating Sheila's death and that one of the suspects was Ray's son, Eric, who may have been in serious debt with the Las Vegas Casinos.

DeeDee frowned. "Oh, is that all? Why didn't you just ask me that upfront? I'd be happy to help Eric out with some money. Harry left me very well off, you know. Do you want some more coffee?"

I wondered just how well-off Harry had left her while trying to get the conversation back on track.

"No, thanks. I'm good on coffee and not asking for money on Eric's behalf. He doesn't even know I'm here. Anyway, he should work off his own debts, or he'll never learn the lesson that the house always wins." I explained to her that an enforcer from the Vegas mob named Victor was searching for Eric, that Ruby Ray told him I could find him, and now the big thug was threatening to hurt me if I didn't find Eric and turn him over to the mob within the next few days.

"Okay, where do I come in?"

I explained that we wanted her to meet Victor under the guise of sharing

Eric's location, but we would really be sending him on a wild goose chase so he would realize he was wasting his time and give up the search. I then told her about STING and how we wanted her to use it to record their meeting so we could have some leverage over this guy with the police if we needed it.

She was in heaven. "Oh, how thrilling. Will it be dangerous?"

"Not really. We will set up the meeting in a public place, and Dean and I will be nearby watching the video from the STING camera so we can swoop in if the meeting starts to go south."

DeeDee frowned again. "Oh, that's too bad. I was hoping for some real excitement."

I must have downplayed it too much. "To tell the truth, I was just giving you the best-case scenario. Dean and I don't want to jump in unless we absolutely have to. You'll be like any good field operative—reading the current scenario and adjusting your strategy on the fly."

That got the twinkle in her eyes going again. "Okay, what's the plan?"

"We want you to tell him that you have a friend in Rochester, and that's where Eric is holed up."

"He's going to want an address or a name or something, so he knows who to terrorize next. Where do I tell him to go?"

Since I was making this up as it went along, the first thing that popped into my head was the jewelry store Dean and I had just visited. "Tell him to be in the lobby of the Grand Hotel in Rochester on Wednesday at noon. Eric will be there."

"Okay." DeeDee furrowed her brow and stared at the dregs of coffee in her cup. She must have thought there was something wrong with the plan. Finally, she spoke up. "I'm not an expert at this espionage game like you and Dean, but won't that just make him mad? Being sent out of town on a wild goose chase? And why would Eric be hanging out in a hotel lobby anyway? We can't say he's agreed to meet this guy there. Otherwise, why wouldn't he just drive back to the Cities and meet him here?"

"Yeah, those are good points." I was working on a new plan when she chimed in again.

"Why don't we send him to the Treasure Island Casino in Welch? One of my lady friends from Bingo goes there all the time. She says they have a great buffet on the weekends, by the way. I could say that you asked me to help search for Eric and that I'd sent a picture of him to my friends. One of them spotted him at the casino. He seems to go there regularly, so he will likely be there on a certain day in the future."

"Hmm, not a bad idea. It's the kind of place where he'd drop in."

DeeDee gave me a big smile for coming up with part of the plan. "So, when do I meet this big palooka?"

Wow. I hadn't heard that term in years. "Well, he's anxious to find Eric, and the longer we make him wait, the worse it will be for everyone. How about Monday of next week? We can have you meet him at the Aussie House. Since Eric's father, Ray, owns the place, we will have the home-field advantage. Dean and I will be in the backroom monitoring and recording your meeting. But he's not going to do anything dumb in a public place."

"No, Monday won't work. I have to get my hair done. How about Tuesday?"

Sure, why not? I'd just explain to Victor that our star witness had a hair appointment. I'm sure he'd be fine with it. "Okay, Tuesday."

"That sounds good, Grayson. By the way, what does the code name STING stand for?"

"Dean told me it stands for Stealthy Tactical INtelligence Gathering."

"Really? That's the best they could do? I'll bet they came up with the name and worked backward to get the words, didn't they?"

All I could do was smile and nod. There was a lot more to DeeDee than met the eye.

Then it was time to go, and since I didn't have a laptop case for her to cram full of religious icons, I was ready for her next ask.

"Grayson, I don't suppose you'd take another box with you. For a good cause, of course."

At least she asked me this time. "Absolutely. I wouldn't have it any other way." DeeDee went to the back bedroom and came out in a flash with a cardboard box that had once held four gallon-sized jugs of Gallo Wine. It was chockful with a mind-bending array of religious detritus, including plastic rosaries, dashboard statues, holy cards, laminated holy cards with crucifixes, praying hands, and mousepads with pictures of the Pope on them. I really had to wonder how many boxes of this stuff she had back there and who was drinking all this wine anyway.

We said our goodbyes, and I put the box in the trunk of the car, fully expecting to donate it to the first dumpster I could find. As I sat in the driveway, I pulled Victor's business card out of my wallet and entered the number into my phone, saving it for future reference. Then I sent him a text.

I have an informant who knows where Eric is. She wants to meet you.

Then I realized he might think she wanted a larger bribe, so I sent him another text.

She's not going to ask for more money. I have her covered.

Just tell me where Eric is. Victor texted back within less than a minute.

My informant won't tell me. She will only talk to you. She wants you to promise her not to hurt Eric.

Where and when? His large size and mob backing must have made him highly confident. The fact he would be meeting a female probably played into it, too.

She wants to meet in a public place – the Aussie House on Highway 13 in Lillydale. Noon on Tuesday.

He texted me back with a bunch more questions that I ignored, and he eventually stopped. I hoped that would hold him for a few days.

Chapter Twenty

Friday Night, June 8

Friday night was date night with Kate, and it was my turn to cook, so I stopped at the Lunds grocery store on Lake Street on the way back from DeeDee's place. I picked up canned, stewed San Marzano tomatoes, oregano, and parmesan cheese and went back to my apartment to make spaghetti sauce from scratch.

When Kate arrived at about six, I opened a bottle of red wine and poured a glass for both of us. Soon, the pasta was ready, and we sat down for a nice dinner together. We hadn't seen each other since Patter had been killed. Sure, we texted and talked on the phone all the time, but being with her in person made me realize how much I missed her.

We got caught up on the week over dinner and dessert, and then we cleared the dishes and moved to the couch to get comfortable. Kate snuggled into my side. I didn't want to ruin the moment, but I needed to ask her about the files on Sheila's memory stick. I also wanted to impress upon her that it was important for me to have a full understanding of the situation surrounding the murders to assess people's motivations accurately. So, I had to tell her that I was aware that the Dixon family was struggling financially.

Kate was shocked. "Where did you hear that? It wasn't from me."

"No, it wasn't from you. Copeland told me first, and Dean confirmed it later. You surely must realize this changes the motivations people have to do things like commit murders."

Kate got the implication immediately and pulled away. "Grayson, I can't divulge my client's confidential information. You know that."

Okay, this wasn't going in the right direction, so I showed her the files.

"Hang on, Kate. I didn't mean to imply that you should have told me. I just wanted to let you know that I need to investigate these things. And I found something in Sheila's office that I'd like to show you." I got up and walked to my home office. Kate followed with a frosty look on her face.

"You searched Sheila's office?"

I figured it was better not to mention that my friend Karl had helped me gain access and quickly glossed over this point so she wouldn't wonder how I got into the office. "Yes. It's what one does during an investigation. Besides, Ray green-lighted me. It's a good thing I did, too, as I found a memory stick taped to the underside of the desktop with painter's tape. The police missed it, and so did anyone else who may have been searching through her stuff."

Before she could protest, I opened the file system to show the unencrypted folder I had copied. As I suspected, any thoughts of my misconduct were forgotten when she saw its name. "This folder was unencrypted. Another one was encrypted so that I couldn't make a copy of it."

I clicked on the file marked 'Financials' and then on the Excel spreadsheet named 'Payments One. ' The file opened to show a list of payments I'd seen before. The balance was over two hundred and fifty thousand dollars, and the payments were two thousand dollars per month.

I clicked on the 'Payments Two' spreadsheet, which displayed a list of payments totaling over one hundred thousand dollars and their dates.

Kate's face turned white, and her eyes opened wide. "Oh my god, I know what these are. I've been looking for them for weeks now." She turned to me and hugged me tightly. I looked like she might cry, which seemed like an overreaction to a spreadsheet.

"So, what are they?"

"Since you seem to know about this anyway, it should be okay to tell you that Sheila has been propping up the business for years without Ray knowing it. He thought he was hiding things from her, but she was much shrewder than that. Sheila swore me to secrecy, so Ray didn't know that she knew the enterprise was failing even though he never told her."

The suspense was killing me. "And?"

"'Payments One' must be the balance in Sheila's Australia accounts. These are regular deposits to the company's account to provide the cash flow the business needs to stay solvent. 'Payments Two' must be the inbound payment someone had been making to her. She would then have transferred the funds from the second account to the first one to be sure she didn't run out of money." Kate pointed to certain cells on the two spreadsheets. "Do you see how the outbound payments from the second sheet match the inbound payments on the first one? It looks like she was transferring funds about every three months."

As I compared the two spreadsheets, I noticed she was right. I had completely missed this key point that was immediately obvious to her. Damn, I loved hanging around smart people, and the fact she was my girlfriend made her even more attractive.

I wondered what else she might be willing to share. "Where were these payments coming from?"

"I don't know. I was unaware that Sheila was working with financial investors or bankers. Maybe it was a family member or personal friend from Australia."

Then, something struck me as odd. "Okay, let me make sure I've got this right. Sheila knew the business was going south and was surreptitiously depositing money from some secret source to prop it up. Not only did Ray not know she was making deposits, but he thought Sheila didn't even know how badly off the finances were."

"Yep, that about sums it up."

"So, he had no idea how badly the business was doing because they seemed to be scraping by somehow. He must be one of those business owners that focuses on the customers and lets the back-office staff worry about the details."

"Exactly."

"Why didn't they just talk about it?"

"Probably for the usual reasons—ego, shame, denial. As long as the business was limping along, it was probably easier to kick the can down the road than deal with it."

It made me consider our relationship and where things were heading. "I hope we could talk about things if this ever happened to us."

Kate hugged me again. "I hope so, too, Grayson."

I was about to close the files system when Kate stopped me. "Wait a minute. What about the other file folder, the one that was encrypted?"

"I handed off the memory stick to Dean so he could hack into it. No luck yet, but he should get in given enough time."

I closed the file system and realized this would be the perfect time to talk about something that had the potential to get in the way of our future relationship. And, since it was Friday night, some additional social lubricant might help the conversation flow. "Why don't we sit on the couch while I pour us another glass of red?"

"Sounds good," Kate said with a smile, kissing me hard.

I poured two glasses, brought them over, and handed one to Kate. We clicked glasses and sipped. After a few minutes, I could no longer hold back. "Kate, do you mind if I ask you about Chadrick?"

Kate looked down. It seemed like she was embarrassed. It pained me to see her this way, and a lot of guys would have probably just left it alone, but I just had to know what had happened.

Kate looked up into my eyes. "No, I knew you would ask me about him. You can't help yourself."

She was right, of course. I was the same way after Dean and I had found out we were adopted. I just had to know who our birth parents were and why they had to give us up. Of course, that curiosity set a series of events in motion that eventually led to multiple murders being committed. I hoped that wouldn't happen here.

"It was a stupid whirlwind romance that never should have happened." She took a sip of wine while gathering her thoughts. "I guess I just got caught up in the lifestyle. Chadrick was so charismatic and charming that he swept me off my feet. We constantly flew to a different city or continent, and the ladies threw themselves at him everywhere we went. He always told them he was already spoken for, which made me feel special. Then, out of the blue, he proposed, and I had a decision to make. It was hard for me to separate my true feelings for him from the great time I was having. I told him I had to think about it."

"Was he getting a little something on the side?"

"I doubt it. Not at that time, anyway. But I'd certainly heard the rumors about his previous relationships and how he seemed to jump from one girl to another. You know how they say some guys suddenly realize it's time to settle down, and then they propose to whomever they happen to be dating, whether they love them or not? The more I thought about it, the more I realized that's what seemed to have happened. I figured all it would take would be one A-list celebrity to show some interest in him, and I'd be left in the dust. I discovered I didn't trust him, but even more than that, I realized I loved the excitement of the relationship way more than I loved him. So, I turned him down."

I nodded. It would be like Kate to lead with common sense in love, like she did with everything else. I hoped I never gave her any reason not to trust me, which is why it was my turn for true confessions. "Kate, I have something to tell you." I poured more wine for both of us while gathering my resolve.

"I figured you were leading up to something." Did I say I loved smart people? Okay, that might have been a bit overstated.

"I saw Chadrick's name on Ray's list of possible suspects and asked about him. Ray told me they had worked together for years. Then he said he would meet Chadrick for dinner soon and asked me to go along. I wanted to see what he was like, so I agreed. I could see how you got swept up in his charm, that's for sure." I hoped throwing her a compliment would soften things up a bit. Boy, was I wrong.

Kate slammed her wine glass on the end table. I was surprised it didn't break. "You asked me about Chadrick and made me feel horrible about not telling you about our relationship, and then you had dinner with Ray and Chadrick and didn't say anything until just now?"

Okay, this was not my best look. "I know, I know. It was stupid of me not to tell you right away—"

Kate got up and started pacing back and forth. "You think?"

I knew people who lived for this kind of drama. They'd go out of their way to create it so they could relish in the adrenaline rush. I never understood that concept. I hated being crosswise with Kate and preferred to get my hyper-aroused thrills from being shot at while investigating a murder.

Just then, all the fears, uncertainty, and doubts I'd experienced while Chadrick was crowing about his book tour suddenly came rushing back, and an even scarier conspiracy theory emerged. What if Kate had somehow managed to 'borrow' money from Ray's business accounts, just as she had done at her previous employer? Maybe Sheila found out about her theft and had to be silenced? I looked at her and wondered how much I really trusted her. What if she turned out to be the killer, and I was the only person to figure it out? Would I tell Copeland and have her arrested?

How much can one person ever really trust another person or even know them, for that matter? I firmly believe in the idea that, as human beings, we are all flawed. We all tell white lies and think unkind thoughts about our enemies and even our friends. But where would I draw the line? Would I cover up a series of murders that were committed by my girlfriend simply because I didn't want to see her sent up the river where I could never be with her again? Wouldn't that be taking the easy way out?

Speaking of parents, I'd found out online that Kate's father, Brett, had been convicted of fraudulently using his clients' funds. Having met her mother, I knew she had a high-end lifestyle. Maybe he wanted to fund their extravagance but couldn't keep up with her demands, so he got a little too sloppy managing his clients' accounts. He'd been barred from ever working in the industry again and died soon afterward. The thought he might have killed himself had popped into my head very quickly. What impact would that have on an impressionable teenager, I wondered.

But then I turned and looked into Kate's eyes and realized how much I loved her and how much I trusted her. Maybe it wasn't logical, but I knew in my heart of hearts that Kate was not a killer or an embezzler. Yes, she'd made that mistake in the past, but it was because she was desperately trying to save her brother from his drug addiction. She'd learned from that mistake and knew there were better ways to deal with that situation now.

I suddenly realized I had about thirty seconds before she would bolt from the apartment, and it was time to apologize. "Kate, it was stupid. I'm sorry. I wasn't purposely trying to deceive you. I just didn't know what to do. I wanted to meet Chadrick to know what my competition was like and to see how well I stacked up. Knowing you had been in a relationship with this guy, serious or not, was driving me crazy." I stood up and got into her pacing path in an attempt at further de-escalation. "I know your mother was right. I'll never be as influential or charming as the Chadricks of the world. But I love you, Kate, and I don't want to lose you. I hope that will be enough."

I held my arms open for a hug. Kate had stopped pacing and was looking at me sideways. The small smile forming on her face told me everything I needed to know. "I love you too, Grayson. Of course, it's enough. Let's try to communicate better in the future, okay?" She hugged me tightly.

Because I really am a glutton for punishment who doesn't know when to leave well enough alone, I had one more delicate topic to cover before we got back to our nice casual evening. "Kate, I'm sorry to have to ask you this too, but have you discussed the robbery or the murder with Chadrick?"

Fortunately, she didn't take offense at that. "No. He hasn't come by the office since I've been there, and I haven't even spoken with him for a few years. Why do you ask?"

"When we had dinner, he seemed to know everything about the night of Sheila's murder. Either Ray was telling him, or he was there when it happened."

"I doubt he was there," Kate said. "Believe me, he always makes such a spectacle of himself. We would have noticed if he was there."

"Do you have any idea how well Chadrick has been doing lately? Is there any chance he needed the money to fund his extravagant lifestyle and wanted to steal the ruby to sell it?"

"I can't see it. He wasn't that kind of guy. Besides, isn't his latest book doing well?"

"Yeah, it is. You've got to love the title. 'Beat Yourself.' Who names their book that?"

Kate suddenly broke off and jumped up. "Wait a minute. What if Chadrick was giving Sheila the money to shore up the business? He wanted to help his buddy but knew Ray would consider any bailout offers to be charity. He didn't want to embarrass Ray, so he slipped the money to her instead. But she needed more and more money to save the business, and he got tired of it, so he tried to stop. She got upset and threatened to go to Ray if he did. So, he had to kill her to shut her up!" She looked at me expectantly. "Well, what do you think?"

It felt good to see her excited about solving the murder and even better to hear her pinning it on her former boyfriend, but that scenario didn't seem very likely. I didn't want to tell her that Chadrick and Sheila had been seen arguing because it would just sound like I was badmouthing a potential competitor to make myself look better. "Perhaps," was my reply. "But we're going to need proof."

"No worries. I will look for some when I return to the office, and I'm sure I will find it."

Kate sat back down, still wearing a big smile. We drank some more wine and made up. Then I had an idea. "Hey, let's take a midnight walk around the lake and go skinny dipping."

Kate laughed and said no, but I eventually talked her into it. We took a walk and had a great time. Unfortunately, no skinny dipping was involved.

Chapter Twenty-One

Monday, June 11

Kate stayed until Sunday evening when she'd told me she was heading back to her place to get an early start on the week. I'd gotten used to having her around and was a little bummed but didn't want to interfere with her plans. Early the following day, Kate called me in a panic.

"Oh my God, Grayson. There's a body in the garden."

"Which garden, where are you?"

"I'm at work. It's in Galland Garden. I'm in the parking lot and can see someone lying on the ground."

"Are you sure they're dead? Maybe they just passed out and need assistance."

"I'm not one hundred percent sure, but I don't see how they could still be alive. The back of their shirt is covered in blood."

"Can you feel for a pulse?"

"No! I can't do it, Grayson. I just can't. I've never been good in these situations. I can't go over there by myself."

"It's okay, you don't have to."

It sounded like there was little doubt that the person was dead. I selfishly wanted to be the first on the scene to examine the body and wondered if I could get Kate to agree to delay in calling the police.

"Kate, you need to call the police, but will you give me a few minutes to get there first?"

"Oh, here we go. You want to be the first to examine the body, right?"

Wow, maybe we'd been spending too much time together. "Okay, yes. But you have to admit, we're getting closer to finding the killer than the police are right now. Once they arrive, it will be too late to search for clues, and I'll have to go groveling to Copeland, asking for a few crumbs. Then, he'll only give me his version of events, which will most likely be intended to send us down some blind alley." I knew I was laying it on a bit thick, but I needed to get there first.

"Fine. It won't make much difference to the poor soul lying there if I wait another fifteen minutes."

"Better make it thirty minutes so I can drive over without getting a ticket."

Twenty minutes later, I pulled up next to the garden and saw the body. It was in almost the exact same spot as Patter's body had been. Then I saw Kate, who was still standing in front of the main entrance. Apparently, she'd had enough of dead bodies for a while. She waved at me and held up her phone, which must have meant she was about to call 9-1-1. I held up both hands with extended fingers to indicate I needed ten minutes first. She nodded and lowered the phone. It was good to know she believed I would be able to scrutinize a corpse for clues without destroying evidence or leaving more behind so I wouldn't become a suspect myself. I'd have to say the trust in our relationship had reached a new level.

As I ran toward the garden, I pulled on a set of rubber gloves I'd thrown in my pocket just for this purpose. The body lay on its stomach, with Reverend Marcel's face off pointing to the side I was on, staring at me with open, unseeing eyes. He was dressed in the familiar black pants and shirt he always wore.

I'd read somewhere that blow flies can invade a corpse within minutes of death, but I didn't see insects of any kind around the body. I bent down next to him, leaned on one knee, and touched his neck to be sure he was dead. There was no pulse, and his skin was cool. He must have died between two and four hours ago.

The cause of death wasn't too hard to discern. As Kate noted, there was a bullet hole that had been oozing blood all over Marcel's back. I could see a seven-foot-long section of willow beneath him sticking out past his head and legs. I had no doubt I'd find the same willow branches formed in the shape of a pentagram if I moved the body out of the way. Based on this evidence, someone had been planting a new pentacle in the ground when Marcel caught them. A fight ensued, and the other person shot Marcel in the chest. He'd started to bleed out, and death would have followed soon after.

It didn't seem like there was much to investigate, and on a whim, I searched through his pockets to see if I could find any additional evidence. The back left pocket of his pants contained a wallet that I examined and replaced. The back right pocket contained a wad of cash that I left alone. The front left pocket was empty, and the front right pocket held a folded-up piece of note paper. It didn't seem like ten minutes had elapsed, but I heard sirens in the background, so Kate must have called 911 already. The paper had writing on one side, so I laid it out with the writing side up, took out my phone, took a picture, refolded it, and put it back exactly as I'd found it. The sirens were getting louder, and it was definitely time to leave. I ran back to my car, got in, and drove off, waving to Kate as I left.

In a mile or two, I was passed by squad cars going in the opposite direction. They had no way of knowing I'd been at the crime scene, so they had no reason to stop me. I pulled over and called Kate to say thanks for indulging me. I didn't want to text her just in case the police decided to check her phone. Again. I told her that the body was Marcel. She asked if I had found any evidence, and I said I wasn't sure and I would let her know as soon as I got back to my place and figured it out. She said the police were arriving and she needed to go, so we ended the call.

Fifteen minutes later, I returned to my apartment and immediately opened the picture app on my phone to see what the paper in Marcel's pocket contained. There were three lines written in scrawly handwriting. "First Bill Goddard, then Sheila Dixon. Life is not fair." Interesting. Whoever wrote this knew Marcel had been accused of Bill's murder in Chicago, and the implication was he murdered Sheila, too. It's funny that Patter's name is not on here, I thought. Maybe there were two murderers?

I called Kate, who had calmed down considerably by this point. "How are you doing?"

"I'm okay. Copeland is here and wants to question me, of course."

"He must be as tired of questioning you as you are of him."

"I know, right? So, what did you find?"

I told her about the picture I took of the note in Marcel's pocket and what was written on it. I also had to explain who Bill Goddard was, as I hadn't had a chance to update her before this. "It looks like someone is accusing him of both murders."

"Do you think he murdered Goddard?"

"It sure seems like it, but I don't know how anyone would ever prove it."

"Uh-oh. Copeland is coming this way, and he's not looking too happy. I'd better go."

"Okay. Love you."

"Love you, too."

Chapter Twenty-Two

Tuesday, June 12

D espite Marcel's murder having occurred in the Garden the
previous day, Ray decided to keep the Aussie House open on
Tuesday, and we decided to press on with the mission. I met Dean
in the Aussie House parking lot at 11:00 am to get set up. Kate had given
Ray and his team a heads-up that we would meet the Vegas mob guy and got
approval to use a back storage room for our surveillance. Ray was excited
and wanted to be part of the action, but Kate convinced him to lay low so
Victor wouldn't suspect this was a setup.

DeeDee arrived at about eleven-thirty, carrying her oversized urn in the
canvas bag, and was shown to the back room. Dean explained how the
STING camera worked and helped her try on the pendant. It fit perfectly,
and the recording would be crystal clear if she kept it mostly pointed in the
right direction. Dean told her that she needed to be sure we recorded Victor's
face so we would have evidence of his extortion racket and be very careful
with STING as it was still an experimental model and was very expensive.

Then, I reminded her that she was only supposed to do two things. First,
she should act as if she were very concerned about Eric's safety and get
Victor's assurance that he wouldn't hurt him. Second, tell him Eric will
be gambling on Wednesday night at the Treasure Island Casino in Welch,
Minnesota. If he asked how she knew that, she should tell him she shared
Eric's picture with her lady friends, who said they saw him there most

Wednesday nights. She should refuse to tell him who it was to avoid getting her informant involved. She should also say she didn't have his cell phone number if he should ask. We figured he would leave as soon as he got the information he wanted, and we could treat DeeDee to a nice meat pie to celebrate.

At eleven-forty-five, I got a text from Kate saying a guy who matched the mobster's description had arrived. He had checked out the restaurant a bit, then entered and sat at a table without ordering anything. She said he wore a dark suit, a white shirt with a black tie, and a black fedora. Classic mobster attire, she texted with a smiling emoji.

I texted back my thanks. Since we were ready, I told DeeDee to go out the back and around the building so she could enter through the front door. She agreed, picked up her bag, and started towards the door.

"Are you sure you want to take the urn with you?"

She clutched the bag close to her. "I'm not going without Harry. He saved my life once already. I may need him again."

Since the whole meeting should be no more than five minutes, it didn't seem worth arguing, so I let her go. Dean and I watched the video as she made her way around and entered the restaurant. The video panned back and forth, so she must have been scanning the restaurant for the big palooka. She soon moved forward to the table where Victor was sitting and put the bag on the chair next to her while she sat at a chair across from him.

"This table is reserved." Dean and I heard him say.

"Oh, so you don't want to know about Eric. Okay, that's fine." She must have made it look like she was going to leave.

Victor immediately stood up. "My apologies. I didn't know it was you. Please have a seat," he said. For a Vegas mob enforcer, Victor Hawkes was nothing if not polite.

The camera panned back towards him, and we heard DeeDee again. "I know you are looking for Eric. He is my friend's son, and I don't want anything bad to happen to him. I want your assurances that all you want to do is talk to him, and there will not be any funny business." I could imagine DeeDee trying to stare a hole in Victor's head so he would know she was serious, as we could see him staring right back without blinking.

"You have my word. I will not touch a hair on his head. We will only talk about the money."

After thirty seconds, the stare-a-thon must have ended. "Okay," DeeDee said. Apparently, Victor had passed the test, but DeeDee must have started wondering if we were getting a good recording of Victor's face as the video image suddenly started moving and becoming a close-up of his face. What are you doing, DeeDee? I thought. You're not supposed to draw attention to the device.

"That is a lovely pendant you have there."

There was a long pause, and DeeDee finally said, "Thank You." She must have let the pendant fall back against her chest, and when she did, the image blurred dramatically. Then it started revolving. I was getting dizzy watching the room spin on the screen. It could mean only one thing.

"Dean, what the bloody hell? The camera must have popped out of its housing because it's rolling down the floor." I whispered even though no one could hear me.

Dean looked embarrassed. "Yeah, that can sometimes happen. We really need to work on that containment unit. Is DeeDee going to get caught or killed? Because we should tell the secretary to disavow any knowledge of her actions."

"Okay, this is not the time to quote Mission Impossible."

Suddenly, the rotating motion on the screen stopped, and we could see Victor's hand. He had picked up the camera and was handing it to DeeDee.

"That is the same pattern that Grayson had on a ring he wore," Victor said.

To her credit, DeeDee picked up on the ring's lion motif very quickly. "Yes, we are related. This is our family crest."

All of a sudden, Victor seemed wary. "You have a badge of loyalty? What kind of family is this?" It sounded like he thought maybe she was part of a Minnesota-based mafia family. Did she realize what she was implying, or did she just get lucky? I wondered. You never really knew with DeeDee. Why this guy believed that anyone like her would have a family crest in the shape of a lion as their family symbol, let alone put it on a fancy ring or in a pendant, was beyond me.

"It is the same family that Eric belongs to. You have already promised not to hurt him. We take promises very seriously in our family." She delivered the line slowly and deliberately, just like Marlon Brando would have. I felt a shiver of fear go up my spine, and I was viewing the whole thing on TV.

Victor seemed to shrink just a bit as he said, "Yes, fine. Agreed. Now tell me where to find him."

"Fine."

Just then, Victor reached into his suitcoat. DeeDee later told me she thought he was going for a gun. She scooped up the urn from the canvas bag and put it on the table between them as protection. We saw Victor barely getting a piece of paper and pen out of his suit pocket when he saw the urn. His eyes got wide as he threw himself back in this chair.

"Why did you bring that?" He demanded.

"I always bring my protection with me," DeeDee replied. She must have thought Harry's new urn would protect her from gunfire, just like his previous one did.

Dean and I could actually see the fear roll across Victor's face. "How many people have you burned," he managed to blurt out.

"I lost count years ago'" DeeDee said with a deadpan voice. The fact that it was true must have made it even more convincing.

Victor was in full-blown panic mode now. He started looking about the room wildly, probably searching for the exit. "This is crazy. You can't be serious."

"That's one of the funny things about burning people. They start to spasm and squirm. Their skin melts off their body. It's a fascinating process." She paused for effect and must have glared at him. "Don't make me use it on you."

Victor spotted the exit, jumped up, and headed out at full steam, nearly knocking over an entire family of five who were guilty only of trying to find a place to eat.

Dean and I looked at each other and simultaneously burst into laughter. I got a text from Kate asking what the heck had happened because the thug ran to his car and zipped out of the parking lot at top speed.

DeeDee happened. I texted back and told her to meet us for lunch.

We were just about to leave the storage room when Dean's cell phone rang. He looked at the screen and said, "You go ahead. I have to take this." He answered, and before I could leave, I overheard Dean say something about the mission's success despite the unexpected pre-deployment of the STING protocol. He must have been reporting back to HQ. I decided to wait to see what else he would say.

He had been smiling, and he must have expected his colleagues to agree with his assessment, but apparently, they did not. They were soon debating the reasons for the accidental protocol deployment.

"No, it was not an operator error." It was a good thing we were the only ones in the storage room, as he was almost shouting. The unit should have been designed so the wearer could not perform an unauthorized deployment."

It sounded like someone was trying to blame DeeDee for their failure, and it was good to hear him defend her. He listened for a minute, then said, "Okay, maybe it didn't go one hundred percent to plan, but keep in mind that the overall goal was to add training data to the knowledge management system, and from that standpoint, this was a very successful mission."

He listened again and started frowning and shaking his head, obviously frustrated with what he was hearing. "You know what, forget it. Let's take this up again when we do the field ops review." Dean signed off the call.

"Were your coworkers watching through the camera?" I asked. Then I realized, of course, they were. They wouldn't have risked losing their precious device without scrutinizing everything it recorded.

Dean didn't deny it. "I tried to tell them that the design of the protocol housing clip was faulty."

"Once again, Dean, as I've tried to tell you in the past, this is what happens when you use engineers to do design work without involving actual designers."

"Well, I still consider it a successful data collection exercise despite the unexpected pre-deployment issue."

That's odd, I thought. Why was the goal to collect training data for a knowledge management system? Then it hit me. X's interest in developing STING was to infuse it with artificial intelligence. He was trying to develop an AI tool that could learn from real-world experiences, not just from online data, which was genius. A system like that could be used for an unlimited number of things, such as training a robot to perform a task just by having it observe a human doing it. It would be worth a fortune.

"X wants to build AI into STING, doesn't he?"

Dean just stared at me. "You can't tell anyone about this." Okay, that was a yes. "We are way ahead of anyone else in developing this technology. You'll be interested to know we've programmed the current AI tool to predict the next step the STING user will take so it will know how to handle unexpected actions in the field. DeeDee's performance varied wildly from those predictions, with much better results. This was fabulous training data."

As fun as it was knowing DeeDee had helped train a future generation of Terminators, we had to get back to business. "That's great, but what about Eric? Victor is only going to be afraid of DeeDee for so long. Then, he's going to gather his courage and call me out. We still need to have some kind of answer for him. I've been wondering where Eric is myself. Maybe we can work something out with the mafia boys if we can get to Eric and find out how much he owes them. I'll look into his background and social media accounts to find places where he will likely hide." I looked at Dean, hoping he would volunteer to search, but he was too preoccupied with STING to notice.

* * *

Kate and Ray joined DeeDee, Dean, and me for lunch at Aussie House. DeeDee was the star, and Ray gladly bought lunch for her and the rest of the group now that Victor Hawkes had been vanquished, at least for the time being. Dean could access the video recording from STING on his phone and replayed the moment Victor fled in sheer terror multiple times. Based on her unintentional impression of a famous mafia boss, we started calling

DeeDee the Godmother, and she didn't seem to mind that one bit. I asked her how she was able to ad-lib that gross description of a burning body so quickly, and she said she didn't have to make it up. That was what actually happened during the cremation process. I was developing a whole new level of respect for DeeDee, but I wasn't sure it was in a good way.

Eventually, Ray returned to his office, so Kate and I walked DeeDee and Dean, who were still smiling, to the parking lot. We hugged DeeDee, and she drove off. Just before he left, Dean pulled Kate and me aside. "I've finally cracked the password to the Writing folder on Sheila's memory stick. You'll never guess what was inside."

Kate squinted her eyes and smiled. "A bunch of drafts of a book called 'The Ruby Ray Story as told by Sheila Dixon?'"

Dean smiled back. "Good guess, but no. There were a bunch of drafts, but they were for a book called 'Beat Yourself.' Sheila must have been ghost-writing Chadrick's book for him."

Kate laughed. "Oh, that's too funny. And I'm not surprised, either. Chadrick told me he used ghostwriters for all of his books because he couldn't be bothered to sit down and write them himself. He didn't have the time or the talent. But he had to use a different one for each book because he was such a pain to work with."

"That makes sense," I said. My mind flashed back to Chadrick's comments over dinner that he used his beat yourself process to improve his focus, such that he was now writing two thousand words a day when his previous personal best had been only one thousand. It turned out the whole thing was a bunch of bull, and he was an even bigger scumbag than I thought. "I'll bet he saw the books on writing and publishing on Sheila's credenza, and he charmed her into writing his latest book for him. From what I can tell, his books are mostly puff pieces anyway. It wouldn't have been that hard. That's why he'd been spending so much time with her. Ray told me he suspected one of his friends of having an affair with his wife. Could his jealousy have caused him to kill his wife?"

Kate offered an alternate theory.

"Or, we know Sheila needed money. What if she saw the success that

Chadrick's new book was having and was blackmailing him for more money? Maybe she threatened to expose him as a fraud and tell the world that she ghostwrote the book unless he paid her a lot more. He refused, but she wouldn't let it go, so he had to kill her to save his empire from collapsing."

It was good to see Kate getting into the investigative spirit. I was going to turn her into a P. I. yet. "Not a bad theory, but that's the problem with the investigation business. We always need to find proof." Then I realized I had additional information supporting her theory and told the two about the partially pantomimed information-sharing session I'd had with Karl.

"You bribed our janitor—"

I held up a finger to correct her. "Maintenance engineer."

"Whatever. You bribed Karl to let you into Sheila's office, and then he told you she and Chadrick had a big argument? That makes Chadrick look as guilty as sin."

"Sure does."

Kate smiled. "Sounds like proof to me!"

"True. Unfortunately, one of the people who could tell us what the argument was about would probably just make up a cover story, and the other is dead."

We said goodbye to Dean and met up with Ray in the office. I asked Ray if he had a minute as I wanted to ask him a few questions. Kate just rolled her eyes and went back to her office.

As we got comfortable, it was high time I confronted Ray about the murder. "Sorry to have to ask you this, but where were you on the night of Sheila's murder, specifically during Patter's set and right when the swing show was starting?"

Ray got thoughtful for a minute, then started. "I didn't want to say this then, but now I suppose it doesn't matter anymore. I was in my office talking to Chadrick on my cell phone. Cheryl told him that Kate would be at the show that night, and he called to ask me if she was alone or if you were with her."

"Wait a minute, Cheryl told him that? The office manager? Ray, haven't you been wondering how Chadrick knew so much about the murder? We just found the mole feeding insider info to him."

The realization seemed to strike Ray, too. "Yeah, you're right." He looked down and shook his head. "Dear sweet ol' Cheryl. Chadrick used to chat her up every time he came in."

I had to know more about their discussion. "So Chadrick called you to check on Kate. What did you tell him?"

"I told him she was spoken for, mate. What else would I say?"

I was about to say we could definitely clear him from the suspect list, assuming all of this was true. And I was about to ask him what Chadrick had said after Ray had told him Kate was with me that night when he started up again.

"Grayson, I'm not about to double-cross you. You've been a real friend to me and Sheila. May she rest in peace. Thank you for that. In order to find justice for her, you need to know the real story. As you know, Ruby Ray Enterprises, RRE, includes both restaurants and the museum, and over the years, we've made a lot of money from all three. And I already told you that Nigel owns twenty percent of the company. With Sheila gone, I now own eighty percent of the business. I suppose you could say that gives me a motive for the murder, but what you are probably not aware of is that RRE hasn't been doing that well lately. No one in their right mind would kill for an ownership stake in this company. I would much rather have my Sheila to spend my retirement and the rest of my life with than a larger ownership of the shell of a once great company."

"Thanks for sharing that..." I started to say, but Ray wasn't finished.

"Here's what happened. When we moved here from Australia, we didn't have any money. The only thing we had that had any value whatsoever was the ruby. Even back then, I knew we could gin up a story around the ruby, and people would come from miles away to see it. But we needed help. So, we formed a financial arrangement with Nigel to get the business off the ground. Nigel agreed to help us in exchange for an ownership stake. And Sheila and I each owned forty percent. We were very much in love, and I figured Sheila would always vote with me. So, we'd always have a majority of the votes for all business decisions.

"This worked great up until a few years ago when the popularity of businesses started fading. People just weren't interested in paying to see the ruby anymore, not when they could see it and a thousand other stones for free on the internet. I wanted to sell out before the business went completely under. I told Sheila and Nigel that I was thinking about retiring. I guess they weren't too surprised. My mistake was not telling them about the true condition of the business, so they didn't know. Sheila wanted to pass it down to the kids so they could run it, which made it even harder for me to tell her there wouldn't be anything to inherit.

"Somehow, Nigel found out and accused me of running it into the ground. Me! Ruby Ray, who built this business with his bare hands." Ray held his thick, rough hands up so I could see them. "Nigel said he and Sheila could run the business without me, so I should go ahead and retire. He even gave me a lowball offer to buy me out. I couldn't believe it. After all these years of him sponging off me, he wanted to kick me to the curb."

"So, what did you do?"

Ray laughed. "I told him no way, of course. Listen, if I had a motive, it would be for killing Nigel, not Sheila. He said he would tell Sheila the truth about the business losing money so she would agree to his offer. I knew she would never vote against me, so we've been stalemated for years. Until Sheila's death, that is."

It was finally my turn to ask a question. "Have you ever thought about selling both the business and the property? They might be worth more together."

"Aren't you the sharp one? Matter a-fact, I've had them valued, and they're not worth as much as it might seem. I do have an offer on the table, though. It's not a very good one, but now that Sheila is gone and the kids have their own lives, it's tempting to be done with the whole thing."

As painful as it was, I was glad Ray finally seemed to be telling me the truth. At least his version of it, anyway. I wanted to ask him how much he had been offered, but that didn't seem polite, so I focused on other aspects of the offer instead. "Ray, one more question, if you don't mind me delving into company business. Who is the offer from?"

"I don't mind. It's from Scott Dimond."

Scott Dimond, that was unexpected. Maybe he was just an intermediary. "Do you mean he was brokering an offer from another investor?"

"Nah. It was from him directly. And it's got a time limit—noon on Wednesday of this week. I have until tomorrow to decide."

I was still trying to wrap my head around Scott Dimond being behind the offer to buy your enterprise and the land it was on. Didn't he say he only buys part of a business as an investment and then stays around to advise the owners on improving their operations and increasing profitability? Didn't Ray tell me Scott promised to introduce him to a marketing guy who would bring Ruby Ray's story to the millennials? But, I suddenly thought, maybe he had a much better marketing plan to keep in his back pocket until he owned the business. Or maybe he was offering Ray less than the company's book value due to the large investment in marketing he would need to make. Either way, he couldn't be the murderer or the thief unless he was extremely good at being in two places at the same time—Scott and I sat at the same table during dinner that night.

I had to know more, so after leaving Ray's office, I texted Scott and asked if we could get together for a chat. He said he would be at RRE around noon tomorrow, and I said I'd meet him there at 1:00. Of course, he'll be there on Wednesday, I thought. That's when he wants Ray to sign his life away.

Chapter Twenty-Three

I t was late morning on Wednesday, and I was leaving the office soon to arrive at Ray's office early. I was just shutting down my laptop when a text from Kate came in. **Call me right away!**

Okay, that was a bit odd as she could have just called me right away. Then I realized the phone was on mute, and I'd missed three calls from her. I called her back right away.

"Grayson! There you are. I've been calling you. Why do you even have that cell phone? I need to talk to you." She was excited about something, and I hoped it didn't involve another dead body. "Hang on one second. I have to close the door to my office." I could hear her close the door and pick up the phone again.

Kate lowered her voice to be sure she was not overheard. "I figured out who was making the payments to Sheila."

I looked at my phone, waiting for more information. She was dragging this out for effect.

"Do you want to know?" she asked. I could hear the smile in her voice.

I tried to sound nonchalant. "I suppose. You might as well tell me as long as we're talking."

"Scott. It was Scott Dimond. He was paying her through a shell company based out of Australia. It took some digging, but I finally figured it out. Okay, I may have gotten some advice from Dean, but I did the heavy lifting. Isn't that exciting?"

This ruined her theory that Chadrick was involved, but that hadn't dampened her spirits. It was definitely interesting news. "Are you sure?"

"Yes, absolutely." She seemed very proud of herself. "it's funny I wasn't getting anywhere with my usual forensic accounting techniques. So, I snuck over to Scott's laptop when no one else was in the office. I found the same payment history there, so I know it was him."

"Wait, what? Didn't he have the laptop password protected?"

"Of course, he did. Dean helped me crack it."

Help from Dean? What was that about? I made a mental note to chastise him at our next coffee meeting. As much as I knew Kate was a skilled CFO, I was fairly certain that hacking into a laptop was not in her wheelhouse, with or without help. You had to remember to leave everything exactly as you found it, or the laptop user might realize they'd been compromised.

"So, what's your theory now?"

"What do you mean? I don't need a theory. Scott was making the payments."

We seem to have lost sight of the big picture. "Right, but what's your theory about the murder?"

"How should I know, Grayson? That's your department. I just got the clue. You solve the murder."

Thanks for the vote of confidence, Kate. Just then, a theory popped into my head about Scott Dimond's involvement with Ruby Ray Enterprises, which was not good. There were too many intersecting threads that all pointed in his direction. I wanted to warn Kate but didn't want to scare her. I couldn't just let it go, either. The feeling was too strong. "Hey Kate, isn't today the day Ray has to decide on signing the contract?"

"Sure is. He's been pacing back and forth all morning. I'm pretty sure he's going to sign it, though."

"Will Nigel be there, too?"

"Nope. Ray told me Nigel gave him signing authority for his part of the business. Now that Sheila's ownership passed along to Ray, he owns eighty percent of the business, so it's his call either way."

"Can you get Ray to hold off on signing until I get there?"

"I don't know, maybe. Why do you want to be here for that?"

"Oh, it just seems like a big deal, and I'd like to offer some moral support. Maybe we can go out and celebrate afterward." Wow, that sounded lame, but I didn't know what other excuse to use. "Will you do that for me, please?"

"Sure, Grayson. I'll ask him right now."

"Thanks, Kate." See you soon." I ended the call and called Dean while I headed to the parking ramp. Fortunately, he answered on the first ring.

"Hey."

"Dean, I have something very important to discuss with you."

"You're not mad about me helping Kate with her investigation, are you? Because you're doing the same thing…"

"What? No. Listen. Kate told me you helped her access Scott's laptop, right?"

"Yea. She was all excited that I found the file she was looking for."

"So, you were driving?"

"That's right. It wasn't easy, either. There was a ton of crap on there. It took over half an hour, which is way off my personal best. Did I ever tell you about a search I did for X? He was amazed—"

"Dean, I need you to focus here. Wait, hang on." I got into my car and switched the call to the car's speakers so I could hit the road. "Did you see any files about the property in Chicago that Bill Goddard bought for his Institute and that Marcel supposedly sold to a developer?"

"Now that you ask, I did see that. There was a folder marked 'Better Life.' There were a whole bunch of spreadsheets and some contracts in it." The gears clicked into place in Dean's head. "Oh my god, Scott was the guy that brokered the Institute's campus sale to a developer. He must have been in on the deal with Marcel."

"Exactly. Thanks, Dean. Talk to you soon."

I hit the highway to St. Paul at top speed.

* * *

Twenty minutes later, I pulled into the RRE parking lot and ran into the building. I asked Cheryl if Scott was there. She told me she hadn't seen him yet, but he was scheduled to meet with Ray at noon, less than an hour away. "What about Kate," I asked. "Have you seen her?"

"Oh sure, she's around somewhere. She was in her office but left a few minutes ago. She got a call and was going to the Supper Club for some reason."

That told me exactly what I needed to know, and right then, I could have reached across the counter and kissed her weary, busybody face in gratitude.

"Thanks, Cheryl." I exited the office as quickly as possible and ran to the Club. I thought about calling Copeland on the way, but I didn't know exactly what I'd say or ask him for, so I just kept going.

I arrived at the main entrance to the Supper Club, inched the door open, crept in, and slowly closed it, trying to be as stealthy as possible. I crept past the coatroom to the clubroom door and slowly opened it to peak in. My heart sank when I realized my fears had been well-founded. In the middle of the dance floor was a figure hunched over a body that I immediately knew belonged to Kate. I just hoped I wasn't too late.

I quickly but quietly took out my cell phone and texted Copeland. **911 at the Supper Club send help ASAP!**

Then I stowed the phone and thanked my lucky stars that Ray had insisted on giving me a tour of his unremarkable museum where I found the venom supply in the warehouse, or Kate would probably be slowly dying from asphyxiation right now if she wasn't dead already. I was unarmed and had no idea what to do or say. I thought about running across the floor and tackling the guy, but we'd probably land on Kate, which would only make her situation worse. I had to stall for time. I hoped Copeland had seen my text and taken it seriously enough to send in the cavalry right now, with him at the lead.

I didn't know how close Kate was to death and couldn't afford to let him do anything else to her. "Scott, get away from her right now!" I said in my best gravelly voice.

He spun around, surprised, but recovered quickly. "Grayson, fancy meeting you here." He extended his hand to show it was empty, then performed a quick bounce, and a gun appeared as if out of nowhere. It was the same trick he did with the business card the first time we met. I made a mental note to look up how he did it if I lived to see tomorrow.

I stood at the end of the dance floor and suddenly realized that yelling at him from behind something large and bulletproof would have been a better-designed plan. I slowly put my hands up.

"You realize I'll have to kill you, too, right?" He laughed. "I thought you were a smart guy. What were you thinking?"

I just shrugged and tried to look non-threatening.

"Well, as long as you're here, you might as well help me." He backed a few feet away from Kate and motioned me over with his gun. "Finish wiring her to the swing, would you?" He smirked. "You can probably figure out how it's done."

What a jerk. As I got closer, I could see that the swing had been lowered to the dance floor, and Kate was lying on top of the seat with the cables hanging next to her. Scott had already wired her to the seat and apparently expected me to wire her arms to the cables, just like Sheila's had been.

I was happy to get close to Kate so I could assess her condition. I was greatly relieved to see she was still alive, but her breath was shallow. Her hair was streaked with blood from where Scott must have hit her to knock her out. I had to keep stalling, and I figured what better way than to flatter his scary serial-killer self.

"Killing Sheila with the cone snail venom was a pretty novel idea, Scott. I didn't realize they teach you how to milk a snail when you get a degree in aquaculture."

"Yeah, thanks." He sneered. "I couldn't believe they actually showed us how to extract one of the world's deadliest poisons. I always wondered if that would come in handy one day."

Okay, this guy was truly nuts. He'd been planning to kill someone with snail venom for years. It was just a matter of when and who would go first. I was slowly wiring Kate's arm to the cable. As long as I kept moving, Scott didn't seem to mind how long it was taking. In fact, he almost seemed to be relishing it. "Why'd you have to kill Patter, though? He seemed like a stand-up person."

"He wasn't as innocent as he seemed. He was playing that stupid piano with a blanket over the strings again, and I didn't realize he was there. He overheard me arguing with someone, and then he told me he would go to the police if I didn't pay him off, as if I would agree to that. What a chump."

"So that must have been when you argued with Sheila, right? She finally realized the business would never recover, and she couldn't pay back all the money she borrowed from you to keep it afloat. So, you gave her the fake ruby and forced her to swap it for the real one."

"I spent over ten grand with a lab in Eastern Europe to make an ultra-high-quality fake ruby using the Czochralski Process. I doubt even Ray would have known the difference. Hey, he was right. You are pretty sharp for a tech nerd. How did you know about that?"

"I didn't until you confirmed it just now. But think about it. If anyone else had wanted to swap in a fake, they would have done it long ago. She was supposed to do the swap on the day she died, right?"

"Right again. I told her a little white lie about clearing off her debt and helping Ray turn the business around as soon as she gave me the real stone so she and Ray would have a fresh start. Once we exchanged them, I told her the truth. She said she would tell Ray the whole story, so she had to go. Hell hath no fury, right?"

Something wasn't adding up. There was no stone in the ruby case when Kate found it. Suddenly, the answer was obvious. "Sheila didn't put the fake one in the safe, did she? She probably suspected you were lying, and she kept it as protection so she could tell Ray or the police what had happened if you double-crossed her. The fake would be her proof."

"You just can't trust people these days, can you? After tying her to the swing that night, I relieved her of the fake. Of course, then you and Kate came swooping in to save the day."

I dropped the spool of wire to buy some time, and it rolled across the floor. I went over to collect it while keeping the story going so he wouldn't yell at me. "So, you planted the spent cone snail in Kate's desk and phoned in an anonymous tip to Detective Copeland saying Kate had killed Sheila and the proof was in her office. Copeland already suspected Kate, so he immediately bought the story."

Scott was smirking again. "Piece of cake."

"Why did Nigel agree to all of this? Did he want to fleece Ray and Sheila, too?"

"Nigel? That big lug? He was too busy flitting off to the Outback every chance he got. He was clueless about all of this."

I finished wiring one arm and made a show of walking around Kate to her other side so Scott would see I was progressing. "Why put the stone in Sheila's body, though? You couldn't count on the medical examiner missing it. You just got lucky there." Then it hit me. "No, wait, you wanted it to be found."

Scott got that annoying grin again. "That was a stroke of genius, my friend! I had been planning to swap out the original and sell it. Ray wouldn't know the one in the museum was fake, not that anyone ever showed up to see it, until the next time they had it appraised, and by then, I'd be long gone. Then I realized if word got out that Ray's infamous ruby was a fake, he would be disgraced, and the value of his business would sink even lower. But I didn't think of that until the next day, and I couldn't just turn it in to the police and say I found it because they would think I'd stolen it."

Was it good or bad that I was thinking the same thing as a madman? I wondered.

"So, I snuck into the crematorium and stuck it as far down Sheila's throat as I could. I figured the crematory operators would find it and turn it over to the cops, who would have it verified to be sure it was the real deal. Even if the operators tried to sell it, they would soon find it was fake and would probably just stash it away somewhere, which would have been fine with me."

"In the meantime, you were planning to fence the real one on the dark web."

"All in good time. You have to wait for the notoriety to die down on these things, even on the dark web."

I was almost done with the second arm but had to keep stalling. "Why did Marcel have to die?"

"That's the funny thing about this whole situation. I didn't kill him. He killed himself."

"What? Why would he do that?"

"I needed a foolproof alibi for the time of the murder, which was sitting at a dinner table with the famous amateur detective, Grayson Dyle. I just needed Marcel to grab the swing key on his return from the restroom. He refused, so I threatened to turn him in for murdering Bill Goddard back in our Chicago days, and he knew I could prove it, too. I planted a few pentacles in the Garden as a warning. He was the only one who would know what they meant. He finally agreed to collect the key, but he got all remorseful. Can you believe it? He didn't even kill her. What a wuss."

So, Marcel really did kill Bill Goddard after all, and the guilt of being involved in another murder and not being able to turn his life around finally got to him. "So, he committed suicide. What happened to the gun?"

Scott scoffed. "No idea. Why would I care about that?"

It was a good question, but I didn't have an answer. I finished tying up Kate and stood up.

"Now we need to get her up to the top. The ropes that pull up the swing are next to the stage behind the curtain. You start pulling her up, and I'll use the guide rope to pull the swing over to the platform." He pointed the gun directly at Kate and added. "Grayson. Don't even think about messing with me. Kate is still alive right now, but that can change in a heartbeat."

I only needed to know one more thing. "Why'd you do it, Scott? Why'd you kill Sheila?"

"Here, I thought you were smart." He was winding himself into a frenzy. "It was for the money, Grayson. It's always for the money."

"No, I get that, but why tie her to a swing?"

"Why?" He sneered at me as if it should have been obvious. "Why not?! Sheila and Ray were obnoxious prats who blew up a perfectly good business while bragging that they were masterminds. They were wasting my money and blaming everyone else for their failures. Sheila especially. Always flirting to get another payment out of me. She needed to learn I wouldn't put up with that crap, so I took the ruby and put her out of her misery."

So, it all came down to Scott feeling Sheila was conning him while he was running a much larger con in the background. With my suspicions confirmed, I walked over to the stage and finally heard some sirens in the background. I had to think of a way to subdue Scott and have the cops arrest him without risking my life or Kate's.

Scott finally heard the sirens and suddenly went ballistic. He pointed the gun back at me. "I will kill you both right now!" He screamed.

Instinct kicked in, and I dove behind the curtain, then did a quick roll, which was fortunate because a bullet went just past my head. I did an army crawl behind the piano while trying to keep his attention away from Kate. "Cheryl and Ray both know you're here. If you kill us now, you'll go to jail for sure."

"I'm going to jail anyway."

I kept moving to the other end of the piano in case I had to get further away. "No, you're not. The cops don't have any proof, and I couldn't find any. You're going to get away with everything if you get out of here now."

The sirens had gotten so loud that the police must have been pulling into the parking lot. Scott wasn't saying anything, so I assumed he was trying to figure out what to do next. I peeked out from behind the piano and saw him wiping his fingerprints off the gun, then throwing it on the floor next to Kate. He started running for the kitchen, taking him across the stage. I waited for two seconds, grabbed the microphone stand, and swung it into his gut as he went by. The sound of him retching told me it was a direct hit. Just then, Copeland burst into the club with two officers behind him. All three had their guns drawn and were yelling at us to keep our hands where they could see them. One of them spotted the gun on the floor next to Kate and kicked it out of the way.

Scott was trying to catch his breath while saying, "Officers, Grayson just hit me with that stand. I caught him trying to kill Kate Larson, and then he tried to kill me. You've got to arrest him right now."

I put down the stand and moved out from behind the piano as one of the police officers pointed his gun at me and repeated the order to keep my hands where he could see them. I was really getting tired of people aiming weapons at me. "Detective Copeland. I suggest you detain both of us until you can sort this out. I'd also suggest you confiscate my cell phone. It just recorded Scott Dimond's full confession."

Suddenly, Kate spoke up. "I heard most of it, too." She must have been playing possum for the last twenty minutes, which I had to admit was a shrewd move.

Copeland asked me to play the recording and listened intently. As soon as he realized who the real killer was, he arrested Scott and confiscated my phone. I knew he was about to ask us to come down to the station when I pointed out that Kate needed medical attention. He reviewed her condition and then summoned the EMTs, who had been waiting until the police cleared the area. They started untying Kate as quickly as they could. When I asked for permission to join her, he hesitated momentarily. Then, he nodded and ordered me to contact him the next day to schedule a meeting. I rode with Kate to the emergency room, where the doctor on duty said she had a mild concussion and should make a full recovery within a week.

I brought her back to my place where I could attend to her every need. Kate suggested we invite Dean and Ray for a mini celebration for catching the killer. She texted them from her burner phone since it was our only one, and they agreed to come over to my place that evening. I asked her to tell Dean to bring the fake ruby with him, and he agreed.

* * *

We didn't have time to make anything fancy, so I ordered a few pizzas from one of the trendy new restaurants in the Uptown area and laid out some beer and wine. Dean arrived a few minutes early so he could pass me the ruby, which I stashed in my bedroom just as Ray arrived. I let him in, and we helped ourselves to dinner and drinks. We found places to sit in the living room to discuss the day's events.

After hearing the story, Ray just shook his head. "You're telling me that

Scott was trying to buy the business for a song so he could turn it around and make a fortune?" It sounded like Ray was still in denial, and I hated being the one to break the news to him.

"Actually, Ray, it wasn't the business he wanted. It was the land. He was planning to raze the buildings and put up condos, which would be very valuable due to their location and the spectacular view of the entire Twin Cities."

"Wait a minute. There wasn't that much land available, and the zoning laws would prohibit new development. The existing buildings had been grandfathered in. But there were issues with the setback distance, and the city council would have to approve variances, which we know they won't do."

Dean was happy to clear things up for him. "Right on all counts. However, our friend, Bishop Tom, told Grayson that he expected a new group of city administrators to swoop into office in the next cycle. He was helping them get elected in case he needed leverage over Marcel's Supper Club Church. Scott must have known who they were and expected them to approve the variances. This meant they could build on most of the property, which would cause its value to skyrocket. Naturally, he withheld this information from you." Ray nodded in agreement, and I wanted to update him on his concern regarding Sheila.

"Ray, there's something else you should know about Chadrick. He had a very good reason to want Sheila gone because she was blackmailing him." Ray was shocked and started to deny it, but I kept going. "He paid her a small fee to help write his latest book. Dean found copies on a file from her desk, and someone overheard them arguing. But, once *Beat Yourself* hit the New York Times bestseller list, she decided it wasn't enough. Scott had been loaning her money to prop up the business, and she was desperate to pay him back. She must have figured Chadrick would be swimming in dough soon, so she insisted he give her a much larger cut. But he wouldn't do that because he needed the funds to save his crumbling empire. She was going to use the drafts she had written to prove she had a claim to the intellectual property rights for the book. But Scott took her out of the picture before it came to a head."

Ray stared at me while trying to process this new information. "So that's why they were spending so much time together. I thought she was cheating on me." A look of relief crossed his face, which turned to anger, and he stood up as if ready for a fight. Only there was no one here to punch.

"It's okay, Ray. You know Chadrick didn't kill Sheila. I'm only telling you so you'd know they were not having an affair."

Ray looked at me and started to relax. He slowly sat back down. "Thanks, mate. I know you meant well." Ray thought about the situation for a minute, then asked, "So, what's going to happen to the ruby?"

"Well, after the police arrested Scott, they searched his apartment and found the real ruby hidden there. I'm sure it will eventually be returned to you once they no longer need it as evidence."

"What about the fake?"

I had to stifle a look toward the bedroom so as not to let on that the fake ruby was sitting in my dresser, safely nestled between my t-shirts. "I'm sure it will turn up eventually. Someone will find it and turn it over to the police. Scott must have paid to have it made, but the police will probably claim it through civil forfeiture. You may be able to acquire it from them." I had no idea if that was true, but it sounded good and was what Ray needed to hear at that moment.

Ray smiled. "Crikey, mate! Just think of how great both rubies will look in the museum. We'll build a second display case and tell the whole story of the attempt to steal the infamous Poona Ruby that was thwarted by none other than the infamous P.I., Grayson Dyle!"

Wow, the force of denial was strong with this one. Did he really believe the public would suddenly start caring about rubies? Then again, maybe the notoriety of the Swing Girl's demise and the ruby's recovery would bring them in by the busloads. "Thanks for the kind words, Ray. But let's just let the police take the credit for this one."

He seemed disappointed that part of his story was becoming less dramatic. "Righto. If you insist."

"Now I have a question for you, Ray. Nigel told me about Halena. What are your plans—"

"Let's just say," Ray interrupted as he leaned back in his chair and laced his fingers behind his head, "that I may be rekindling an old flame that never really died out."

Chapter Twenty-Four

Thursday, June 14

The story hit the national news cycle the next day. It immediately went viral online, and it was the lead story on all of the local media feeds and most of the national news shows. Detective Copeland was beaming at a press conference as he touted the tireless efforts of the fine men and women of the St. Paul Police Department in solving two murders and a suicide by tracking down and arresting the killer. The previously undisclosed story of the theft and recovery of the infamous Poona Ruby was prominently mentioned, much to Ray's delight. It was sure to drive substantial new traffic to his establishments. I was slightly disappointed but not at all surprised to see that Copeland forgot to mention he had received a bit of help in solving the cases. I considered texting him to remind him that he owed me another one but decided against it. I hoped I would never need to call in that marker, but if I did, Copeland wouldn't need a text to know exactly what favors I had done for him. Again.

Kate and I were listening to the clips from the press conference on the radio in her office and occasionally fist-bumping when they talked about the recovery of the ruby.

"Does Ray realize he will be able to develop more of his land once the new city council gets elected?"

Kate laughed. "Are you kidding? He's been talking about it all morning. Unfortunately, he'll need a large cash infusion to make it work, and his only

VC guy will be in prison for a very long time. He keeps asking me if I know anyone he can build with, but I don't. Do you know anyone?"

I thought about it for a moment and shook my head. "No one comes to mind immediately, but I can ask around. Maybe the owner of our office building can make a referral."

Just then, the main entrance door to the enterprise offices banged open loudly. We ran out of her office to see what had caused the ruckus, only to find Victor Hawkes looming large in the doorway with a rumpled suitcoat, no tie, and his hands balled into fists. Based on his look of frustration and anger, I had to admit I was scared of him just then.

"For the last time...where is Eric?" If his slow growl was meant to be intimidating, it had worked.

Kate was immediately horrified by the sight. She came over to my side for moral support. "What are you doing here?" she demanded.

I quickly got over my initial fear. "It's okay, Kate. I know why he's here."

Kate stepped back to look at me quizzically. "You do?"

"I do." Knowing we were not in any real danger from this big palooka, as DeeDee referred to him, helped my blood pressure return to normal. "Come in, Victor. We should talk in the conference room. Would you like something to drink?"

Victor shook his head, so I led the way to the conference room while Kate was undoubtedly staring daggers in the back of my head and wondering why I was being so nice to a mobster.

After we all took a seat, I started in. "Eric doesn't have a gambling problem, does he, Victor?"

"Not that I am aware of. Why?"

"We all assumed you were an enforcer from a Vegas casino looking for Eric because of the tremendous debt he'd built up at the slots or the roulette wheel."

Victor smiled for a moment, which looked a bit odd, if I was honest. "Okay, that explains a lot."

I turned toward Kate and continued. "Eric told me he was writing marketing campaign music for companies in Vegas, but that didn't seem quite right, so I did some research and found out that a whole cottage industry has sprung up around writing music for slot machines. I know it sounds unbelievable, but the soundtracks are designed to make players overestimate the number of times they win, which convinces them to keep playing. The music designers made a fortune, and I figured Eric was one of the best. Ray filled him in last night about Sheila's killer being caught, and he called me this morning to thank me for helping the police solve the murder and to apologize for being rude." At least someone is giving me some credit, I thought.

"I confronted him about Victor and the casino business, and he confirmed my suspicions. He said he started out writing TV and social media jingles for Minnesota groups, and then he was recruited by a company in Vegas that developed new slot machines. They offered him crazy money, the latest audio software, and sample instrument libraries, and he would rub elbows with some of the best composers, designers, and audio engineers in the business."

"Everything was going great, but then he visited some Minnesota casinos to see how well his machines were doing. When he saw the deplorable condition many of the gamblers were in, he decided he didn't want to contribute to their addictions anymore. So, he quit. Victor has been searching for him not because Eric owed them money but to coerce him into writing more music."

Kate scrunched up her forehead. "Wait a minute. You told me that Victor left Ray a voicemail threatening to hurt Eric if he didn't pay up."

"That's what I assumed when Ray first played the message. After listening a few more times, I realized when Victor said he wanted to 'discuss a financial arrangement,' he didn't want to extract payments from Eric. He wanted to give him a lot more money."

"Okay, that does explain a lot." Kate turned toward Victor and asked, "Why didn't you just tell us why you were looking for him?"

Victor was obviously embarrassed and just looked down, so I answered for him. "Victor didn't want to tell us the real reason he was looking for Eric because he figured we wouldn't help him if he did. The incremental amount of money the House took from the machines using Eric's music must have been huge because Victor was willing to agree to whatever amount Eric demanded. Only Eric wanted out of that world. He didn't want his family or friends to discover what he'd been doing, so he went off-grid, hoping the casinos would eventually give up and leave him alone."

I looked at Victor, who just nodded. He probably thought we were at an impasse and would keep looking until he found Eric. I needed to disabuse him of that.

"Victor, do you remember the 'family crest' pendant our informant wore when you met her at the Aussie House? It was the same as the one in the ring I was wearing when we met."

"Yes, but I won't fall for that trick again. I'm not scared of you or her. You're not part of some 'Minnesota Mob.' She just made that up."

"Good call, but I think you should know that the pendant actually contained a recorder and a microphone. I have a very clear recording of you bribing me to find Eric. I have a copy on my phone. I'd be happy to play it for you if you like."

Victor's venomous look reminded me he could still seriously damage Kate and me if this discussion went off the rails.

"Eric assured me this morning that he has no intention of working for any casino in any capacity ever again. All he wants is to be left alone. And I have no interest in keeping your money. So, here is my proposal. I will return all the money you 'loaned' to me. In exchange, you and the rest of your team will never contact Eric again. If you don't agree to this now or if someone contacts Eric in the future, this video will be released to the FBI, the news media, and every social media platform I can find." I had no idea if the FBI would be interested in what may or may not be extortion. But I was confident the casino industry didn't want their music manipulation business to become common knowledge. "Do we have a deal?"

Victor shifted nervously in his seat while he mulled it over. He was probably trying to devise a story to explain why he returned empty-handed to his boss. I had one card left to play. "My informant still has room in her funeral urn. Don't make me sic her on you."

That was all it took. "Fine. We have a deal." Victor got up and left without so much as a goodbye. Kate and I looked at each other and had a good laugh. "Now I know why I love you," she said.

"Hey, here's a crazy idea. It's almost time for lunch. Let's grab a bite somewhere and then take the afternoon off. We can go back to my place, have a lovely stroll around the lake, and then have a nice, quiet dinner."

Kate came over and hugged me. "That sounds wonderful." She texted Ray that she would be out that afternoon, and I texted Paul the same message. I didn't see how either of them could complain after everything that had happened.

I scooped her up in my arms again, just as another idea popped into my head. "Tell you what, I'll even make you another deal."

"Yeah, what's that."

"I'll go to dinner with you and your mom sometime in the next few weeks, but it has to be at the restaurant of my choosing."

Kate's eyes lit up, and she was about to say something, but I kept going.

"That's not all." Why did I suddenly sound like Monty Hall on Let's Make a Deal? "I want you to come down to Rochester to meet my mom, too."

"That sounds like fun, Grayson." She gave me a passionate kiss and then flashed her trademark smile. "Will your mom tell me about all the girls you've dated before me?"

All I could do was shake my head and laugh as we gathered our belongings and walked hand-in-hand to the door.

* * *

It was a fine afternoon and an even more enjoyable evening hanging out with Kate. The weight of Kate's being a lead murder suspect had been lifted, which made us both feel lighthearted. But I knew the spell would be broken when I met with Detective Copeland the next day. I texted him in the morning to see if he was available for a meeting. He said he could meet me in his office at ten, which was good enough for me.

I drove to the police station in St Paul and entered a few minutes early.

Copeland must have told the receptionist we had an appointment because she paged him when she saw me walk in. "Have a seat, Grayson. He'll be right with you."

I took my usual spot on the bench, wondering if it was good or bad that I was on a first-name basis with police personnel. Copeland soon arrived and showed me in. We grabbed a cup of coffee and went to his office for a private discussion. He questioned me about every conceivable topic related to the murders, including the events in the Supper Club, Scott's confession, the fake ruby, the real ruby, and the cone snail poison kit.

Copeland got a bit testy when I presented him with the fake ruby. I was hoping to conceal DeeDee's involvement in recovering it from Sheila's cremated remains, but, in the end, there was no way to avoid telling him the truth. To say he was irritated would be putting it mildly, but he eventually realized he couldn't do anything about it as no laws had been broken. It was the fake ruby she'd found, and because Scott owned it and planted it in Sheila's body, technically, it wasn't stolen property. After two hours of intense grilling, we were tired of each other's company, and he said I was free to go.

But I had a few items of my own to discuss. "Detective, there are a few loose ends I'd like to clear up if you don't mind."

He looked at his watch. "Ten more minutes is about all I have right now, Grayson. What can I do for you?"

"I was just wondering what the police had on Rev. Marcel and why you thought he was dealing drugs out of the church."

Copeland stared at me for a minute, his brown eyes trying to drill a hole through my head.

"You seem to be well informed. You tell me what we have."

"This is only speculation, but someone in the St. Paul Narcotics Unit must have suspected that Marcel was dealing out of the Supper Club. They probably thought he was using the club as a cover.

"Then, someone who didn't like his success with the community started a rumor about him turning his church group into a cult." I had no proof, but I'd wager that my old friend The Fixer had started that nasty gossip. Who else had an interest in casting doubt on what Marcel was doing? "The police heard that and assumed he was using the cult to control his superstitious followers, many of whom come from countries where beliefs like Santería are commonly practiced.

"In the meantime, the Chicago Police had been conducting a cold case investigation into the murder of the Institute for a Better Life's leader, Bill Goddard, during Marcel's time there many years ago, and they contacted the St. Paul police to see what Marcel had been up to. When they found out he might be involved in a cult here, they asked the local police to look into it further. After Sheila was killed, their combined interest in Marcel took off. Since you were the investigating officer for her murder, you were briefed about their suspicions, and during a subsequent discussion, you implied that I should look into him."

The look on Copeland's face told me I was right. It was time for him to come clean. "Well, I figured you'd be out beating the bushes anyway, despite my telling you not to, so there was no harm in pointing you in a new direction. Besides, you kept Marcel focused on the murders while we investigated the drug running. If he were dirty, we would have been able to figure out who else Marcel was working with."

"But he wasn't dealing, was he? He was just doing his thing, trying to make a difference that would benefit the community. But between the neighborhood, the Catholic Church, and the police, he had too many people plotting against him. Then, Scott came along and gave him an ultimatum: help me clean up after Sheila's murder, or be exposed as a cult leader and leave in disgrace. Eventually, he caved in despite his best intentions. Then, he succumbed to the guilt and killed himself." I paused for effect. "And I'll bet you found the gun that killed Marcel beneath his body, and I'll bet it will match the one used to kill Bill Goddard, too."

Copeland just shrugged his shoulders. "We did find a gun there, but that doesn't mean he killed himself or Bill Goddard. You can't possibly know what he was thinking."

I took a page from police procedure and ignored the comment, mostly because he was right. I didn't know all that, but I'd be willing to bet that was exactly how it happened. Still, I was disgusted at being used by the police. "You let me do your dirty work for you, didn't you? You owe me one, my friend. No, wait, you owe me two, no three, because I solved the murders, too.

"By the way, you will find all the evidence the Chicago Police will need about the shady deal that Scott and Marcel made selling the Better Life property on Scott's laptop if you haven't already gotten there."

"How could you possibly…" Obviously, he had not gotten there yet, but he still wouldn't give me credit for anything. "Tell you what, Grayson. You stick to the design business and let me worry about the murder business."

* * *

On Monday morning a few weeks later, I found myself at the same place as when this whole affair started—waiting to pick Kate up outside St. Celestine's Rectory. Like last time, Bishop Tom walked her to the car, and I got out to talk to them.

"Morning, Father," I said to the Bishop as we shook hands. I laughed to myself at the double entendre. After all, some of these jokes were just for me.

"Things didn't work out as anyone expected, but we did look into Reverend Marcel for you." Tom was getting used to my weird sense of humor and let the comment slide.

"Yes, I've already spoken with Detective Copeland and received a full briefing."

You and the rest of the country, I thought. It was all over the news.

"Thanks for looking into it," said Tom.

"Have you considered making arrangements to continue the mission that Marcel started at Galland Garden," I wondered.

"Of course. Marcel had a good thing going even though it ended badly for him. I've already been in touch with some representatives from his community. We'll ask the group to join our flock at St. Celestine's. It's right down the road, and they can continue the community engagement that Marcel started by working on the garden."

That's my dad. Never one to pass up an opportunity.

Speaking of which, Paul had already created some stunning jewelry designs for Lindsey Brazzer, who was in the process of acquiring them. We also completed the design work for our new café table. We had a local furniture fabricator build a few prototype units that worked out great. The legs could be loosened and retightened to handle any variation in floor height of half an inch or less. We figured any bar, restaurant, or coffee shop whose floors varied more than that probably needed to invest in new flooring instead of new furniture. Kate had already placed an order for forty units for the Aussie House and for the Supper Club, where business was still booming due to the notoriety of the murders and the theft and recovery of the ruby.

Ray had reopened the museum and was now displaying both the real ruby and the fake one side-by-side in a secure case beneath a large sign asking visitors if they could spot the differences. That didn't seem like the best approach to me. If the average person couldn't tell the difference, why bother having a real one? But it wasn't my decision to make.

"That's great to hear, Tom. Ready for lunch, Kate?"

"Sure, but let's not go to the Aussie House. I've had enough of that place for a while."

Acknowledgements

To my Agent, Dawn Dowdle, who encouraged and supported me and was taken from us way too soon.

To my Publisher, Shawn Simmons, thank you for believing in me.

Thanks to the following family and friends who assisted with plot development and editing: Alexa Golemo, Melissa Logan, Mary Ann Cockriel, Calvin Morrison, Billie Logan, and Grant Hiesterman.

Thanks also to Anthony Scarpelli for his subject matter expertise in police procedures.

Any errors are my sole responsibility.

About the Author

When he's not working on his next murder mystery, Joe is a Partner with a Management and IT Consulting firm. He is originally from Chicago and holds a Chemical Engineering degree from the Illinois Institute of Technology and an MBA from the University of Minnesota, Carlson School of Management. After school, he moved to Minnesota to work for IBM and fell in love with the Land of 10,000 Lakes. Joe has been married for over 30 years and has two adult children and a crazy dog named Marco.

AUTHOR WEBSITE:
www.joegolemo.com

SOCIAL MEDIA HANDLES:
https://www.facebook.com/JoeGolemo/ (business page)
https://x.com/JoeGo7
https://www.linkedin.com/in/joegolemo/

Also by Joe Golemo

Design Flaws, Level Best Books

www.ingramcontent.com/pod-product-compliance
Lightning Source LLC
Chambersburg PA
CBHW020721130726
47899CB00011B/599